PRAISE FOR *THE HUNT*

"Imagine if Megan Abbott penned a chilling yarn about an annual Easter egg hunt in backwoods Arkansas, and you're getting close to what Kelly J. Ford's pulled off in her next novel. *The Hunt* perfectly captures the strangeness that lurks behind the guise of so many small-town Southern traditions. Nobody does buried secrets better than Kelly. But this dark rural noir conjures up more than just old ghosts—it shines a fresh new light on the truth."

—Eli Cranor, author of *Don't Know Tough* and *Ozark Dogs*

"Ford's *The Hunt* cements her as not only one of the best Southern fiction writers around but also one of the best contemporary writers period. There's a macabre playfulness to *The Hunt* as each unpredictable twist builds to an ending no one will see coming. But despite the dark humor, this is ultimately a story about how guilt can consume and destroy, especially in small towns, where empathy can be in short supply and gossip is a sport. Ford knows how to put her characters' humanity front and center even as they repeatedly stumble down dangerous paths. These are damaged people you want to see win."

—Heather Levy, author of the Anthony-nominated *Walking through Needles*

"Kelly J. Ford is a modern master of the rural noir—dragging the elements of a classic tale and reshaping it with a tone and viewpoint that is undoubtedly modern and alive. *The Hunt* is loaded with tension and razor-sharp plotting but also lets readers engulf themselves in the all-too-human characters Ford is so adept at creating. A small-town suspense novel that evokes tales like Megan Abbott's *The Fever* and Gillian Flynn's *Sharp Objects* with Ford's trademark voice. A winner."

—Alex Segura, bestselling author of *Secret Identity*

PRAISE FOR *REAL BAD THINGS*

"Acclaimed author Kelly J. Ford spins a propulsive, sophisticated, and fearlessly queer tour de force in *Real Bad Things*. Ford's richly drawn characters and breathtaking storytelling create an inescapable undertow of menace that will not let go until the final, shocking page. This is gothic suspense at its most haunting."

—P. J. Vernon, author of *Bath Haus*

"Ford's follow-up to her devastating debut novel, *Cottonmouths*, is a moving meditation on misplaced loyalties, love, and the legacy of violence and abuse, all wrapped in a mystery filled with guy-wire tension."

—John Vercher, author of *Three-Fifths*

"A powerful, grounded, and dark dose of rural noir, *Real Bad Things* is a tale of a homecoming gone wrong. Kelly J. Ford evokes the work of superstars like Gillian Flynn and Daniel Woodrell in this story of dark secrets coming back to roost and pulls it all through the prism of her own potent voice. This is a down-and-dirty crime novel that nods to the masters while keeping both feet firmly planted in the present. I loved it."

—Alex Segura, acclaimed author of *Secret Identity*, *Star Wars Poe Dameron: Free Fall*, and *Blackout*

"This absolutely gripping and gorgeously written Southern noir grabs hold and does not let go until the very last page. Ford's darkly atmospheric writing transports you right to the underbelly of Maud Bottoms—where the water teems with dead bodies, hidden secrets, forbidden love, and past betrayals—and pulls you inescapably into its ominous current, then shocks you with its final twist. *Real Bad Things* is Southern gothic perfection."

—Elizabeth Chiles Shelburne, *Holding On to Nothing*, winner of the IPPY Gold Award for Southern Regional Fiction

"At the start of this gripping suspense novel from Ford, Jane Mooney, who's been living in Boston, returns home to Maud Bottoms, Arkansas . . . The truth slowly unfolds as the plot builds toward a surprising conclusion foreshadowed by a trail of skillfully disguised clues. Ford delivers the goods."

—*Publishers Weekly*

"A confessed killer's return home brings long-buried secrets to life with a series of seismic jolts."

—*Kirkus Reviews*

"Beautifully written and socially astute, *Real Bad Things* delivers on the promise of Ford's debut, *Cottonmouths*."

—CrimeReads

"With layers of storytelling portraying generational trauma, small towns, and the unbearable confines their scrutiny can place on anyone who feels different, as well as the unbreakable bonds that adversity can forge, *Real Bad Things* is sometimes a hard read but always an excellent one. Readers looking for slow-burn mystery with unforgettable characters and an unforgettable atmosphere will find here exactly what they need."

—*Mystery and Suspense Magazine*

"This atmospheric, suspenseful novel will keep you guessing and page turning all the way to the end."

—*Good Housekeeping*

"Some writers seem to have a natural affinity for originality and the kind of narrative-driven storytelling that immediately engages and then holds the reader's total attention from first page to last. Clearly, with the publication of *Real Bad Things*, Kelly J. Ford has proven herself to be one of those novelists."

—*Midwest Book Review*

PRAISE FOR *COTTONMOUTHS*

"Ford's novel features a lesbian protagonist, yet sexuality is only one facet of her strongly drawn character. Emily suffers from unrequited love, from betrayal, and from a longing for meaning and acceptance. Her struggles, as well as those of her family and community, are universal struggles set in a brutal reality where choices are scarce. Read this debut novel for its ability to go beneath the surface, striking impressive depths of character and setting."

—*Los Angeles Review*, the Best Books of the Year, 2017

"Refreshingly, *Cottonmouths* refuses to romanticize unrequited love . . . *Cottonmouths* is not a love story: it's a tale of resentment, venomous betrayal, and the wounds hidden beneath familiar surfaces. Through a kaleidoscope of characters, Ford's dark novel shows us the choices people make when the world denies them good options and the consequences of complicity."

—Lambda Literary

"Filled with foreboding and anguished desire, *Cottonmouths* is a perfectly paced drama of the perils of loyalty, love, and homecoming. A terrific novel by an exciting new queer voice."

—Christopher Castellani, author of
All This Talk of Love and *Leading Men*

"Gripping and atmospheric. A tense tale of the specific gravity of the places and the people we come from and can never fully leave behind."

—Kate Racculia, *Bellweather Rhapsody*

"A taut page-turner trembling with desire and regret, Kelly J. Ford's debut, *Cottonmouths*, strips away nostalgia for person and place when the return of one young woman reveals the rotting core of a small Southern town, unraveling with the ferocity of addiction and forcing a painful lesson—she must learn to let go of her delusions in both love and friendship before it's too late."

—Michelle Hoover, author of *Bottomland*

"Kelly J. Ford's *Cottonmouths* is a fierce first novel—startling in its grip and authenticity. It's a novel about desire and desperation and the perilous danger of loving broken people in broken places."

—Travis Mulhauser, author of *Sweetgirl*

"A compelling story of unrequited love, identity, and the power of letting go."

—Heather Newton, author of *Under the Mercy Trees*

"Part noir, part Southern gothic, *Cottonmouths* is far more than the sum of these parts—an original story that haunted me after I read it. Kelly J. Ford's unflinching prose plunges readers into the town of Drear's Bluff, where what's familiar isn't what's safe and where desire proves deadly."

—Stephanie Gayle, author of *Idyll Threats*

"With prose as lyrical and languid as a hot Arkansas summer, Kelly J. Ford explores the myopia of desire—and its tragic aftermath. I found myself torn between wanting to rip through these pages to find out what would happen and a need to slow down and savor Ford's sentences. A remarkable debut."

—Lisa Borders, author of *The Fifty-First State*

"Kelly J. Ford delivers a sharp punch to the gut with this tightly spun modern noir tale. I can't wait to read more from this author."

—Tiffany Quay Tyson, author of *Three Rivers*

"Ford's debut novel traces the sobering struggles of small-town meth addiction, sexual identity, and the choices people make when good options are in short supply."

—*Los Angeles Times*

"Kelly J. Ford's novel *Cottonmouths* captures life in backwoods America like a fish in a frying pan. Ford takes her young, raw, flailing characters and rakes them over the heat of a high-octane plot until their vulnerable insides sizzle on the page."

—*Shelf Awareness*

"*Cottonmouths*, another book that seems to sample the new territory wrought by David Joy and Frank Bill, is an original addition to the meth-and-magnolia genre . . . This debut novel from Kelly J. Ford is sensitive yet brutal, with Ford giving her protagonist, Emily, believable flaws while nailing small-town Southern culture in the new world that has replaced Welty and Connery with Joy and Crews. A terrific new voice in the genre."

—Shelf Discovery

"*Cottonmouths* paints a disturbing picture of deep darkness lurking just below the surface of small-town America."

—*Mystery Scene* magazine

"A Southern gothic queer masterpiece."

—S. A. Cosby, *Do Some Damage*

"We talk about the need for diverse books in America; *Cottonmouths* shows us a version of our country seldom given its own narrative. Kelly J. Ford writes with honesty, subtlety, and grace."

—Patricia Park, *Re Jane*

"*Cottonmouths* is an astonishingly assured debut from Kelly J. Ford, a writer who daringly plumbs the depths of both love and despair in a new and chilling South rendered with taut and pitch-perfect detail. Trust me, this is a book you will remember."

—Kimberly Elkins, author of *What Is Visible*

"Kelly J. Ford's *Cottonmouths* is a heartbreaking debut about the lies we tell ourselves to brave the past—and the truths we hide that hurt us most. An honest, unflinching portrait of yearning and loss."

—Andy Davidson, author of *In the Valley of the Sun*

THE HUNT

OTHER TITLES BY KELLY J. FORD

Real Bad Things

Cottonmouths

THE HUNT

KELLY J. FORD

This is a work of fiction. Names, characters, organizations, places, events, and incidents are either products of the author's imagination or are used fictitiously. Otherwise, any resemblance to actual persons, living or dead, is purely coincidental.

Published by Thomas & Mercer, Seattle

www.apub.com

ISBN-13: 9781662500107 (paperback)
ISBN-13: 9781662500114 (digital)

Cover design by Rex Bonomelli
Cover images: © oxygen, © mdesigner125, © Feifei Cui-Paoluzzo / Getty Images; © Rex Bonomelli

Printed in the United States of America

To KISR 93.7 for the hunts and the hits.
And to Glen Ford for the night terrors.

AUTHOR'S NOTE

Though the following is based on real events, people, and places from and near my hometown, this book is a work of fiction.

Shared Google Doc / The Hunt

Last edited June 1, 2021

VICTIM #1

Put your research/notes here. We can organize later, so don't worry about that. But PLEASE add dates and details as much as possible, and DO NOT delete anything. If something looks off to you, just add a comment or something and we'll review together. Finally, DO NOT share this document with anyone, PLEASE and THANK YOU! 🙂 We don't want to share with others until it's ready.

Since KCLS 103.9 FM's inaugural Hunt for the Golden Egg began in 2005, sixteen citizens of Presley, Arkansas, have either died in a mysterious manner or disappeared within seven days of Easter, starting with Garrett Holcomb, white, nineteen years old, who went missing on March 22. His body was found on Easter morning, March 27, by a duck hunter along Lee Creek, a sixty-four-mile river in Arkansas that also flows through nearby Oklahoma. The death certificate lists the cause as accidental drowning. There is no record of an autopsy being conducted.

Locals in Presley are split into three camps:

1. The deaths are accidental and unrelated.
2. The Hunt is cursed.
3. Something—and someone—more sinister is at play.

In 2013, eight years after Garrett died, the family and friends of Annalee Raleigh, white, sixteen, another alleged victim, began to question the deaths that inexplicably plagued Presley around Easter every year. They believe someone is responsible for the deaths and ensuring the deaths look like accidents. They call him the Hunter.

Is the Hunter real or a story that locals tell to frighten themselves and their children? What's really happening in Presley?

We may never know. The Hunt for the Golden Egg continued, uninterrupted, until this year. In March 2021, the Hunt for the Golden Egg was canceled by KCLS due to unforeseen circumstances, which locals believe was related to the ongoing pandemic.

Many in town, including the victims' families, are hopeful that the Hunt will cease to exist in 2022.

KCLS 103.9 FM Commercial Transcript

First aired Tuesday, March 1, 2022

Hey, listeners, Rod Halstrom here from KCLS 103.9 FM, Arklahoma's station for classic-rock hits from the '60s, '70s, and '80s.

I think we can all agree that 2020 sucked. And 2021 REALLY sucked. But 2022 is here, and so is our most popular event, after a year off: the annual Hunt for the Golden Egg. This year we're giving away more money, more free tickets, and more prizes than ever before. You don't want to miss out.

So dust off those boots, get your allergy and eye prescriptions checked, and stay tuned to KCLS 103.9 for the first set of clues, coming your way March 18.

One

Nell

Thursday, March 24
Afternoon
Twenty-four days before Easter

By the time Nell Holcomb pulled up for her shift at Mayflower Plastics, the KAOK news van had parked in her spot. Adding insult to injury: Maggie, the office manager, stood in front of the camera, chatting them up. Wearing her new bedazzled *Hunt* T-shirt that clashed with the fake tan she'd maintained since her sorority days that still showed her white skin in the underarm creases. Talking about how "causation does not equal correlation" and "accidents happen."

Tell that to the families, Nell thought. Maggie never would, though. Not to her face or anyone else's. But she'd go on TV and tell the world and call herself and other people like her "Eggheads," like they were a fun little group and there weren't any deaths associated with the Hunt every year, serial killer or not. If Nell didn't know any better, she'd guess that Maggie worked for either the radio station or the Chamber of Commerce.

Nell walked on by Maggie and the news crew without saying a word, hoping they wouldn't recognize her as the little sister of Garrett Holcomb: white, young, handsome, smart, and dead.

When Nell opened the plant door, Lloyd startled her. He hiked his pressed khakis, looked outside, and cast down his eyes.

"Sorry about all this." He gestured in the direction of Maggie and the news crew. "Nancy asked me," Lloyd offered as an apology. He was your average white, middle-class guy from a flyover state. Not wanting to stir up any trouble but doing it anyway. "Said it would be good to present both sides. Let people know how we feel. And with Maggie so . . ." He searched for the word. "Excitable. And Nancy so against it, well, I guess they thought it'd make for good TV. Otherwise, I wouldn't have." He checked his watch, struggled with his words. "They were supposed to be here hours ago." He looked genuinely torn up about it. A young Asian woman wearing a KAOK vest and carrying a clipboard gestured for Lloyd to join her. "I can tell them no. Have them go on home."

After Garrett died, there wasn't much attention. Not like now. There was a brief mention at the back of the newspapers. It wasn't until Nell had been working at Mayflower for five years, and after earning everyone's trust that she wasn't a dumbass and knew how to fix things, that Maggie told everyone else. That changed everything.

"No, no. Don't worry about it." Nell tucked a loose strand of unwashed hair back under her slouchy beanie hat and pretended like everything was fine and nothing bothered her because that's the only way she knew how to cope with what had happened to Garrett and anything affiliated with the Hunt. "I appreciate it," Nell said. "But I think Nancy's right. Good to get both sides." She thumbed toward Maggie. "Especially to counter folks like her." Nell laughed, although it was forced. "Thanks again. I appreciate you. And Nancy." She checked a fake watch on her wrist. "Eek. I should clock in before my boss discovers I'm late." She clapped Lloyd on the arm at the joke; then she smiled brightly and broadly and hoped Lloyd bought it because she didn't like people worrying about her or plain even thinking of her.

The break room was no better. She knew what she would find—the whole lot of them sitting at the table, their little ragtag night crew: Marcy, a white, bumbling-but-well-meaning label operator straight out of high school; Viv, an older white Christian conservative woman who had become a grandmother at the age of forty-five; Phonesavanh, a Laotian immigrant mother of adorable twin boys; Juanita, a third-generation Mexican American woman who hated living in Arkansas and couldn't wait for her husband to be stationed somewhere, anywhere, else; Kasey, a white male hipster college student who drove forklifts and listened to emo bands; and Ada, who was equal amounts smart and smartass and the proud Black mother of a future engineering student.

As Nell made her way through the long hallway, their voices grew louder: who was their biggest competition, who won in previous years, strategies for searching, and warnings not to go alone. *Don't let the Hunter get you!*

Louder than the others was Ada Johnson—Nell's "work wife," according to everyone at the factory—boasting the most about how she'd come so close last year, and without needing any of them. When she saw Nell walk into the break room, she stopped talking. Didn't even pretend to be talking about something else or look at her. Nell guessed most people didn't know how to talk to people like her without worrying they'd say something wrong.

She understood that. Hard enough to say, *Sorry your brother died of mysterious circumstances on the side of the road.* Harder still to say, *Sorry everyone thinks your brother was the first victim of the notorious serial killer who's been stalking Presley's annual Hunt for the Golden Egg.*

If it were up to her, no one would say shit and they would just go about their business like they didn't know her personal history.

"Afternoon, folks," she said and walked right on by them to enter the plant floor. She tried to sound light and cheerful to cover the irritation that had once been a brightly burning rage. But she'd had to deal with this long enough. There was no use in fighting it. The town wanted the Hunt. It didn't matter what families like hers wanted. Still, she wished Ada wouldn't talk about it at work like all the others.

Out on the floor, the machines roared and pressed and molded hot plastic in all colors—red, blue, green—into caps meant for milk jugs and gallon water bottles. Nell wandered over to Janie, a white woman who operated the press on the second shift. Her knuckles and fingertips were always covered in either blood or Band-Aids, thanks to dry skin. Janie stretched and yawned and shivered dramatically after giving Nell the updates on the presses, which were as fussy as ever.

Despite a few balmy days the previous week, the early-spring chill had returned, overtaking the sun and its warmth like a thief intent on taking everything, all at once, so the factory door had remained shut to keep in what warmth they had this time of year. Everyone zipped up their sweatshirts as high as they could go and cinched the strings of their hoodies around their heads in a dramatic fashion, the tight circle of facial features making them look like cartoon characters. They took to briskly rubbing their hands together when Nell walked by.

Nell pulled a large five-gallon bottle cap from the cardboard box to examine it. She could tell that the mold was almost shot. But this cap was good enough to pass inspection. She considered the journey it would embark on once it left the plant: the gravel road out of the plant's parking lot, the rural route, a state highway, an interstate, a town, a bottling company, and then back out on the interstate, the tires rolling for hours and days until the bottle cap ended up in a smaller warehouse and a smaller truck and was carried by some driver down a carpeted hallway and placed on the floor until some guy in a suit and a tie, or maybe a janitor, would remove the empty from the cooler and then take off the lid that Nell had held in her hand. That person, whoever they were, would toss the plastic lid in the trash, and everyone in that office would fill their cups and not give a thought to where that cap had come from, that one forklift driver, one label operator, five press operators, and Nell had both sweat and shivered inside Mayflower Plastics in Presley, Arkansas, on a twelve-hour shift for shit pay and what you could barely call benefits. And insurance that ensured nothing but more debt on top of what they already had when something went wrong. All for the luxury of clean water, all while Presley was still feeling the effects from when the crude oil pipeline that ran from Canada down to the Gulf burst and infected their water supply almost ten years prior, causing widespread panic about short-term drinking water and long-term health.

What a world, there in Nell's hand. And her inside the plant, small, insignificant. Maybe that cap would never make it out of Presley. Maybe that cap would end up in the hands of Garrett's killer.

"Why can't this shit break down in summer?" Janie asked, hands on her hips, exasperated by another broken press. She was waiting on someone to retire or die so she could get onto the third shift with Nell's crew because it paid more and she wanted to hang out with Viv and Phonesavanh.

"Dunno." Nell flipped the cap in the air, where it twirled a few times before landing in her palm. She handed it back to Janie. "Cursed, I guess."

"Well, fix it!" Janie said.

"Tell Maggie to buy me the parts I asked her for a week ago, and I will."

"It's cold!" Janie complained as Nell walked away.

"So buy some goddamn gloves," Nell yelled back at her. Janie tossed the bottle cap at Nell's head in response. They both laughed.

There was not much else they could do but wait for the press to break down completely so upper management in Illinois would have no choice but to pay attention to their rinky-dink plant in the middle of the woods.

When Nell had first come on at Mayflower Plastics, she'd also wondered about the problem with the machines. Maybe the metal seized up with the change in temperature. Or it had something to do with physics. Nell didn't know. At the time, she hadn't yet enjoyed the challenge of fixing something broken. She'd been too new. Too eager to convince everyone that she knew what she was doing. That she wasn't Lloyd's pity hire.

All that mattered was proving herself worthy of the job, of Lloyd's trust, after he'd found her in the casino, drunk and unemployed. There were others like her. A mostly homeless, mostly harmless-to-everyone-but-themselves gang of teenage alcoholic gamblers. But she guessed what set her apart from the others was her tragedy. Good guys like Lloyd ate that shit up.

He'd heard before most people about what had happened to Garrett. Eventually, everybody in Presley did. Didn't matter what side of town they lived on. Nell and Lloyd had talked about it over coffee in the casino cafeteria. Not all the details. Not everything about that night. At least not that she remembered. There was a lot about those days Nell didn't remember.

A bit before midnight, she squirreled around for spare change in her truck and found something to gnaw on from the snack machine, followed by a Rolaid or three. She'd been going through them like hard candy lately, the chalkiness turning her tongue dry and gums itchy.

Nell's pocket buzzed. She could feel disappointment spark her fingertips when she opened up her most recent text: I miss you.

Sorry, Nell replied. Work's been busy.

The lie left her stomach feeling as hollow and hungry as when she ate drive-through leftovers. It was only half a lie. Still, the text exchange sat in her intestines like a stone.

After devouring a bag of Doritos, she left the plant for her usual spot at the picnic table under the giant oak tree next to the gravel parking lot. She pulled her vape pen from her jacket. A nasty habit. She knew she should stop. But stopping bad shit that felt good wasn't exactly in her DNA. She liked the smell and the action of sucking something in, letting it out. Therapy was kind of like that, she guessed. She'd picked it up after trying to quit smoking when Elijah, her nephew, moved in with her all those years ago. His mom had been pregnant at the time of Garrett's death but hadn't known it. She had managed to keep herself together until Elijah turned five. But then, all that sorrow, she'd said, just broke her. It was either Garrett's family or foster care for Elijah. Been twelve years now.

A cold breeze spiked the air and rustled the leaves. Nell pulled her jacket collar up, crossed her arms, and leaned forward. A short time later, Ada sauntered out the break-room door in that way of hers, like she had no place of importance to be yet the whole world awaited her arrival. She wore jeans, thick double braids that cascaded to the middle of her back, and the "Aggie Maroon" Texas A&M hoodie she'd bought online as soon as Anthony had confirmed his college choice.

There was plenty of room on the other side of the table, but Ada sat right next to Nell, like a heat-seeking missile.

"Give me some of that," Ada said and nodded toward Nell's vape pen.

Nell groaned but acquiesced. "You don't even smoke."

"Well . . . ," she said, not offering anything more.

Nell shook her head and handed it over. "One of these days, I'm gonna quit and you're gonna have to get your own."

"You ain't ever gonna quit. And neither am I." Ada smiled before taking a long drag. Nell liked the way Ada tilted her head and then let the smoke ease through lips she'd done up to match the shade of her hoodie, and twirl in the air before disappearing. Even without the vape pen, Ada always smelled like a sunny day at the beach somewhere far from Presley.

What a looker she'd been back when Nell started at the plant. Still was, even after hard work and night shifts had worn lines into her hands and hung exhaustion around her face. They'd both come on at the factory young, Ada a few years before Nell. At least Ada went to college for a bit. Nell just got her GED.

Nell would be lying if she said she didn't once or twice consider asking for a little bit more than friendship, but Ada had made it clear she didn't eat where she shits. Nell wasn't sure if Ada was sparing her feelings so she wouldn't have to say she didn't date women, let alone a white woman, given how Ada's white college boyfriend had taken off a year into their marriage and barely contacted Anthony afterward. Feeling the warmth of Ada's thigh next to hers on that picnic bench in the quiet night air would have to do, as it'd done so many times over the years. What they had was safe, comforting, someone to turn to when the bad thoughts pressed. But Nell had found a different harbor of late, and Ada was nothing if not curious.

"Thought for sure I'd find myself alone again, given you've been MIA a lot lately," Ada said.

Nell tried to laugh. "I have not."

"Bullshit. We've been sitting out here how many years? And suddenly you're nowhere to be found? In the middle of the night? For weeks now." Ada took a drag off the vape pen and then placed her arms on the table—her interrogation pose.

Nell had always gotten a little thrill when she did that. She'd been enamored by the attention of this "older woman" at work. It was safe. There wasn't anything that would happen between them. She'd never in a million years have believed when she'd started at Mayflower that her work crush would become one of her best friends. Maybe her best friend.

"What have you been up to?" Ada asked.

"Nothing." Nell didn't have to look at Ada directly to know she had a spark in her eye, that dog-on-a-hunt energy that vibrated off her body. Nell had known that she was walking a fine line, messing with their routine. But once a gambler, always one. "Just running errands."

"In the middle of the night?"

Nell shoved her hands deep into her pockets. "Some errands need night doing."

Ada laughed, heavy with innuendo. Nell smiled that the line had landed the way she wanted it to. This was the best part of her day. This dance between them. Even with the Hunt being an occasional sore spot.

Before this past December, that is. Now she had other things, someone else, to look forward to. How could Nell even explain her?

"Aren't you supposed to be off today anyway?" Ada asked.

"You keeping track of my calendar now too?"

Ada lifted an eyebrow.

Nell had been picking up more shifts, and everyone had started to notice. Not just Ada. Maggie had bugged her about it earlier that day, after her time in the spotlight with KAOK news. Warned Nell that she couldn't keep working every night. She had to take a day off. Not because Maggie cared. She didn't want the plant to get into trouble for labor laws or whatever. Like Nell was a pilot and could fall asleep at the wheel, kill everyone. The worst that would happen if Nell dozed off is Viv or Phonesavanh would yell at her to fix something.

She couldn't tell anyone why she'd been working so much. They wouldn't understand. And if Ada did, there was no guarantee she wouldn't slip and tell Elijah. There was no way he could know. He'd never speak to her again. Avoiding him was the only thing she could think to do. She wasn't good with lies. Maybe because she'd used it all up for the Big Lie.

"Elijah's been at my house a lot lately," Ada said, as if reading around the edges of Nell's mind, catching the characters if not the content of what had plagued Nell of late.

"Sorry. I can have him come home."

"No, that's not what I meant. I'm just . . ." *Worried about you.* That's what Ada was probably going to say before she stopped herself. Nothing Nell hated more than to hear that phrase. "Sorry I mentioned it," Ada said after a stretch of silence.

"I need the extra cash. For bills. That's all."

Ada picked at something on her jeans, a distraction. "Sorry about earlier."

Nell's stomach tensed at the reminder of Ada's boast, but she waved a hand in the air. "I don't care about that."

Ada pursed her lips and turned away. "Anyway."

Here they were again. Different year, same awkwardness. Ada clung to her tradition. They had agreed to disagree and never talk about it again so they wouldn't end up like Ada and Maggie, former friends forced to work together out of pure economic necessity. Nell guessed she couldn't put the blame squarely on Ada. Everyone was talking about the Hunt.

Every year—as the Hunt commenced unaltered, even with all that speculation about the deaths—Nell had to live through the torture of remembering the last time she'd seen her brother alive. The only abatement, the pandemic. The Hunt canceled for the first time in seventeen years. And not even because of the pandemic itself so much as Rod, the white, well-off KCLS station owner and Hunt creator, getting so sick he couldn't manage it—and refusing to let anyone else from the station manage it for him. She remembered the relief and the feeling that maybe, after seventeen years, she could finally breathe a little easier in April. But now the Hunt was back. And bigger than ever.

Nell just wanted it to finally end. To never have to hear Rod's clues on the radio or see people out searching the ground. Or never to walk into a room of strangers who knew that Nell's brother had been killed, even if they didn't agree on whether he was the first victim of a serial killer or the subject of a tragic accident. Nell couldn't avoid the topic and everyone's perception of her as the sad little sister. The last one to see Garrett alive.

All she had to do was make it through Easter. And then make it through the handful of weeks after that. And then everything would go back to normal until the next April. And maybe, if she was lucky, Lloyd and Nancy and the church groups and all the others would get their way after all these years and the Hunt would end forever.

She didn't put much weight on that. Nothing spoke as loudly as money. And money in the city and local businesses' pockets was the one thing that no one contested the Hunt was responsible for. Rod gladly took all the blame for that.

The plant door opened, and Maggie tugged her purse over her shoulder and came down the steps. Nell and Ada stared at her. They knew what was coming. Happened every night.

"Oh! Y'all about scared me to death! Again!" She held a hand to her chest and laughed like it was some bit they were all in on. "One day you're gonna do it for real!"

They didn't respond.

"Well," Maggie said. She tugged at her thin cardigan to try to hide this year's customized, bedazzled *Hunt for the Golden Egg* T-shirt with her team's name: *Maggie's Miss Thangs*. Didn't even make sense, Hunt-wise. But she never made any kind of sense any time of year.

"Here kinda late," Ada called over to Maggie. Ada's tone was deep and accusatory, still harboring a grudge Ada had never shared the details of with Nell.

Maggie smiled at Ada in that fake way of hers. "There's always something to do and catch up on. I can't ever seem to get ahead." Probably because she spent all her time making tacky T-shirts and trying to get on the news. Maggie clicked her key fob, and it squeaked out into the night. "See y'all tomorrow!" She waved and then sat in her car with the headlights on, like always, nearly blinding them for sport. She was always waiting, looking, watching Nell and Ada. Hunting for gossip, her favorite feast.

Nell nodded her head toward Maggie. "Maybe she's the Hunter." Making fun of it was sometimes the only way that Nell could get back at all those people who kept hunting, feverish with dreams of winning something that might make their lives a little less dim than the day before. People like Ada.

Ada shifted uncomfortably on the bench, tightening her limbs like the roly-poly bugs in the flower planters at the house.

"Think about it," Nell said. "She's always here. But she's always in the office. She can sneak out anytime. Nobody knows anything about her."

"She only works late because she has no life," Ada said, all agitated.

"If you say so." Nell loved to get Ada riled up, watch the little veins pop along her temple and her jaw clench tight. She also knew it was the surest way to get rid of Ada. You couldn't work that closely with someone for that long and not get a little irritated, crave a little space.

Nell's pocket buzzed, and Ada stood.

"You better get that," Ada said, using the same tone she'd used for Maggie, a parting shot. Still, she paused, like always, after these little tensions between them. "Before your girl breaks up with you."

"She's not—" Nell cracked her neck, scratched at her arms. She hated how her body betrayed her. "It's complicated."

"You gonna put that on your Facebook status?"

"Fuck you." Nell laughed. "You know I hate that shit."

Ada narrowed her eyes. She had been joking, but there was an edge to it that bordered on irritation. "Do I know her?"

"No," Nell said. "I don't think so. Maybe."

"Is she married?"

"No."

"Then why keep it a secret? Give me something. I need to live vicariously through you."

Nell pursed her lips. She wanted so badly to tell Ada, but she was worried she'd hate her if she knew. Nell held her head in her hands and rubbed her forehead.

"I like her," Nell said. "Maybe too much."

"Well, shit. That doesn't sound like a problem. I'd love it if someone loved me too much. Hell, I'd go for loving me just a little at this point."

Ada talked about men, but she rarely dated, as far as Nell knew. She knew Ada had never wanted to bring anyone around Anthony when he was little. Nell didn't know why she would care now. He was already eighteen. Maybe Ada was keeping secrets too.

"Anyway," Nell said.

"Anyway," Ada mimicked, like Elijah did to Nell. Nell wondered if maybe Elijah was spending most of his time hanging out with Ada instead of Anthony when he hung out at their house. "Been having trouble with press one."

"What kind of trouble?" Nell got a giddy little spark whenever a problem presented itself. All the problems at work had solutions, unlike everything else in her life. "Janie mentioned something earlier about her presses too."

"A bit of flashing around the edges of some of the caps. Not many." Ada looked off toward Maggie's car and considered.

Maggie still sat there doing who knew what. Probably journaling about her day or writing another letter to the editor about how great the Hunt was for local businesses—some goofy shit like that. Or maybe puzzling out the latest Hunt clue from Rod on KCLS on her phone's Notes app, like Ada did when she didn't know Nell was watching.

"The caps are probably fine to pass inspection," Ada said. "But I don't trust Viv not to notice when she covers for me."

"Could be the mold's degraded. Or the temperature needs to be adjusted," Nell added. "I'll take a look at it when I head back inside."

Ada nodded and stood. "You staying out here?"

Nell offered a little mm-hmm but didn't make a move. Ada liked to talk big about how she didn't believe in the Hunter. But she always seemed to hesitate whenever Nell stayed outside alone.

Sometimes, Nell let her thoughts wander to the possibility that the Hunter was real. But then she'd remember how much time they'd spent knowing that it'd been an accident. Almost seven or eight years before talk of the Hunter went mainstream in Presley. It was hard to shift perspective. Guilt. Considering he'd been murdered only made Nell feel worse.

There were those steady buzzes from the phone in Nell's pocket, begging for attention. "I'll be there in a minute."

"Suit yourself," Ada said and sauntered back the way she'd come.

Ada stopped right in front of Maggie's car headlights, waved dramatically, and yelled bye. Finally, Maggie put her car in reverse and left the parking lot. Nell laughed.

Ada offered a devilish grin and then bowed for Nell—a sign they were good again—before leaving her alone to the quiet night.

As soon as the door closed, Nell pulled out her phone and scrolled to the last text she'd received.

It's okay. I'm tired anyway.

That tightness in Nell's chest squeezed a little harder. She shoved her phone into her back pocket and stepped out of the origami-like position she'd put her body in to sit comfortably on a bench not made for tall, long-legged folks like her. She grabbed her vape pen off the table and proceeded toward the building.

Gravel crunched behind her.

She whipped around, blood jackhammering her veins.

The wind rustled the darkened cathedral of pine trees that ringed the factory. She held still, scanned the ground for signs of a chipmunk or rabbit, maybe a feral cat. Sometimes, she heard things. Sometimes, she thought it was the Hunter, watching her, waiting. Sometimes, she thought maybe it was Garrett, his spirit coming back to taunt her. He'd loved ghost stories around the fire. Tales of terror. Egged their dad and uncles on, begging for more. Nell had pretended to love it too. But she'd never slept right after a night of those stories. She never slept right on nights when she heard what sounded like his footsteps following close behind.

Soon, the wind picked up, muting all else, muffling even the jagged breaths that escaped her. She stared at the tree line until her adrenaline eased and logic took hold.

"There's nothing there," she muttered to herself and turned toward the plant, all the while blaming her sleep schedule, busted after all that time spent working, that time spent with, or thinking of, Tessa.

The noise from inside the factory grew louder the closer she walked toward the building's door. By the time she opened it, she'd refocused on the machine that Ada needed fixed and shut the dark thoughts and the unidentifiable sounds behind her.

Facebook Post: Nancy Barker

I CANNOT believe that YET AGAIN, we have to sit by and watch as this dangerous annual event takes another life. Rod Halstrom, the city council, the Chamber of Commerce, and MANY business owners should be ashamed of themselves. They've put their love of money over the lives of innocents! No matter if you believe in the Hunter or not, one fact remains: THE HUNT FOR THE GOLDEN EGG IS A HAZARD TO THIS CITY. What will it take for people to recognize this danger for what it is?? How many more people will have to die before people open their eyes??? How many more families like the Raleighs and the Holcombs and all the rest must suffer before someone pays attention? What do we have to do? We can vote out the councilors, but what about the rest??? I could spit I'm so mad! I'm planning on protesting at the radio station TOMORROW at NOON. If you feel the same way, I URGE you to join me and Lloyd. We'll meet at First Baptist Church of Presley on Main Street and will proceed from there. Feel free to bring signs and loud voices. OUR COMPLAINTS WILL BE HEARD!!

Two

Ada

Saturday, March 26
Morning
Twenty-two days before Easter

"What on earth are you wearing?" Ada asked. Elijah was decked out in camo, head to toe. "You look like a damn fool."

Elijah smiled and strolled to the car from where he'd waited at the end of his driveway, intentionally swinging his hips left to right. He did a twirl and stopped dramatically, head cocked toward the ground, eyes directed at where she sat in the driver's seat.

"Going hunting doesn't mean you have to leave the fashion at home," Elijah said.

Sometimes, it still startled her, the way Elijah looked so similar to Nell. Their white skin and pointy little noses and thin lips looked like they'd stepped out of an English gothic novel. The only thing that kept them from looking full-blown vampire was when they smiled or wore something besides black. His hair was shaved on one side, long on the other. Black. Blue on the ends. To top it off, he also wore eyeliner. The polar opposite of Anthony, who was usually in his red hoodie and gray basketball shorts if it was cold. And Anthony always wore his thick, curly hair in a high-top fade. And he'd never, ever wear eyeliner. Not that he thought there was anything wrong with it! It just wasn't for him, or his grandfather and some of their male relatives. And, well, Ada was a little bit thankful she didn't have to worry about what might happen to him if eyeliner was for him on top of everything else that came along with raising a Black son, if she was being honest. But she'd support him if he wanted to wear it. And she'd fight anyone who had something to say about it.

She shook her head. "Get in the damn car before Nell sees you."

Elijah opened the door and stuffed an oversize backpack on the floor. "She won't. She's already in bed."

"You didn't tell her, did you?" she asked.

He leaned into the car and stared.

"Okay, okay." She looked up the driveway to check for Nell. "Did you tell Anthony you're hunting with me?"

"No," Elijah said, easing himself into the passenger side. "You told me not to tell anyone. Remember?"

"I know. I'm just checking." She paused, thinking on Nell up at the top of the hill. Guilt coursed through her. Anthony had given her that Disappointed Dad look when the topic of the Hunt came up over dinner a few days prior and Elijah had offered to go with Ada. Elijah wouldn't have offered if Anthony hadn't made fun of her. And he wouldn't have offered if Anthony hadn't gotten a job at the Best Buy fixing computers. But he ended up enjoying his coworkers, and the money, and took on extra shifts whenever they asked. Just like Nell.

Ada didn't need the company, but she liked it.

"You can change your mind, you know," she said.

"Do you want me to change my mind?" He tilted his head just so, teasing her.

"If Nell found out, she'd never speak to me again."

Elijah smiled, all sass. "Would that be so bad?"

She shook her head and drummed her nails on the steering wheel. "You're just about the worst."

"Look. I know you have, like, feelings capital *F* about this because of Nell," Elijah said. "But I heard this year is major. And I love money. So, I'm, like, one hundred percent on board with whatever you want me to do. Even if it's just holding your snacks and seltzer while you do whatever it is you do on these things. I've never, ever, been able to go, thanks to . . . you know." He swiped a hand in the air. "But Nell doesn't get a say in the matter. I'm almost eighteen. And she doesn't have to know. Unless we find it. And then who cares? We'll have fifty thousand dollars."

Elijah settled into his seat and adjusted the seat belt across the camo jacket he wore. A hint of brown T-shirt showed above the buttons. He even wore military boots.

She nodded toward his pants. "Where'd you get those?"

"They're my dad's," he said, nonchalant. As if wearing a dead man's clothes were no big deal. A dead man who had gone missing during the very event she was whisking the dead man's son to with the hopes that she'd win a prize. And without telling Nell, his guardian.

Ada had looked up Garrett once online. Back when Facebook wasn't a place where old people got radicalized into right-wing militants. Elijah was the spitting image of his dad. All these years later, Garrett still had a Facebook page and photos and posts of going to parties off campus at the U of A. His friends still posted on his page, telling him how much they missed him, reminiscing about deer camp and football games and dumb kid shit they'd done they couldn't talk about publicly, as if Garrett had moved to another town, another country, could laugh along with them and then feel sad about how those times were gone.

She promised herself and God that if she found the egg—which she was certain she would this year—she'd give some of the money to Nell as a peace offering. And, of course, she'd give some to Elijah, depending on how helpful he decided to be. So it wasn't like she was being 100 percent selfish. Only a little bit.

Elijah finally buckled in, and Ada set Google Maps to her destination. She had been listening to Rod's clues on the radio and thought that the far end of Presley's Creekside Park would be a good place for them to start. Sometimes, it was better to wait to hunt, anyway. Otherwise, you were circling the same patch of ground for days for no good reason. Ada suspected that Rod withheld hiding the egg so soon after starting the Hunt anyway. Otherwise, the sponsors and the city would see their investment as a waste of money if it ended too soon.

While she drove, Elijah futzed with various things in his backpack. She watched him out of the corner of her eye. So far, she'd clocked an extra pair of pants, black nail polish, scissors, and a bunch of notebooks.

"What's all that, anyway?"

It took a moment for Elijah to catch her meaning, but then he looked down at the backpack between his feet. "Supplies. In case we need them."

"In case of what?"

"I've never been on a Hunt. I don't know what you need to bring. And from all I've heard, it can be . . ." He paused and turned to her, face serious. "Deadly." He drew out the words and released what sounded like a 1930s monster cackle.

"Oh, hush," she said and took off down the road, pretending not to believe in all that. But she did, even though she swore to everyone she didn't.

Finally, Elijah pulled one last item from his backpack, what looked like a homemade machete. "I always dreamed about using this on that son of a bitch who killed my dad," he said.

"So you don't believe it was an accident?" Ada wasn't sure she should be talking about Garrett. She already felt like shit for taking Elijah out for the Hunt without Nell knowing.

"TBD," he said, inspecting the machete's dull blade. Wouldn't slice a banana, but she wasn't about to tell him that. No telling what damage he could accidentally do with a sharp weapon.

"Do you believe he was killed?" he asked.

"I don't know," she said, not wanting to believe in all that, even if the possibility nagged at her sometimes. She could understand why people got caught up in the myth of the Hunter. Her grandfather loved to read true-crime paperbacks and kept them all on a shelf in the living room. Ada's parents didn't approve, but they couldn't tell Grandpa what to do in his own home. When everyone was outside in the yard during family get-togethers, Ada would sneak one of the slim volumes with her into the bathroom, terrifying herself with the stories and pictures, especially the one about the hooded Phantom Killer. He'd terrorized Texarkana for ten weeks and caused hysteria and a rash of false confessions. He was never apprehended. Same as Presley's alleged Hunter.

Yet, with all that knowing, Ada couldn't stop herself. She wanted that egg. She wanted it so bad, sometimes she wondered if she felt what junkies did, the cravings so strong you might just do anything for a hit. She wouldn't know. She liked a little light beer now and then, but that was it. She had tried to set aside the idea of going on the Hunt this year. But the way Nancy and the Raleighs and everyone else were carrying on after the Hunt was announced, she never knew when it would be the last year. Without even realizing it, she'd begun her process of running through all the previous Hunt clues and locations of where the egg had been found in the past. She mapped out her next moves, the first spot she'd look. She wrote down the clues she heard on the radio. She wrote them repeatedly, like a delinquent kid at a chalkboard. Somehow, writing it over and over helped her think.

She flicked her head toward the machete. "Did your dad use that to hunt?" She couldn't imagine for what.

Elijah placed the machete in his lap and stared out the window. "Yeah. She and my dad and Grandpa used to go out a lot. But that's all I know. Nell doesn't really like to talk about him. She just cries." The Holcombs could get so moody. One wrong word and the world turned upside down.

Nell always held in her emotions. Made jokes. Pretended to be unbothered. Nell never really said anything about the before or after of her brother's death, other than a brief mention that she had been homeless for a time. Ada couldn't judge Nell either. If Ada's brother had died, even though they weren't as close as Nell and Garrett had been, well, she might've gotten too sad and too drunk and stupid too.

"That must be hard," she said.

He shrugged. "Did you know my dad?"

"No. I went to Eastside." Nell and Garrett had gone to Westside, like Elijah and Anthony, on the "better" part of town, where they had sidewalks and lawns that never burned brown from the sun due to a lack of city-planted trees. Early on, she wondered if maybe she should've moved and enrolled him at Eastside High, where there were more Black and Latino kids. Maybe he wouldn't be so comfortable being so mouthy. But she'd wanted him to have a better shot at good classes. And he had gotten into the Texas A&M engineering program, so no one could say she had failed in her efforts.

They rode a while in silence. They passed a few groups of Eggheads on the way. Mostly teams of two and three people. All focused on the ground. With a $50,000 payout this year, she guessed she couldn't expect to be the only ones out at 7:00 a.m. None of them were in team T-shirts, so that was good. Teams had been at it longer than most. Years. They knew that it was too early in the contest to win, but she thought it'd be good to get a feel for how she and Elijah would work together.

"What's our team name?" Elijah asked, pointing at the Eggheads. Before she could answer, he flicked his head to the side dramatically. "We'll call ourselves the Golden Egg Girls."

She rolled her eyes and let him have his way. As long as he didn't ask for a custom T-shirt, she didn't care.

She tried to swallow her irritation at seeing other Eggheads along the route and not having Anthony with her, but it was hard. Those people were looking in the wrong places anyway. All they'd find were free tickets to see a washed-up '80s hair band at the fairgrounds.

"Any news about this mystery woman Nell's been seeing?" she asked, trying to get his mind off his dad and all his disappointment in Nell. She wasn't a gossip. She wasn't like Maggie. Whenever Anthony wasn't around, she and Elijah would chat like this.

Nell had had plenty of girlfriends over the years, from all backgrounds and ethnicities, like a Benetton women's wear ad from the '90s. No one serious. No one secret. It's not like she was in the closet. Ada sometimes even teased Nell and called her a dog, like a man, even as Ada toyed with Nell herself, sitting right up close, with no intention of taking it further than that. But after so long without, Ada couldn't resist Nell's attention. It felt good to feel like something other than a caretaker. Not knowing who Nell was running around with made Ada's insides twist with what she realized was jealousy, a feeling she hadn't felt since she couldn't even remember. A feeling she didn't altogether understand when it came to Nell. They were friends. And Ada didn't date women. At least she hadn't.

"She's sneaking around like it's *Romeo and Juliet* or some shit," Elijah said. "It's embarrassing."

"I'm sure she has her reasons." Not everybody could be happy-go-gay like Elijah, even if it was a veneer. Still, Ada wondered why Nell was sneaking around—and why she hadn't told Ada. "She's been through a lot."

"And I haven't?" Emotions clouded his face. Just like his aunt Nell.

"I'm not saying you weren't affected," she said. "But Nell and your dad were close. And she was so young. It changed her life."

"It changed mine too." He paused and looked off to the distance. "As soon I graduate, I'm getting the fuck out of here."

"Mouth," she said, and he smiled, his sulkiness retreating. When he was barely six years old, he'd started testing out whatever dirty word came his way.

Unlike Anthony, Elijah had not gotten an acceptance letter because he hadn't applied. Elijah wanted nothing to do with college. He had his sights set on New York. Waiting on tables and living on the streets like it was some sort of education for artists. Who knew what kind. He never elaborated when she asked, just said, *You know, art shit.*

"Have you tried telling Nell why you want to talk about your dad?" Ada asked, deciding to go all in on the conversation, given Elijah's sulkiness.

"Yes, I've tried." He shrugged again, one of his few gestures when he got in his head, like Nell. "It's too hard. For her, that is."

Ada had tried to talk about it with Nell several times, early on when they were getting to know one another, but Nell always stopped when it got to be too much.

Elijah reached for the radio dial. She thwacked his hand and turned up the volume.

"Ow!"

"Hush," she said. "I barely touched you."

Another day has dawned with the morning dew.
It's Rod from KCLS, here with another clue.

In the valley of the shadows, the choir did sing,
Their voices will lead you to a letter in a ring.

"That is, like, the corniest shit I've ever heard," Elijah said. "Did Rod study poetry in college? If so, he should get his tuition back."

Ada ignored him and repeated what Rod had said out loud, trying to parse the meaning.

"Make it make sense," he said, interrupting her recitation.

"It makes sense if you pay attention and you know what's where in town. It's not about geography and looking at the ground. It's a mind puzzle. You have to figure out one clue and then the next, and it all adds up to a bigger picture," she said. "I mean, sometimes there are prizes at the clue locations. So some of those folks we saw, if they go to the right church, which it obviously is, and then go to the right spot for that clue, then there might be an envelope with a gift certificate to Lowe's or Country Kitchen or something. I got a lot of those over the years, but I usually leave them for others so they can have something. It's not—"

"Wow." He laughed. "Anthony was right. You really take this seriously."

For years, she'd put up with her family's and friends' judgment of her desire to find the golden egg that Rod hid around Presley's perimeter. But coming from Anthony? When it had been their thing, ever since Anthony was a baby, barely able to lift his head? That hurt.

She loved Rod's puzzles, stretching her mind to connect one hint to another and then to a place in town where she would scour the ground, hoping for a little glint in the sun that could change her life, if only a little bit. Anthony gurgling behind her in his carrier, drooling onto her neck, helping her forget how she usually felt. Low down and done all wrong. Wondering why William, a sweet but tortured white boy from Oklahoma that her parents had not been pleased about, had decided that a hard life without them was better than a hard life with them. But with the Hunt, her hurt settled.

At first, the grand prizes were only $500 or so. Nothing to someone who had something, but a lot to her. That could buy some necessary—and some fine—things. She'd walk and dream about a new couch. A new bed for Anthony. Christmas presents. Moisturizer that smelled like what her favorite actresses would wear.

Each year, she got closer and closer to the prize. And each year, Anthony would toddle along with her, and then walk, looking with the same fervor as Ada. Adding his own desires to her dreams: a train set, Iron Man pajamas, a karaoke machine, a laptop. But then everything changed the summer before senior year. He got moody, slept in late, wanted to be alone, and then wanted only to be at work, with his new friends—and when he couldn't be, he'd slip in the AirPods she'd bought him for his birthday and shut her out. Hunting without him felt like the last loss before he left her for college.

When she'd threatened to go hunting alone this year, he'd told her to keep him posted about where she went "in case you end up going missing. I need to know the details for the report."

Casual cruelty had become his senior-year specialty. Some of the older women at work had said that was normal. That making their mamas cry was in a teenage boy's DNA. That he'd grow out of it. She hoped they were right.

"Are you okay?" Elijah asked. He could morph from over the top to mature and empathetic in the blink of an eye.

She'd barely noticed that the car was sitting still through a green light, so lost she'd been in her memories.

"I miss Anthony," she said, oddly comfortable in confessing such a private thought. He didn't laugh or make fun of her or roll his eyes. He smiled sweetly.

"I wouldn't take it personally," he said. "Guys are total assholes at this age. Ask me how I know."

"You seem to be doing mostly okay," she said. "What's your secret?"

"I'm wearing my murdered father's clothes for a clandestine meeting with my aunt's coworker she's been hot for forever. I'm not sure if Nell would be more mad at me going hunting with you or spending time alone with you." He laughed and pulled at his jacket. "Aside from all that, I'm hardly okay. I'm barely hanging on."

Ada paused and then laughed to cover her mild shock at what he'd admitted. Nell's attentions hadn't gone unnoticed. But Ada had brushed it off as mild flirting, a little fun among friends. Work wives, everyone had teased. Nothing serious. Or real.

"What do you mean barely hanging on?" She eyed him. "Do I need to worry about you?"

He flicked his eyes her way and then back to the road. "No."

For the remainder of their fifteen-minute ride, they sat in silence. She let him commandeer the radio despite not wanting to miss a clue. Her mind raced with a silly schoolgirl's obsession, Rolodexing through her interactions with Nell, wondering why they'd never done anything more. Maybe because Ada always talked about men. She'd never been with a woman, although she'd thought about it, what it might be like. But it didn't matter. Nell had someone. A secret lover. She couldn't help but think of that Atlantic Starr song. Her mom had played it over and over when Ada was little, swaying in the kitchen while washing dishes.

"This is it," she said and then parked the car along the side of a mostly barren road along Lee Creek, its adjacent empty park, and the park's mostly overgrown trails. Nobody else was around.

The only time the park got any use was for the annual Lee Creek Fest. Nothing like the river festivals down in Little Rock or even over in Fort Smith. Just a sad little show of arts and crafts tents and local bands full of middle-aged men who preferred volume over melody. Face-painted children whose parents took advantage of free activities in the kid zone to get a childcare break.

In the distance loomed the paper factory, pumping out toilet paper and paper towels and tampons since she could remember. Barbed wire protected its grounds. Beyond the scattered treetops lay Oklahoma, where William had disappeared after their divorce. Back home. She wondered what he was doing now. Where he was at. If he ever thought of her and Anthony. She'd done fine without him. Hard, but she'd done it. She hadn't had much of a choice.

"We'll start here," she said, "and then make our way down to the water."

Outside the car, Elijah stretched his long arms to the sky, as if they'd been in the car all day instead of half an hour. "Will it shine?"

"What?" she asked.

"The egg." He looked to the sky. Dark clouds that held the promise of a storm creeped closer to them.

The egg was a closely guarded secret. "I don't know," she said. "Keep your eyes on the ground. Look for something gold, I guess. Or shiny. And walk slow."

They started at the front of the car.

After five minutes, Elijah asked, "Would Rod hide the egg right here in the open? Wouldn't he hide it in the bushes or something?"

She shook her head. "Only the winners know for sure, but Rod would hide it anywhere. So you've got to look everywhere."

They inched forward for a while. She could tell that Elijah wasn't as into the act of hunting as dressing up for the Hunt. Occasionally, he'd pull out his phone and run his index finger across the screen. But they had little service.

"If you're gonna check your phone, then you need to go back to the car."

He rolled his eyes again. "Okay, Mom."

To keep him focused on the task, she asked him about school and other things, like Nell, even though she knew she was pushing it. Getting insider details, like a jealous schoolgirl. But it only made him dig down on his current gripe about Nell working all the time and the usual gripes about being abandoned by his mom.

"Might as well have put me in foster care or something."

"Oh, 'cause that would've been easier? A better life than the one you've got?" she asked and paused to bend down to the ground and move around a clod of what turned out to only be dirt. "She could've walked away when your mom showed up on her doorstep with you in tow. At least she didn't abandon you at the fire station."

"That's so old fashioned." He thwacked another section of tall grass. "My mom could have had an abortion and saved us all the trouble."

Anytime she heard that word, it sank her, reminded her of a hard, long day with a fussy baby, feeling equal measures of gratitude and guilt that she could leave her baby with her mom and go to work. Only half joking with Maggie later that night that sometimes she wished she had gotten an abortion. Because it was hard. Harder than she knew anything could be. And sometimes it didn't feel like the reward that church and society and her mom all said it was. How it felt like she had to simmer and put on a smile so no one would think she was a bad mother. She'd thought she was telling these thoughts to a friend. The closest she'd had since quitting college after getting pregnant. She'd thought she was safe. But Maggie had joked about it one night at the break-room table, unrelated to anything. Everyone—Viv, Janie, and others—talking about motherhood. As if it were no big deal. As if it were Maggie's story to tell. As if it weren't something that Ada had told Maggie in private, in a vulnerable moment. Just venting. What right did she have to share that?

"You think getting an abortion is easy for everyone?" she asked.

"Actually, it is. You can get a pill at Planned Parenthood."

"If it's not been outlawed." She gave him a look. "Most people couldn't get that pill seventeen years ago. Some people didn't even know about it. Then or now. And you think it's easy? Making that kind of decision?" She didn't regret Anthony. Not one bit. But she wished she'd had access to that information. And she bet Elijah's mom had too. Regardless of the outcome, they deserved to know.

"I'm just saying, there are options when shit goes sideways." He whacked at the grass with a long, thin stick he'd found. "It doesn't matter. I'm leaving soon. And then nobody will be annoyed by me wanting to know more about my dad." He looked around. "I'm gonna go take a piss."

She smacked him on the arm. "You sound pitiful."

He grimaced. "How am—"

"You're not the only one who grieves. Not everyone handles shit the same way you do. And you can't force someone to talk about something they don't want to talk about. That's not how life works. So put on your big boy pants or get over it."

He looked like a forlorn puppy, bopped on the nose for eating the furniture. She didn't feel bad for that. She was right. And he needed a bop on the nose more often than not.

"I'm going to relieve myself now," he grumbled. "If that's okay with you."

"You don't need my permission," she said. "But don't go far. And remember your spot. You'll need to start there. And don't miss anything."

"Yes, ma'am," he said and saluted her like a sergeant. He never stayed mad long. She admired that about him. So rotten, but she loved him like her own. A nephew, maybe. But she didn't like how that would make Nell her sister or sister-in-law. And she didn't like how her mind kept drifting over the ground and into thoughts about how she was allegedly someone that Nell wanted to sleep with.

As her mind wandered into areas untoward, she lost her place and had to backtrack a few times. The temperature fell and rose as the sun shifted with the clouds that spit occasionally. But she'd come prepared. Late March in Arkansas meant sweat on your skin one day, sleet the next.

She checked her watch. She'd been out there for an hour. A shocking amount of time, even for her. She'd let herself daydream for too long and couldn't be sure that she'd paid attention to the ground.

She looked up and around her to an unfamiliar landscape, no car in sight. No Elijah. Trees and brush surrounded her, seemed to reach out to snag her clothing. The dark clouds had darkened further, casting everything in shadow. She tucked her hands into her jacket pockets and tried to get her sense of direction but couldn't make heads or tails of which way she'd come. Her phone was no help with one bar of service, when she had that. She tried the compass app, but that didn't help much, considering she didn't even know from which direction she'd come. The ground all around her was flat and full of trees choked with spiraling vines boosted by spring rains, the brush creating green nests that encapsulated everything within reach. Bugs antagonized her. When she tried to backtrack, a thorny bush captured her jeans. She yanked at it until it let go, only to be caught by another during her escape.

How had she not figured out how to use a compass? In all these years of hunting? But she'd gone out with Anthony, who knew where he was at all times. Unlike her, directionally challenged. Anthony, tall and broad shouldered, always a few steps behind, but never completely out of sight. He never left her side, even when he started wearing his headphones to hunt.

The crack of a branch stopped her in her tracks. She spun, slowly, taking in everything. Her pulse beat too loudly and stuffed up her ears.

"Elijah?"

She checked the time on her phone. She'd need to get back to the car soon. Get to the grocery store. Then the pharmacy for Anthony's acne prescription and her Prozac (a prescription she'd fought her doctor for and that her mother told her not to tell her dad about because he'd be disappointed in Ada). Then all the things that had to be done around the house before her shift. The endless cleaning and meal prepping for Anthony while she worked the night shift so he wouldn't eat pork rinds and Dr Pepper for dinner because he was too preoccupied with homework or video games to find something more nutritious. And then her nap. She still had to sleep. She'd come straight from work, and the long night was catching up with her.

"Elijah!" she called. "Cut it out!"

If Elijah had followed her to scare her, then she would beat the living crap out of him. But then she'd have to admit she was scared.

She never should've let him out of her sight. She took a deep breath. Tree limbs creaked. Squirrels and birds ran up and around and down them. She stepped on things like broken tree limbs and underbrush. Leaves.

There had been plenty of tricksters over the years. Some folks had even admitted to trying to scare people away from the Hunt so the odds would be better for them. Getting their kicks by making people even more afraid to hunt. Following them, making people nervous. She'd always had Anthony with her, so no one had bothered them. But she'd heard the stories.

There were schemers, she reminded herself. People who liked to play on others' fears about a killer out there somewhere.

The wind picked up. That's what made the trees whisper. Nothing more.

"Fine. I'm going back to the car." She lifted her voice into the air. A branch. Another crack. Nothing. "Sorry about that. I got caught up thinking about some work thing."

She didn't recognize that rock or that tree. They all looked alike.

A noise. Indistinguishable. Not human. A small animal?

"I need to head back now." Her voice, she had to keep it calm, steady. She had to channel Anthony. "I've got work tonight."

A laugh from behind a bush.

She spun around, heart not keeping pace with her desire for calm. *Don't lose your grip. You're tired. Overtired. Hearing things that aren't there. That happens when people get tired.* She'd read it in a book about sleep. *Hallucinating. Or hearing things and thinking there's danger when there's not. Don't freak out. There's nothing there. And if there is someone there, it's an Egghead, fooling with you.*

Nothing around her but shades of green and a few patches of brown grass that had yet to revive with the changing season. She looked to the sky.

"It looks like rain." Her voice shook. She glanced around her. "We better run to the car to avoid getting soaked."

Nothing. Nothing but her pulse pounding in her ears, her throat. Screaming, *Run.*

Shared Google Doc / The Hunt

VICTIM #9

In 2013, Annalee Raleigh, white, sixteen, was found dead in a pasture off Sixth Street and Morrilton Road from a gunshot wound to the head. Based on evidence collected at the scene, authorities determined the wound to be self-inflicted. Annalee's parents, Alice and Aaron, who are active members of First Baptist Church of Presley and respected community members, requested a new autopsy, indicating they believed Annalee's death could be attributed to a pattern of deaths surrounding the annual Hunt for the Golden Egg, lending credence to rumors that have plagued the Hunt for the Golden Egg almost since its inception. They insisted the gun found on the scene—whose serial number had been removed—did not belong to Annalee, nor did they recognize it from her family's collection. The second autopsy results were inconclusive. Upon the denial of the authorities to open a new inquiry into Annalee's death, Alice Raleigh rallied others in Presley to shut down the Hunt, to no avail.

Since then, a growing number of people have come out in favor of ending the annual Hunt for the Golden Egg, while an equal number of fans, including local business organizations and the Chamber of Commerce, insist the Hunt is a safe, family-friendly event that brings an infusion of much-needed tourism dollars to local businesses in Presley.

Annalee Raleigh searched for the egg with three of her friends the day before her death.

Three

Ada

Saturday, March 26
Morning
Twenty-two days before Easter

Ada flew through the brush, cutting at it with her arms like Elijah's machete but feeling the rip of thorns and sharp vines at her wrists where her sleeves rode up. Her feet crashed against the hard ground. They already ached from standing on the concrete floor at work all night. She stumbled, no grace, no speed. Just barreling through, away. She ran and ran, sweat soaked and itching from the brush. So long her lungs and legs burned with exertion.

She paused to catch her breath and caution a glance behind her. She had no idea where she was.

When she looked up, she found her escape.

She hadn't climbed a tree since she was a girl, probably never would have again. But fear and desperation would make a person do dumb things. She grasped onto the branches and lifted herself up above the brush. She wasn't sure she'd be able to get back down. But it was better than standing there doing nothing, vulnerable as she tried to get her bearings. At the top she caught her breath. She was able to focus long enough to see past other trees. There, off to the right, in the opposite direction, was the road. And farther up, her car. All she had to do was walk back the way she'd come, through the woods. First, she'd have to let her adrenaline cool down. Her heart still felt about to beat out of her chest.

She waited, listening. Had she dreamed the laughter she heard? Her mind so scattered and scared it'd created a bogeyman out of nothing? She watched the ground for what felt like hours, until she couldn't wait anymore. She had to pee and she was hungry and she had to get back home and eke out some sleep before another night of work.

Finally, she eased herself down, bear-hugging the tree trunk the whole time until she reached the last sturdy branch and hung by both arms. She looked around her before letting go and dropping to the ground.

The climb had invigorated her, made her less fearful. Still, she found a stick that already had a sharp point to it and took off on a fast walk in the direction of the road and her car. She swore to herself she wouldn't run. She wouldn't let some unfounded fear commandeer her mind again.

When she finally reached her car, every part of her was damp and hours had passed.

She looked all around and shouted Elijah's name.

"Shit." Maybe he'd gone home when she had gotten lost in the woods—a fact she'd never mention to anyone, ever. But a deeper fear wriggled its way into her head: the Hunter.

She closed her eyes, breathed deeply to settle her nerves.

Foolishness. That's all that was. Elijah had probably gotten bored. Probably walked home or, God forbid, hitched a ride with someone.

She checked her watch again. The sun beat down on her, much warmer than it'd been when they'd first left the car. She wandered down to the edge of the woods again to see if maybe he was there, feeling more defeated than she liked and more anxious each step she took. She didn't want to go back into the woods. But what could she do? She couldn't leave him. Maybe he had called Anthony. Or he'd called Nell. If so, Ada would never hear the end of it.

Worried, she looked out into the trees and the bushes. So spring green and bright on the outside, dark and foreboding within. "Elijah!"

Nothing. She called out again and again.

As time passed and sleep and hunger pressed on her, she reconciled herself to having to call Nell. But her bladder had waited long enough, and it couldn't wait any longer. The pain was at a high point. The air had become thick with humidity. A cold sweat prickled her skin. She swiped a hand across her brow and scanned the options. She could pee by the side of the car, but cars had come and gone from around the curve with no warning. With no other option, she headed toward the woods again, her bladder pressing ever more urgently. As she ran toward the woods, she tripped in a hole. A little bit of urine seeped out, and before things could get worse, she jogged, all the while undoing the buttons on her jeans and then the zipper. She went for the first tree, pushed her pants and underwear down, and accidentally peed in her underwear, again, before she could get them down all the way.

"No, no, no!" A hard and warm stream wet the leaves beneath where she squatted. She tucked her jeans and panties between her thumb and forefinger and tried to push them away from her so they wouldn't become wetter than they already were. The relief of release was greater than her mortification, though, and she finally sighed. After what felt like forever, she finally stopped. She felt around in the crotch of her panties and jeans, already damp from sweat. The jeans wouldn't be comfortable, but they were dark, so at least she could disguise them. But the panties were soaked. She pulled them both up and quickly decided to ditch the underwear. She got both legs out of her jeans and pulled off her underwear. She rushed to stand and pull up her jeans. She had gotten them up around her waist when she turned and bumped into something hard. She jumped back and screamed, falling to the ground in the process. Ready to punch and kick.

She covered her eyes, and they better adjusted and focused in on someone, tall. Lean.

Elijah. Eating a burrito wrapped in foil. Laughing with a mouth full of food.

"Are those your underwear?" he said, pointing to the discarded cloth on the ground. "You really shouldn't litter."

Shocked at the intrusion, she scrambled to get her focus, her bearings, her jeans zipped. They were covered in dirt. Last pair she had clean too. Add that on top of the other irritations of the day. She picked up her wet underwear, shoved them in her pocket, and hurried away from the woods, from Elijah. She could have died right there. This new embarrassment was worse than climbing up a damn tree.

"Hey, wait up," he yelled after her.

Bringing him had been a mistake. He'd been nothing but trouble. No egg, and now she had wet underwear in her pocket.

"Ada," he yelled after her, laughing. "Stop, or I'll tell Nell that you peed your pants."

She spun and faced him. "What are you? Five?" He must not have expected her to react, because he looked like he'd been slapped, and that only made her want to yell more so he could feel as mortified as she did. "Do you know how long I've been looking for you? Worried about you? And here you are, eating a burrito and threatening me? Laughing at me? How dare you." Before she would let him have a say, she turned on a heel and headed toward the road, that fire inside her raging ever brighter.

He caught up to her, but she wouldn't look at him. Finally, after they walked a spell, he spoke.

"I'm sorry. Your pants were already on. I didn't see anything. Just your underwear on the ground. I swear. I'm not some creeper." When she didn't answer, he continued. "I was walking around looking for you. I didn't see anything. I swear."

"What in the hell were you doing sneaking up on me like that?"

He wiped his mouth with his sleeve. "I was looking for you. Where'd you go?"

She glared at him. "I went into the woods. You were supposed to follow me. We were supposed to go together."

His earlier laughter had morphed into indignation. Brows up and eyes wide. "I told you I had to go pee."

"I waited right there for you!" She hadn't, though. She'd been lost in her thoughts about Nell, falling into the routine she'd had with Anthony.

He looked at his burrito as if he not only had no more appetite but was disgusted with it and then applied the same look to her. "I didn't go anywhere but to pee, and then I came back and you were gone." He let the burrito hang from his left hand and looked off in the distance before reproaching her again. "You left me. And I couldn't find you. And I got hungry. But you have all the snacks in your little fanny pack or whatever."

"Don't you have your backpack?" She was livid. "For emergencies?"

"Yeah, but I didn't bring any snacks because I thought you would. You always have snacks. I walked to the 7-Eleven I saw on the way and bought myself a burrito. But thank you very much for accusing me, a teenager, of somehow being the one who wandered away and got lost in the woods instead of you."

Sometimes she hated how adult he was. How perceptive and correct. How offended and able to turn his attacks onto others to make them feel bad for what they'd done in a way that no other teenager could manage to do. Anthony would never. He could get mouthy with her, but he'd be mortified to talk to any other adult the way Elijah did. But Elijah never let anyone think of him as a kid. He demanded respect.

She rubbed at the back of her neck. "You're probably right—"

"I am right." He never took his eyes off her, placing the blame square on her shoulders.

"Sorry. I must've gotten carried away thinking." She hoped he didn't remember what they'd talked about earlier in the car. About Nell.

When he didn't respond, she said it again. "I'm sorry. But you did scare the shit out of me. I forgive you for that." She poked him in the arm, something she also did to Nell when she got her back up over something dumb Ada had said without thinking first. "Tell me you forgive me."

He screwed up his mouth and finally rolled his eyes. "Fine. I forgive you."

She smiled because she knew he meant it. He never said anything he didn't mean. He never made you think he felt any way other than exactly how he felt about you.

She nodded her head toward his hand. "What kind?" She wanted to veer away from the topic of her underwear, how he'd probably seen her with her pants down despite his insistence he hadn't.

He looked down. "Bean and cheese. Nothing fancy." Without her needing to ask, he offered it, and she took it. Wordlessly, they walked back to the car. The burrito tasted like salvation in that moment. Only on the walk did she realize how hungry she'd been, how amped up and anxious about having to tell Nell that she'd lost Elijah. Like Nell had lost her brother.

She couldn't let those thoughts intrude. They were fine. Elijah was fine. She was fine, if a little ego bruised. Still, she shook her head in confusion once they were at the car, on opposite sides, looking over the hot roof, the metal creating wavy illusions between them like a mirage. "I don't know how I missed you."

He twirled in his camo.

She laughed before exhaling long and deep. "We should call it a day."

Elijah nodded and proceeded to enter the car. She didn't have the energy to clarify that meant calling it off entirely. She couldn't risk another terror like losing him again.

Facebook Post: Nancy Barker

Sunday, March 27

Friends! I'm happy to report that the pressure we have applied to shut down the Hunt for the Golden Egg is WORKING. Please see the video of our protest at KCLS below for PROOF that we are making an impact. In case you somehow did not know, that's Rod Halstrom, KCLS station owner. Fast-forward to the :58 second mark to see how he lashes out and calls us foul names, like a child. What self-respecting man flips off a bunch of churchgoing fellow citizens who are simply SICK of him and the city IGNORING our requests that Presley shut down the Hunt, which has been responsible for SEVENTEEN DEATHS?!

While Lloyd and I—and our dear friends, the Raleighs—are thrilled by the online response, I PERSONALLY am less than thrilled with the turnout. Please please please, if you RSVP, SHOW UP! We need all the support we can get right now to SAVE OUR CHILDREN. Don't let another mother and father bury their child this year because of the greed of Rod, the so-called Eggheads (WHAT A STUPID NAME!!), and the small business owners in Presley who should know better.

LET'S KEEP UP THE PRESSURE!!

Four

Ada

Thursday, March 31
Evening
Seventeen days before Easter

The break room had gotten noisy now that it was going on ten till clock-in time. Viv was telling everyone about her upcoming three days off after Easter. Janie, who should've been cleaning up from her shift, and Marcy and Phonesavanh all oohed and aahed. Juanita didn't pay much attention to anyone, choosing to ignore them all as usual. Viv planned to head up to Eureka Springs to see the Great Passion Play and the Christ of the Ozarks, as she did every year. Didn't even talk about Eureka Springs. Probably didn't set foot in town on account of all the rainbow flags.

"Oh, I've been there," Ada said when Viv finally stopped to catch a breath. "Did you know that statue was put up in the sixties by some white supremacist who didn't believe the Holocaust was real?" That thing was also covered in bugs. Every church youth group, including Ada's, got dragged up there at some point.

Viv's glare could've burned holes in Ada, but she didn't care. She just smiled.

"That was a long time ago," Viv said.

"Not that long." Ada chewed her spearmint gum and pushed back in her chair. She glanced at Nell, but she wasn't paying attention or was intentionally ignoring Ada, which panicked her for a moment. Nell usually had some smart remark about Ada getting people stirred up before shift and leaving Nell to clean up the mess. Maybe Elijah had told Nell that they'd gone hunting.

"Anyway . . . ," Viv said and kept going about the boring details of the "darling" B and B where she and her husband always stayed. Probably still had a **Whites Only** sign in the office as a "joke." Only Phonesavanh and Marcy stuck around for it; Janie finally went back out onto the floor, and Juanita wandered to the restroom. But even Phonesavanh and Marcy looked like they wanted to get out of the conversation. They were too polite to interrupt her, though.

The only reason they were talking about Viv's trip instead of the Hunt was because Nell sat at the table with them, scrolling through her phone with a frown.

"What's wrong?" Ada nudged her while Viv carried on.

Nell clicked it off and shoved it in her back pocket. "Nothing."

Before Ada could bug her any more about it or confirm that Nell was mad at her, Lloyd walked in.

"Evening, folks!" He grabbed an Ensure out of the fridge.

"Whew. Tying one on early, huh?" Ada joked.

Lloyd laughed; Nell didn't.

Lloyd patted his stomach. It wasn't even big. "Nancy's got her meeting tonight, so supper's gonna be late."

Ada wanted to ask why he didn't stay home and make supper for Nancy instead. But Ada didn't like Nancy all that much, what with her going around talking about the Hunt like it was the work of the devil. The meeting was likely about that. She got real into it, taking notes from the Satanic Panic in the late '80s and '90s. Ada was never sure if Lloyd believed the Hunt was a bad thing, too, or if he didn't have the energy to fight Nancy on it. But he was kind enough to know April was a hard month for Nell and Elijah. And a lot of other families. He always went out of his way to ensure Nell was doing okay.

One time, Nell and Elijah had gone with Lloyd and Nancy to church because Lloyd had done something nice for them and then Nell felt kind of obligated to go when he asked. Ada couldn't judge, she'd done the same when Lloyd did something nice for her. When it came time for the prayer-requests portion, Nancy pointed at Nell and Elijah, called them out in front of everyone as the first victim's family. Everyone then rushed to lay hands on Nell and Elijah.

Ada about died laughing when Nell told her. She told Nell if she wanted to go to church, she should log on to Ada's. They streamed Sunday services over Facebook. You could take a pee or do chores or even work out while listening. And that was before the pandemic. Her parents were still miffed she'd stopped going in person.

Ada must've sighed loudly and not noticed because Lloyd asked her if she was feeling okay. She told him she could use a vacation, to which he laughed. She was always trying to get more days off out of him for fun, even if it never worked. But it didn't hurt to try.

"How are you doing today, Nell?" Lloyd asked after Ada's unsuccessful bid for additional days off.

Nell smiled warmly and lied about how she was doing fine. Ada knew it was fake. Nell never asked for days off. If anything, Lloyd had to force her to take them.

"The latest clue is—" Maggie said when she entered the room and swiftly cut herself off when she saw Nell, who raised her eyes to Maggie but kept her frown. Nell left the break room and walked out to the plant floor. Viv wandered off too. Probably found someone on the first shift she hadn't talked at yet about her Jesus Adventure.

Lloyd ignored Maggie, probably because he had to sit next to her all day and needed a break from her face. "I'll be in my office for a bit longer if you need me," he said. "If I don't see y'all before I leave, have a good night!"

They all said good night in return, and he wandered back into the hallway where his and Maggie's offices were located. He'd probably stay until about 7:30 p.m. or so, then pack up to meet Nancy at home after her meeting.

As soon as he left, Maggie reanimated. "Oh, I wish Viv hadn't wandered off. I was gonna say, the latest clue dropped."

Ada hadn't heard it yet. Rod usually didn't drop one in the middle of the workday. Sometimes, that meant he was drawing things out for sponsorship reasons, creating confusion to get folks off track.

"I texted y'all what it said and my thoughts based on our last outing." Maggie glanced at Ada and then the rest of the women. All but Ada and Juanita had joined Maggie's hunt team. "Don't let anyone sneak a peek," she joked.

Phonesavanh immediately checked her phone. She scrolled and stood and walked out of the room, eyes fixated on the new clue. Marcy followed soon thereafter.

That left only Ada and Maggie in the break room.

Maggie scooted out a chair and sat right across from her. She peeled the top off a fat-free yogurt from the mini fridge she kept near her desk because she was too fancy to use the common one in the break room.

"How's your Hunt going?" Maggie asked.

After the shit show with Elijah, Ada hadn't been back out again. But Ada told her it was going fine because she didn't want to hear it.

"Hmm," Maggie said and swiped a spoon through the creamy mixture. "Anthony's working at Best Buy, right?" She placed the spoon in her mouth and then turned it upside down to lick the curved side while thinking. She widened her eyes and lasered her focus onto Ada. "Does that mean you're going it alone this year?"

"Yes," Ada lied. She wasn't one of those Jesus teetotalers. A little white lie here and there didn't do too much harm, if you considered the context and didn't aim to hurt.

"Why don't you join us?" *Us* being Viv, Phonesavanh, Janie, Marcy, and Maggie. "It'd be a lot safer."

Ada raised an eyebrow. "Thought you didn't believe in the Hunter."

Maggie had gone back to her yogurt. She scraped the sides of the little plastic container, trying to eke out every last drop. "I don't. But there's no denying that it can be a hazard if you're not careful."

"I'm careful, so you don't need to trouble yourself."

Maggie reached out a hand to Ada. Ada stared at it there on the table and then grimaced.

"We'd be more than happy to let you join us," Maggie said. "Even though that'd cut into some of our winnings."

"This isn't the lottery," Ada said. "And I'm not about to split my winnings five ways. I'm doing just fine on my own."

"You're awfully sure of yourself!" Maggie laughed.

"With good reason," Ada said, seething. Thankfully, it was time to clock in. She let the break-room door close behind her and the noise from the presses fill her ears to ward off the urge to go out hunting alone, which she had been considering but kept putting off.

The next five hours inched by. Everyone yawned, probably on account of the sedative that was Viv's story. Even Nell wasn't up for chatting, ratcheting up Ada's worry. Ada hated nights like these. Normally, she'd put on her headphones, but even that wouldn't alleviate the boredom.

She replaced a full cardboard box of milk caps from press number one with an empty one, taped up the sides of the full box, and then placed it on the pallet. Same thing she'd done for years. She stretched and yawned and decided to take her lunch break a little before midnight. No sense in seeking out Nell. She was back on her bullshit, sneaking out to see her secret lover after that one-night reprieve.

Ada hollered over at Viv to watch her press. They couldn't really hear each other over the noise, but Viv gave her the thumbs-up.

She grabbed her lunch container and headed out to the bench.

The temperature was milder than it had been. Nell had let them pull the plant doors wide open. Otherwise, Ada wouldn't have come out to the bench alone right before midnight.

That last outing with Elijah had spooked Ada. She always told Anthony and anyone else—and Nell, though in a softer, more sensitive tone—that the Hunter was nothing but a bogeyman, conjured from boredom by townsfolk. But deep down, she knew there was something off about it. Why would all those people turn up dead? And right before Easter? Her mouth said one thing, but her heart and mind had been fighting her all these years. Telling her that she was a shitty person for going out searching for gold while people died.

Moments later, she made for her car, where she kept a bottle of mixed medicine, from pain relievers to Pepto. She dry swallowed some ibuprofen. Before she could shut the car door, the front door to the plant opened, and Nell stepped out. Ada couldn't help but smile at the unexpected opportunity to hang out again.

But then Nell looked around and rushed behind the building.

"What the hell?" Ada whispered.

Despite the darkness and her earlier fears, Ada tiptoed around the building. Nell was nowhere behind it. She searched the area and saw the beginnings of a trail that led into the woods, the weeds and ground tamped down and the branches pulled aside. In the distance, the sound of running. A motor. Her heart thumped.

She walked for a few minutes before finally coming to a clearing she hadn't expected to be there. She shouldn't have been surprised to see Nell there, given she'd followed her through the woods behind the factory, but she was.

She couldn't see much, but she could see enough to know a white woman with long dark hair sat on the open tailgate of a boxy car, legs wrapped around Nell, whose body leaned into the woman's. Nell clasped the woman by the rear and yanked her closer, a move that elicited a laugh from the woman and then a gasp as Nell's hands wound their way beneath the woman's shirt and up her back, deftly removing the woman's shirt as she went. Nell tangled her fingers into the woman's hair before cupping her face and kissing her like lovers did in the movies.

An indescribable feeling rushed through Ada. She had to catch her breath.

Nell grabbed the bottom edges of her own T-shirt and pulled it off.

Branches thwacked Ada as she rushed to get away, back to the factory, snagging one of her braids. A knot grew in her stomach at seeing with her own eyes the reality of what she'd suspected and maybe had not wanted to believe.

Behind her, the chatter and laughter stopped. She heard an unfamiliar voice ask, "What was that?"

A hoot owl came to Ada's rescue, calling out and relieving Ada of the need to haul ass back to the plant to pretend she hadn't seen what she had.

Shared Google Doc / The Hunt

VICTIM #13

Adam Acosta, Mexican American, forty-one, was reported missing by his wife, Lisa, white, forty-one, when he did not return from his bowling tournament on April 13, 2017. Lisa arrived at the bowling alley and discovered that there had been no bowling tournament since the previous year. The cops told Lisa to "go home and wait twenty-four hours" in case Adam "got lost and was trying to find his way home from the bar or something." Lisa said she was furious by their inaction and proceeded to call all her friends and family, including members of Presley's anti-Hunt group, of which Lisa is an active participant, to create a search party.

The search party found Adam three days after Lisa reported him missing to the authorities. Autopsy reports indicate that Adam died from bleeding out after stepping on three animal traps while out hunting for the golden egg, an activity he kept hidden from Lisa due to her objections to the Hunt.

The traps were presumably hidden from view and did not have owner-identification data on them, as is required by Arkansas law.

Additionally, the traps appeared in an area that had previously had trespassing signs posted, as noted by the landowner and neighbors. Though the police report stated that the signs had been present when they arrived, we spoke with the landowner, who noted that it looked like someone had "fooled with the signs." When asked for clarification, he pointed out that the signs looked like they'd been taken down and put up again based on the way the bark and nails looked.

Also, police were unable to fully explain the existence of additional footprints on the scene, saying that they "could have been anyone hunting there before Adam that day."

Five

Nell

Thursday, March 31
Before midnight
Seventeen days before Easter

Nell pulled back the branches and stepped into the clearing from the little midnight trail she'd created from walking back and forth from work to the woman who sat on the open hatchback of her car.

Tessa, white and white-collar, black hair skimming the middle of her back, body by Anytime Fitness, where she spent most days outside work and away from Nell.

Elijah's mom.

If he found out, he'd never forgive Nell. Not ever. But the roaring in Nell's head couldn't compete with those other urges. At least not tonight.

Nell and Tessa had only come out here a handful of times. Neither liked the idea of renting a room by the hour or making out in the back forty of the Walmart. When Nell had first suggested this copse of oak trees out near work, Tessa had hesitated, despite Nell's reassurances they'd be safe.

Tessa had shaken her head, her skin going so pale she looked like a ghost. "You don't know that."

They'd gone out on similar nights. Nell and Tessa and Garrett, summers and then when Garrett was home on the weekends from college at the U of A. Nothing else to do, so they drove back roads in Nell's used Nissan. Drank wine coolers because it sounded like the kind of dumb fun that would pass the time. Until that night.

"What's that?" Tessa asked, looking off into the woods from where she sat bare chested on the tailgate of her Honda, Nell wrapped between her legs. Despite Nell's repeated assurances that no one would see them, Tessa still got jittery every time they met out in the woods. She never wanted to show up before Nell. They'd heard too many stories of the bogeyman as kids and then the Hunter as adults.

Nell paused and reluctantly removed her mouth from one of Tessa's nipples. She placed her head to the side to listen. "I don't hear anything." An owl, maybe. That's all it was.

"What about him?"

Him. Tessa didn't need to say who.

Tessa had been talking about him a lot lately. "Do you think he killed Garrett? The Hunter?"

Nell had never thought so. But the more Tessa talked about it, the more Nell considered if the rumors could be true, after she'd spent all those years thinking otherwise.

"Movie villains do like to kill people having sex," Nell said by way of distraction, inching her way back up Tessa's body. "So maybe you should keep your hands off me."

Tessa finally turned away from the woods. "They usually only kill teenagers, which we're not." In high school, they'd rented and watched every single horror movie Presley's local Blockbuster had to offer.

"Well, Presley's famed serial killer usually only picks one person to kill at a time," Nell said. "And the Hunter always ensures it looks like an accident. At least that's what they say. Assuming he's real. But we should put our shirts back on. In case he changes his MO."

Tessa laughed quietly and then turned her attention to a rusty nail on the tailgate, picking at it with a fingernail. "We shouldn't joke about it."

Pretending not to be bothered by anything had been Nell's coping mechanism since she'd modified her other coping mechanisms—excessive amounts of alcohol, drugs, gambling—when Elijah came along. She didn't think it'd be a good idea to break down as a guardian. Though she wanted to. Sometimes she did. In the shower. Usually when she knew she was in the house alone.

"What else are we supposed to do, then?" Nell asked.

"I don't know." Tessa crossed her arms over her bare chest and looked out into the woods before turning back to Nell. "But I guess we can't have sex."

"I didn't say we can't!" Nell grabbed Tessa around her waist and pushed her farther back into the hatchback. She hopped up and straddled Tessa, their heads up against the back seat, their legs hanging off. It'd be easier in Nell's truck, but she didn't want to explain to Ada or anyone else where she was going during her thirty-minute lunch break. "I said we shouldn't if we don't want a *Friday the 13th* situation on our hands. I'm willing to take my chances. Aren't you? I mean, if it's our last night on earth, wouldn't you want to be doing this?"

Tessa laughed. "I suppose."

She didn't say what they were probably both thinking: If it were their last night on earth, they wouldn't want to get caught with their pants down, together. She didn't want to add more death without an explanation to Elijah's plate. One was enough.

In those years since Tessa had dropped Elijah at Nell's house, Tessa had gone back to school. Worked in marketing at an IT company in Fort Smith. Deposited money into Nell's savings account every month, which she then deposited into Elijah's savings account. He knew where the money came from, but he never wanted to talk about that. She guessed she could understand his point, but she had hoped that he might come around one day.

"Have you thought more about what we talked about?" Nell asked. "The letter?"

Tessa shook her head.

Nell had suggested that Tessa write a letter to Elijah to get her feelings down on paper before trying to talk to him. Nell often wondered if the delay was because she and Tessa had started sleeping together. If it had put a pin in all Tessa's earlier plans. Like knowing Elijah through Nell might be enough for her. 'Cause then she wouldn't be rejected. She could just know him from the sidelines.

"I don't know if I'm ready." She paused. "Has he said anything?"

Nothing good, so Nell said no.

"I'm sorry," Tessa finally said. Her voice had gotten lower. She sniffled. "I know it's not fair to you. Talking." She paused. They were both thinking the same thing, and it wasn't about the talking. "And asking you not to tell him."

"Don't apologize. You're trying. That's what counts."

Nell knew Tessa was trying to figure out a future that included all of them. But Nell didn't know what kind of future was possible, especially with Elijah's feelings about Tessa. But Nell had loved Tessa. Still did. That's what made it so goddamn hard. Sometimes, Nell wished they could slip back into that space they'd occupied before everything had become so complicated, the normalcy of the before. Where the day went exactly according to plan. The days when Nell had a good mom and a good dad and a good brother and she didn't have any troubles. All Nell had wanted was to be in that warm, good place where everything was great and nothing was wrong and her whole life was still ahead of her, not this messy after-and-also-in-between state with all this baggage.

Eventually, Tessa's fingers wandered inside Nell's jeans and between her legs, not letting the denim get in her way. Guilt crackled within Nell. Sometimes it felt bad to feel so nice with her, given they had only reconnected because Tessa wanted to see Elijah again.

Nell had gotten calls from this one number. No voice mails. Finally, she had picked up. Hearing Tessa's voice had shocked her into silence.

While Nell breathed into the phone, Tessa broke down. She apologized for leaving Elijah. Nell sometimes still got mad about it. But she couldn't be all that mad. Tessa had saved her, in a way. Nell probably would've ended up dead by now if she hadn't had Elijah to worry about.

They talked on the phone more after that. Then they met up in person, followed by too-long, too-tight hugs. There were quick kisses on the cheek that eventually slipped closer to their lips. And then there was that first night out here in Tessa's car. Colder than cold, even with Tessa's emergency blanket wrapped around them. But it had felt right. Like they were teenagers again, finding lost time. Tessa had come out of nowhere, after so many years, needing comfort, a friend, someone who didn't need a map and legend for her pain.

Tessa moaned against Nell's neck. That was the greatest sound Nell had ever heard. A sound she had dreamed about and never thought possible in high school. Being with Tessa now felt like time traveling. Sneaking around, keeping their mouths quiet while their bodies crashed into each other and swelled and swelled like they might explode.

Afterward, Nell pulled the blanket tight around them, trying to trap the heat from their bodies even as their feet dangled off the edge of the tailgate. They couldn't lie there long. Nell only got thirty minutes for her lunch break, and it took five minutes to walk to their meeting spot from the plant. Five minutes back. That didn't leave much room for romance.

"We should've done this a long time ago," Tessa said after their bodies stilled, her voice sleepy and sweet.

"I tried," Nell said. "Trust me." *But you chose my brother,* Nell thought.

"Sorry I ruined it." Tessa sounded serious.

"I'm joking." Nell kissed her on the head. "You didn't ruin anything. This is perfect."

"Yeah, if your idea of perfect is absolutely fucked up," Tessa said. "If only—"

"Shh." Nell kissed her. She didn't like thinking or hearing about how things could've been, because they weren't time travelers. They were adults who had lived their lives and had to deal with what they had, not what they wished they had.

They were only together now because of something awful.

Early on, when she and Tessa had become friends, her mom had said, *That girl ain't nothing but trouble wrapped in good packaging.* She had laughed when she said it, but there'd also been something else that Nell hadn't understood at the time.

Nell had thought a lot over the years about her mom's warning. Nell and Tessa hadn't come from wholly different backgrounds or belonged to different cliques in high school. They weren't the "good girl, bad girl" combo. They hung around the same people. Went to the same church. Liked most of the same things. Listened to PJ Harvey and Hole and Liz Phair on repeat on shared headphones to and from football games. Their parents were friendly.

It wasn't until later that she understood her mom's meaning; she knew that Tessa would break Nell's heart. But her mom didn't know that Garrett had broken her heart first, sneaking around with Tessa without telling Nell. Her best friend and her brother, a brother who knew how Nell felt about Tessa, how Nell wanted more than friendship, who had listened to all of Nell's obsessive crush wonderings and what-ifs about Tessa. A brother who knew how much it would hurt Nell. Nell's mom didn't know that her daughter's completely normal yet over-the-top teenage jealousy would be the thing that tore their family apart. That would tip Nell over the edge one otherwise uneventful night, when she had gotten so mad, so suddenly, with the secret and the lies, that she'd forced Garrett out of the car and taken off, Tessa screaming the whole time as the outline of Garrett's body faded and then disappeared in the red taillights. Nell finally pulled over the car. Cried and carried on, jealous for reasons she couldn't admit to Tessa at the time. And Tessa in hysterics, convincing Nell to go back and get Garrett. So they did. But he wasn't there.

Nell and Tessa were the last ones to see him alive.

Tessa didn't blame Nell outright and out loud after it happened. But it was loud enough to Nell, who could feel it in the downturned eyes, puffy with tears. Eventually, Nell dropped out of school and began her career as a casino kid, begging for change, sleeping wherever, and getting drunk on the bottom-of-the-glass leftovers of other patrons. Nell had never expected to see Tessa again. Not ever.

But then Tessa came back with a kid—the spitting image of Garrett at that age—clinging to her legs, looking up at Nell, all scared. Turns out Garrett had forgotten his condom, and Tessa hadn't expected a baby to pop out months later. Hadn't expected that she'd have to take care of that baby alone. That that baby would look so much like Garrett that the only thing she could think to do was tell his daddy's sister, her ex–best friend, that she couldn't live with that face looking at her every day or she might go mad. Tessa hadn't looked like a junkie or an alcoholic or anything like what you hear about women who abandon their babies. Nell had never seen someone so broken.

So now Nell had to look at her dead brother's features on Elijah's face every single day instead and try to reconcile why she wasn't just talking to Tessa after all these years but doing the things they did on Tessa's tailgate. Even after Tessa had abandoned Elijah.

Tessa zipped up her jeans, sat up. Nell followed suit. Her stomach grumbled.

"Sorry for taking your lunch break," Tessa said. She rearranged her shirt so it wasn't all twisted around her body.

"I'm not." Nell positioned herself around Tessa. Wrapped her legs and arms around her. Squeezed tight. Nell's chest against Tessa's back, their breaths synchronizing. Buried her nose in her hair. She'd always smelled like she'd come fresh from the shower. Even after cheerleading practice. Even after sex.

"Do you think Elijah will ever talk to me?" Tessa finally asked.

Nell tried to stay positive as a general rule. She wanted things to work out for Tessa and Elijah. She wanted them to have a relationship.

She didn't know how they could. Elijah and Tessa were like oil and water.

"I don't know," Nell finally said. "It might take some time." It's what Nell always said because she didn't want to lie. Anytime they spoke about Elijah in this way, instead of general information about who he'd become and what he was like, Nell punted the conversation to something else. She'd check her watch and claim she needed to leave. She knew what they were doing wasn't gonna last long. How could it?

Tessa let out a little breath, like she wanted to speak but decided not to. Nell guessed there were still too many words that Tessa couldn't say. Tessa choked a little but gathered herself. "It's hard to explain what I did." She waited for Nell to say something. When she didn't, Tessa continued. "I love you. You know that, right?"

"I know," Nell said. She couldn't think of what else to say. Words seemed stuck in her chest. She squeezed Tessa a little tighter.

"Are you mad at me?" Tessa asked after a while. Maybe because Nell hadn't said she loved her back. She'd said it before. Many times.

"Why would I be mad at you?" Nell kissed her cheek and offered a hint of a laugh, but her voice cracked.

"Because I fucked up so bad." Tessa fussed with the ring her parents had bought her when she turned sixteen. A delicate gold band. Could've been mistaken for a wedding ring. Nell had even joked and asked if it was a purity ring from Tessa's dad.

"You didn't fuck up." Nell unwound herself from around Tessa's body and sat next to her instead. Everything in her was screaming at her not to ruin what good they had found in a horrible situation. But there was that lump in her throat she'd been swallowing down since Tessa had first called her. "You did what you thought was right for Elijah."

Time was running out. Tonight. And otherwise.

KCLS 103.9 FM Commercial Transcript

First aired Thursday, March 31, 2022

Hey, headbangers! It's Rod Halstrom here with the latest from the greatest classic-rock station in Arklahoma. We'll be down at the Wu Subaru dealership this coming Saturday from 10:00 a.m. to 4:00 p.m. for their big pre-Easter cash bash, where you can spin the wheel for discounts ranging from 5 percent to 10 percent off your purchase price on a new or used Subaru, and all your favorite station swag, including tickets to the hottest events in Presley. And this year, you'll want to take a spin because we're giving away one FREE, exclusive, and private clue for our annual Hunt for the Golden Egg, which has all of Presley abuzz.

That's right! Despite what you may have heard, the Hunt for the Golden Egg is still on!

With prizes this hot, how can you stay home? Come see us this Saturday at Wu Subaru!

Six

Ada

Thursday, March 31
Before midnight
Seventeen days before Easter

Ada peeked around the corner of the factory to ensure no one was outside. She didn't want to have to explain what she'd been doing back there, especially to Maggie. Maggie would tell everyone Ada had been sneaking around outside in the middle of the night, and would laugh and make jokes and come up with stories for why. Nell would guess what she'd been doing in a heartbeat. But Ada also didn't want to go back inside. She still had twenty minutes left on her break.

She wandered back to her car and turned on the ignition. She fussed with the section of braid that had been snagged. Roy Orbison crooned from the speakers, talking about crying, lulling her into feeling the same, even though she shouldn't. Nell was just a coworker. A friend. A good friend. Ada didn't even date women, though she'd wondered about it before on dark nights in her room once the hormones hit and she had to hold her stomach tight. Thinking of all those bodies on display in the girls' locker room had made her as uncomfortable as she'd felt at school dances, the boys circling the girls, who were ripe for the picking. Maybe she liked both. Maybe she needed to go on a date and stop acting ridiculous. It'd been forever. She was a little horny, was all, she thought and laughed at herself.

A commercial break interrupted her thoughts. She knew what was coming next. Another clue. The one Maggie had been so secretive about.

She welcomed the opportunity to get the image of Nell and that woman out of her head. But the other thing she was wrestling with was no better: Should she hunt alone? Or should she forget about it? Let those dreams go? They were dumb dreams, she told herself. No better than wishing for a secret relative to leave her money when they died or finding a pot of gold at the end of the rainbow.

That creepy background music played for a few seconds, and then Rod's voice came over the radio to reveal the next clue:

> Peek between the cracks, and you might see some truth.
> But don't linger too long, for the Hunter is on the loose.

"Hunan Palace. Fortune cookies. Duh," she said to the empty car. Rod had used a similar clue in the past, thinking he was being clever. She thought it was in poor taste to mention the Hunter, but Rod was nothing if not an opportunist.

She sat in her car a while longer, enjoying the slower songs KCLS played at this hour, before hauling herself back in to work for the next six hours. In the break room, she fixed herself a third cup of coffee, even though it'd tear up her stomach.

Right after Ada had poured her coffee and grabbed the sugar bowl, Maggie walked into the break room suddenly. Ada jumped and dropped the glass container she'd been holding. It shattered and covered the floor in little white granules and glass.

Ada looked at Maggie accusingly. They used to have little sugar packets, but Maggie insisted it was more economical to buy in bulk.

"Oh no!" Maggie rushed over, cheeks flushed, worry splashed across her face. "I'm so sorry I startled you!"

Ada closed her eyes, tightened her shoulders to her ears, and then released them. "It's fine."

Maggie could be a fierce competitor in the Hunt and a real gossip, but Ada reminded herself that she usually meant well. Gave Ada lots of hand-me-downs when Anthony was still young. Said they were from her sister's kids over in Dardanelle. Brought in brownies with sugar that cracked between the teeth and made twelve hours go by a lot quicker than without them.

And they'd been friends once. Ada had thought she was nice. But she'd also been young. Maggie was one of those women whose best days were behind her. Probably was on her high school and college reunion committees or some shit. Everything else was just a scene in which to reminisce about how great things had been and tell stories about being a teenager in Presley. Ada had been one too. It didn't require reminiscing.

Ada shoved her coffee cup aside and took off to find a broom in the supply closet. While Ada was busy with that, Maggie had stayed put, standing in a pile of sugar for no discernible reason than she had something to say to Ada that was meant to agitate.

Ada swept with such vigor that she hit Maggie in the leg. She hadn't meant to, but not hunting and not having anything to fill the hole and then seeing Nell making out with that woman had put her on edge.

"Geez, Louise." Maggie laughed when Ada held up her hands in apology. Finally, she shifted her feet away from where Ada was sweeping and wandered over to the soda machine. She jingled coins while perusing her options. "What's got you so riled up?" She looked at Ada sheepishly. Whispered, "This about Nell?"

Ada's insides flared with anger and other emotions she would prefer to purge. "Why would I be any kind of way about her?"

"Okay." Maggie dragged out the vowels in a manner that would've made anyone listening think Ada was someone who didn't have a grip on reality.

Ada took the dustpan and brushed a pile of glass and sugar into it. A thick shard of broken glass steps from Maggie's foot glinted back at

Ada. She hoped Maggie would step on it, cut right through her white fashion sneakers, turn them red.

"What are you even doing here so late? It's after midnight." Ada couldn't keep the irritation out of her voice. "Don't you have a life?" Pretty much everyone assumed Maggie was a spinster who only got out for Friday-night bingo with the church ladies—when it wasn't Hunt season, that is.

Maggie stepped back, her eyes so soft and kind. "I don't mean no harm." Maggie's tone was the kind you'd use with a sullen child. Her warm hand clasped Ada's shoulder. "Is this about the other day? The news crew?"

Ada shrugged it off and glared at her. Ada knew women like her. All smiles and honey words to your face. But she talked shit to anyone who would listen.

"I feel just awful about KAOK showing up so late, and Nell being here," Maggie said. "I figured maybe she—"

"You feel awful about them being here?" Ada asked. "Not about calling them up and asking them to *come* here? When you wear your stupid little shirts and rub it in her face? You're just so darn broken up about it?"

Maggie held a hand to her chest. "I didn't—"

"That wasn't a question." She held the broom handle toward Maggie. "We all know why you do what you do."

Ada flicked the broom handle in Maggie's direction, and Maggie stepped back, so close to that glass that Ada decided to leave it there for spite while Maggie still hovered.

Maggie's eyes moistened with incoming tears. "I—"

"You keep your mouth shut about Nell and everyone else whose business doesn't concern you."

A flicker of indignation crossed Maggie's face. "I'm sorry," she said. She left whatever she had intended on eating in the snack machine and rushed down the hallway toward the front exit, nearly knocking Nell over in the process.

Ada hadn't heard her come in. Nell looked flushed, like she'd been running. She probably had. But that wasn't all she'd done. Red-hot jealousy fired within Ada. The recognition of it as such nearly made her lose her balance.

Nell looked at Maggie and then at Ada. "Everything okay in here?"

Maggie didn't answer. She apologized to Nell in a quiet voice and then rushed outside. Didn't even slam the door behind her. Probably because she knew it'd make her look less guilty and mean if she let it shut quietly.

"What happened?"

Ada could feel the nerves tighten and twist her stomach. "Dropped a sugar bowl and broke it. Guess it was an heirloom."

Nell narrowed her eyes.

Ada rushed back out onto the plant floor and her presses before Nell had a chance to reply or interrogate her.

Shared Google Doc / The Hunt

VICTIM #6

Susan Wisniewski, Asian American, thirty-nine, was last seen at the Holiday Laundromat on March 30, 2010. Earlier that day, according to her husband, James, white, forty-one, she had prepared breakfast, gotten her three grade school–age children ready for school and on the bus, and planned a day of housecleaning. James left for work at 8:30 a.m. and was confirmed by his executive assistant to have been in back-to-back meetings all day until 4:00 p.m., at which point he shut his office door and caught up on emails until 7:00 p.m. He arrived home at 7:30 p.m. Susan's car was not in the driveway, and the lights in the house were off. Upon entering the house, James found several voice mails on the machine from a neighbor who had allowed the children to stay with her while they waited for Susan to return home. James proceeded to search the house for Susan. In the basement, he noted that the washing machine was pulled away from the wall and the laundry detergent and fabric softener were gone. Given their recent washing machine issues, James assumed Susan had gone to the laundromat, as she had done previously.

At midnight, and after several unanswered calls to Susan, James drove to the Holiday Laundromat. James found Susan's car in the parking lot. Inside, he found their laundry basket and two dryers of their clothing, with one clean load piled on a folding table, presumably because another patron had needed to use one dryer. Along with their clothing, James found a paperback novel that belonged to his wife. He recognized the book because Susan had told him about it, a past-life historical romance novel, while preparing for bed a few nights prior to her disappearance. No other trace of Susan was found in the laundromat or anywhere else since.

After a lengthy search and calls for help on KAOK, Arklahoma's regional news station, the family's story eventually faded from the spotlight until 2013, when Annalee Raleigh's family questioned the authorities on the series of strange deaths that occurred in the days leading up to the annual Hunt for the Golden Egg.

In the police interviews we reviewed, a neighbor of Susan's had spotted Susan and the children hunting with an unidentified man two weeks prior to her disappearance. When asked about it, Susan's children mentioned that their mom had asked the man if he wanted to join them, as he was alone and "a noise from the woods had scared her" earlier that morning. The children described the man as "friendly" and "familiar."

The man hunting with Susan and her children has never been identified by police or mentioned in any of the follow-ups. James and his children moved from Presley the year after Susan disappeared.

Susan remains the only active missing person among the Hunter's alleged victims.

Seven

Nell

Friday, April 1
Morning
Sixteen days before Easter

Nell walked into the house at 6:30 that morning, like she did after every shift. The smell of bacon and coffee pulled at her. It used to be that Nell had to practically drag Elijah out of bed on school days so he wouldn't miss the bus. Now he left for school on his "Blood Money Dirt Bike" with five minutes to spare.

"It's not blood money," she'd told him the first time he used the term. "It's child support."

"Same diff," he'd said.

She set her work bag on top of the dryer as she went into the kitchen. Her bones ached from being on her knees and back most of the night trying to fix another broken press. And there was also the tailgate sex. Her eyes burned from being awake too long without enough sleep in between. She couldn't sleep most days, though. She was too wired from all that anxiety over Elijah and Tessa bouncing around her head.

Elijah stood at the stove with chopsticks. He moved the bacon from the pan onto a paper towel–covered plate. She wondered where he'd picked that up. Nell wasn't much of a cook herself, preferring frozen dinners or takeout. That was before Elijah came along and required nutrition. As a kid, she'd been more likely to be found outside with Garrett and her dad fixing cars and old machines than inside with her mom learning how to make a pie or cook a small piece of meat like a good southern girl.

She wandered over to the counter and picked through bacon slices to find the ones that had a bit more give to them than the extra-crispy options.

Elijah lifted the cast-iron pan with Grandma's faded strawberry-patterned pot holder and began to pour the bacon grease down the sink.

"That's gonna clog," Nell said and popped a piece of bacon in her mouth. Whoever had taught him how to cook bacon hadn't taught him to leave the grease in a jar on the stove. Use it for rolls, pinto beans, anything but the drain. Elijah must've read the package and gone from there.

Elijah made a face. "It's not gonna clog."

"What do I know? I only work with grease and oil and broken parts every day."

"Yeah, I heard shit's been breaking a lot," Elijah said and proceeded to add the remaining grease to the sink. He could be a real shit sometimes. When he'd first come to live with her, Nell hadn't known what to do. She still wasn't talking to her parents all that much back then.

They about lost their minds when Nell showed up with Elijah. Her dad grabbed her mom after she'd fallen to her knees, Elijah watching like it was some bizarre TV show. They both sobbed and welcomed Elijah into their home. Nell said she'd be back to pick him up whenever they liked. Her dad texted the next day, asking her to come get Elijah. The boy's presence, her father said, "made your mom cry." There were visits after that, and less crying, but nothing overnight. Nothing too long.

Nell didn't want to bother her mom with things like how to take care of the grandkid she didn't even know she had. She'd had to lean on

Ada for the basics, like how do you even talk to a five-year-old? She'd probably leaned on Ada too much. Ada and Elijah had become tight over the years, what with Elijah spending all his time over there with Anthony. Tight enough to trade stories about work, apparently.

After Elijah turned from the sink, Nell ran the hot water as hot as it would go and poured some coffee into a cup. That was one thing she had been able to teach Elijah. He'd started drinking it young. About as soon as he came to live with her. She figured there were worse things than giving the kid coffee with too much cream and sugar. His father was dead. Coffee didn't seem so bad.

"Aren't you vegan?" she asked. The bacon wasn't bad, considering. He had to want something in exchange.

He filled the sink with hot water and added too much dish soap. Bubbles went everywhere.

"Thanks for remembering," he said. "I made it for you."

"Why?" She knew it. "What are you up to?"

"Nothing." He grabbed the skillet handle with the pot holder again and plopped it into the sink.

"You can't put a cast-iron skillet in dishwater!" She grabbed the sudsy pan out of the sink and plunked it onto the counter and then shook her hand from where it had burned her. "It'll ruin the seasoning."

He lifted an eyebrow. "Do you even know what that means? You only cook with the microwave."

She sighed and wiped down the skillet with a towel. "It's common sense."

"If it's so common, why don't I know?" Elijah stared at her with a forced lack of emotion. He probably thought that made his emotions unreadable, but Nell had been around him long enough to know that it meant he was pissed, and she'd have to tease the why out of him. "Sorry I don't know common sense shit. Maybe if my dad hadn't been murdered, my mom wouldn't have dumped me on your doorstep. And maybe if she hadn't abandoned me, I would know all this shit you apparently think I should know, even though there's no one here to teach me."

Nell froze at the mention of Tessa and the circling hell of how things might have gone differently if she had behaved differently that night. Elijah would have a mother in his life. Garrett would still be alive.

"You could ask me," Nell said. "I'm here."

"Barely," he muttered.

The comment stung. It's not like he was always around either. When she did have a day off, he was usually at Anthony's playing video games or at the library, presumably studying. Though his grades certainly didn't show it. "Who told you Garrett was murdered?"

Elijah glared at her. "The whole town." He held up a hand. "And before you say it: yes, I know that it's a rumor. But has it ever occurred to you that it might be true?"

She returned the skillet to the stove and focused on cleaning bacon grease from the counter. She swallowed other words she needed to say. She could barely handle small talk, though; Elijah might be able to puzzle out where she'd been just by her rattling off a grocery list, let alone this conversation.

"The cops looked into it," she said. "They said it was an accident."

"And you believe the cops?"

At the time, she'd had no reason not to. But she'd grown up since then and now knew better.

"You're welcome for the bacon," Elijah said. "By the way."

"Thank you. Sorry. I appreciate it. It was really nice of you." He had the darndest way of keeping track of minor infractions.

For his own breakfast, he grabbed his vegan, fat-free yogurt from the fridge. An apple. A brand of granola she didn't recognize. He licked the spoon he'd used to scoop out the yogurt and then tossed it into the sink. Water went everywhere.

"You don't need to use your money for groceries." She grabbed a towel and wiped it up. "That's my job."

"It's my money," he said. "I can spend it on what I want. Besides, you always complain about me being expensive."

"If I said that, I meant teenagers are expensive in general. Not you specifically." She wondered if maybe it was something he'd heard Ada say and attributed it to Nell.

He put his hand out like one of the models on *The Price Is Right* showing off a brand-new car. "Do you see any other teenagers here?"

"I can buy your damn groceries. You should save your money for special things. That's why your mom sends it to you."

"She sends it to you. You give it to me. I've seen no indication that she gives a shit what I do with the money."

"Well, I know that's what she wants."

He leaned up against the counter and faced her. "How do you know what she wants?"

Nell blinked excessively and then grabbed another piece of bacon. There were trip wires inside Elijah, pulled tight, and Nell didn't know where they were set and when they might go off and how long that might last.

After a painful interlude of silence, Elijah returned to his breakfast yogurt with a new, clean spoon. "Probably makes her feel better for dumping me on your doorstep."

He ate his yogurt and scrolled through his phone while she grabbed some mayonnaise, lettuce, and fancy full-of-good-grains bread Elijah had requested she buy and sat down at the table.

"Nell," Elijah said. He had an uncanny ability to ignore her and then flip a switch to wanting something, with a sweet voice. "I know you don't like to talk about it, but with the Hunt here again, I was thinking about Dad."

"Okay." This conversation always came. Every year. Nell's phone buzzed. She glanced at the number. Tessa. She put her phone on silent.

"You were the last one to see him alive. You and my mom. You've never told me what happened that night."

Her phone buzzed again. Early on, Tessa's rapid-fire texts had alarmed Nell. She'd dropped everything to answer them because Tessa had never been the girl who called too much or cared too much. She'd made everyone else wait for her call. But Nell quickly learned that Tessa was no longer the girl she had been.

"I told you." Nell hated when Elijah brought it up. She didn't know how to say what she wanted to say to him: she was the reason his dad had been out alone on the road that night. She didn't know how to admit that to him. She was terrified he'd leave and never forgive her. "We were out drinking."

"Yeah, I know. But did my mom have something to do with why Dad disappeared? Is that why she abandoned me?" he asked. "Were they fighting?"

He'd asked this same thing, in various ways, so many times. All he wanted was for someone to tell him something. And she had. But it was never enough. He always wanted to know more. If they'd been out hunting for the egg. If they'd seen anyone else. He wanted to know every detail of a night that still terrorized Nell.

Nell squeezed dramatic circles of mayonnaise on the bread before adding the bacon and lettuce, squashing it all down, and shoving it into her mouth. It would've tasted better on white bread.

"I don't remember," she said, mouth full. "We were drinking. A lot. Which was stupid, by the way." The grains and seeds that "enhanced" the bread scraped down Nell's throat. Her first instinct was to turn on the TV, create some noise to drown out the thumping she was sure he would be able to hear, her jugular racing with the blood beating inside her. "We were young and dumb. We stopped the car. And then he was gone." She tried to step around the truth without admitting everything. Even her parents didn't know the full story. And certainly not the cops. Only Tessa knew.

"But why did you stop the car?"

Nell tore the ends off the bread and squished them into balls. It was something she could do with her hands while she thought about what and how to say what she'd been thinking. "I don't know. Probably to pee."

"Where did he go? Did anyone request another autopsy?"

Nell stared out the kitchen window. The temperature would reach seventy degrees, according to the forecast. Spring actually sprung. Nell should mow the lawn. Trim back the trees that were getting a little too close to the power lines. Do something. Something to get away from the awfulness growing in her gut and what felt like accusations that she and her parents had not done enough to ensure Garrett's death was not a murder but an accident.

"Nell." Elijah's voice interrupted her.

"What?" she asked.

"Why do you always zone out as soon as I ask about my dad's murder?" He glared.

"That's not true. I don't. And he wasn't." The words came out far too quiet and sheepish for Nell's comfort. She ran her tongue along her molars, extracting the gummy bread. She abandoned the balls of bread, scratched at her nose. "We were somewhere out on Highway 59. We were all drunk. He left the car to go pee. Your mom and I couldn't find him. And when a hunter did a week later, the cops and coroner said it was an accident. End of story." She took a quick breath and cut off whatever Elijah was about to say. "There's nothing else to know. Even if there was, it doesn't change anything."

The color in Elijah's face drained, and Nell worried if maybe she was walking that thin line again, the one that separated Everything Is Okay from Everything Is Going to Hell, the same line she'd been walking since Tessa had called in December.

"It was a long night at work," Nell said. Tessa's moan lingered in her ear like tinnitus. She had to get her shit together. "I need to get some sleep." She shoved away from the table, flung what remained of the sandwich into the garbage and her plate in the sink full of soapy water. The splash hit her in the face.

"You really believe that?" he asked.

"I do." She couldn't control her sudden tears and the little gasps in between wiping her eyes and then her nose. "I know it's not what you want to hear, but it's what happened. No matter what the whole town says. They weren't there. I was."

Elijah's sigh was filled with frustration. "You can't talk about him without crying." He sat back in his chair, dry eyed and accusatory.

Nell's mouth went dry, her head fuzzed from the lack of sleep, the constant thoughts, the sneaking around. "It's hard for me, Elijah."

He stood and grabbed his wallet off the top of the microwave.

"Where are you going?" she asked.

"School," he said, annoyed. "It's a weekday."

"I mean after." She hadn't meant that; she had trouble keeping track of the days lately. "You going to Anthony's?"

"Why? You'll be at work. What do you care?" Awful words she'd said to her parents as a teenager. She never knew how annoying and hurtful they could sound. "I need to be alone with my thoughts."

What kid even said that? He was seventeen.

"What do you need?" she asked, following him to the back door. "What will help you?"

"Venting to you without you giving me the third degree or trying to send me to therapy again."

"I simply asked." She rubbed her face. "Will you text me to let me know where you're at?"

Elijah didn't say anything. And Nell didn't offer more before Elijah shut the door behind himself, the waves of his discontent rushing to meet her.

◆ ◆ ◆

It seemed like no sooner had Nell gone into her bedroom, pulled off her pants and shirt, lain in bed, and begun to fall asleep than a racket from the kitchen woke her. She'd always hated the trailer layout. Who put the main bedroom right next to the living room, let alone the cable hookup right on that wall? What kind of sense did that make? She yanked the pillow over her head and tried to drown out the noise.

She'd gone to sleep unsettled and woke up irritable. Her brain processing pain and guilt and filtering it the best it knew how while she slept.

Nell closed her eyes and recalled a time the year prior, before Tessa had called her up out of the blue. Nell would come home and go to bed. Elijah would eat breakfast and then head to school. They'd sit down to their frozen dinners and watch some *Jeopardy!* and then the latest must-see limited series on HBO. There were no arguments, no slammed doors. No hurt feelings. No chest tightening. There'd been no Tessa.

She hadn't been back in Nell's life all that long, but the idea of her not being there left Nell feeling rootless.

A door opened and closed. A cabinet door slammed.

"I'm trying to sleep in here," Nell said after finally opening her bedroom door.

There was no one in the living room. All the lights were out. Storm clouds brewed outside and gloomed the space.

She could have sworn she had heard someone. She scrubbed at her face and blinked a bit, her eyelids heavy, her eyes raw. She wandered to the hallway.

"Hello?" Her voice echoed off the walls.

She checked the kitchen table. No note. Elijah was almost always home when she woke up in the afternoon. And if not, he always left a note. Always.

A shot of anxiety pulsed.

She pulled the kitchen curtain aside cautiously to stare out the window. A memory of the night before, Tessa thinking she'd heard someone in the woods, lingered. She checked the locks on the doors and windows. The guest bedroom they used for storing crap they didn't use was empty.

Elijah's bedroom was empty as well. Bed made. All his hair products and skin products and cologne arranged neatly on the dresser. His closet door shut.

She walked to the closet and opened it quickly. As if that would spook someone more than her. If someone were hiding in there. Which they were not. Because why would someone be hiding in his closet?

Still, even though her body thrummed with exhaustion, that thread of fright persisted. She slowly pulled open one of his dresser drawers.

One night at work, Nell had read a magazine Maggie had left on the break-room table. There was this story about a gay kid who got kicked out of his house by his parents when they learned about the true self he'd hidden from them. All night after reading that article, Nell thought about what Elijah might need to hide from her. They were both queer, so she couldn't even understand her own worry. But she did worry. She worried if he ever worried whether Nell would kick him out for some reason. If she'd abandon him like Tessa had. If he'd have to head down to Sixth Street like a lot of kids before him.

Later on the next day, Nell had straight up told Elijah that no matter what, she'd never kick him out. Not ever. Not for anything. Not even if he had a boyfriend who needed a place to stay because his parents had kicked him out. Or two boyfriends. Friends, whatever. They'd clear out the spare bedroom. They'd make it work somehow. Nell would never be like those parents in the magazine.

She'd never be like Tessa.

Relief rushed through her when she found all his clothing still in his dresser drawer.

But there was still that worry there, that one day she'd open that drawer and it'd be empty, and she'd be the reason why all his clothing was gone.

KAOK News Report

Tempers are high in Presley today as protestors of the town's contentious Hunt for the Golden Egg clashed with fans, who call themselves Eggheads. The trouble started at the Wu Subaru dealership yesterday during their annual pre-Easter sales event, when protesters, led by Presley's alleged Hunter's victims' families and friends, held signs and chanted, disrupting shoppers and KCLS 103.9's fans alike.

Of the claims that the annual Hunt is a danger to the community, KCLS station owner Rod Halstrom had this to say when we spoke to him earlier today at the station: "No disrespect to the families who have lost loved ones, but the Hunt is not to blame for what happened. Look," he said, "we've got families and friends, and strangers even, who are out there having the times of their life. Some people even create teams." Rod pointed to a group of women in matching neon-green T-shirts. They all cheered and waved. "If you look at the evidence, every single death can be attributed to accidents, despite what some other ghoulish people would have everyone believe." He went on to add, "Ask who the police believe. I think you'll see that they agree with me."

Despite the tension, the Hunt goes on for now. As for the police, they have no comment.

Eight

Ada

Wednesday, April 6
Midday
Eleven days before Easter

Ada hated grocery shopping. Absolutely loathed it. And that was before everyone was told to wash their groceries because of the pandemic. And she had to do it on her day off. The last thing she wanted to do. That made it all suck more. But if she didn't, there'd be nothing in the fridge. Anthony wasn't going shopping, even though he should. And with Elijah coming over all the time, it seemed like all she did was shop.

Rather, Elijah had been coming over. It'd been more than a week since he'd last shown up for dinner.

"I told you. He's pissed off at me," Anthony had said the previous night when she'd asked him about Elijah. The sound of simulated gunfire ricocheted off the walls and into her brain. He said it helped him decompress, even though it was all shooting and killing. But his grades were good, and he seemed to be normal and no danger to others or himself, so she let it go. Mostly.

"Turn that down!" she yelled behind her. When he'd sat down to play his video game, Anthony had turned off the soundtrack to *Jesus*

Christ Superstar that she played on the Bluetooth speaker he'd bought her. She liked to listen to it regardless of the season. But she liked it most near Easter, especially the 1973 version, which her mom also loved.

It hadn't felt much like Easter that year without the Hunt.

Anthony clicked his head up, but his eyes stayed glued to the TV. His hand didn't make a move toward the remote on the coffee table. Something blew up on the TV and shook the glass measuring cup on the counter.

"Anthony!" She squeezed her mouth up tight, indicating that Anthony was to do as she said. Right now. Anthony glanced at her, grumbled, and then lowered the volume. But barely.

"Why's Elijah mad at you?"

Eyes still on the TV, thumbs all over the controller, he said, "Because I don't want to do dumb shit with him anymore."

"What's that supposed to mean?"

"Mom." Sometimes, Anthony sounded too much like her dad. Ada was supposed to do something with her life, be more, do more. But she'd fallen in love with a sad boy named William, gotten pregnant with Anthony, and ended up working in a factory. Not exactly what her parents had planned. Anthony's voice and mannerisms reminded her of that almost every damn day.

Ada hadn't pursued the issue with Anthony, because she figured his fight with Elijah was about Anthony's job. They'd spent all that time together growing up, and then Anthony had gone and found new friends and other things to occupy his time. But Ada also wondered if there was something between the boys. Anthony swore they were just friends. But then where were the girlfriends? Or even other boyfriends? They were too handsome to be alone. Maybe they had been together and then broken up? She had only mentioned this to Nell. She could never mention it to her parents, especially not her dad.

It annoyed her how much she related to those emotions. The former, not the latter. Ada and Nell were friends, she told herself. It was normal to get upset when your friend stopped coming around or having midnight lunch to sneak off with some naked mystery woman in an ugly car.

She turned up the radio in the car. That helped soothe her irritation for a while, but then Rod came on with his latest clue and she had to punch it off. She couldn't listen anymore. The past week had been like trying to detox. Every time Rod whispered the latest clue in that low voice with the creepy music box soundtrack, she got lured in as if by a siren.

She'd asked Anthony to go hunting again that morning, just to see if he'd been in a bad mood the other times she'd asked, and he'd laughed at her. Asked if she needed to go to rehab. That was rude.

What was she supposed to do? Hunt alone? She wanted to. She'd tried. She'd gone early, after work, and driven to a place that seemed to match the last clue she'd heard. She'd parked the car. Put on her bug spray and her sunscreen. Ensured her backpack had water and snacks. Walked for a bit, taking care not to let her mind wander, as it usually did. Even in that wide-open pasture with mowed grass, with no one able to hide among trees or overgrowth, she couldn't focus. It was too quiet. No cars came by. The birds weren't even singing. All she could think about was another Egghead coming across her lifeless body a day before Easter and screaming. The headlines calling her the latest victim of the Hunter. And her dad shaking his head next to her mom and Anthony and Nancy and Lloyd at the funeral, telling everyone, "I told her so."

She got so mad thinking about it, on top of everything else. Maybe she'd join Nancy and Lloyd and the Raleighs in their efforts to shut down the Hunt. If she couldn't go, then why should anyone else?

That was dumb, of course. She was being selfish and a scaredy-cat.

Maybe she hated herself most of all. She'd let everyone else's stories and fears infect her. It didn't matter, though. She wasn't hunting this year. She'd already made her decision.

She'd have to change the radio station, and she'd have to ignore all the Eggheads she saw on the way to the grocery store, staring at the ground. There were more of them now that Easter was so close and the protests had gotten so much attention on the news. At a stoplight, she gripped the steering wheel and focused on the bumper ahead of her and not the young white guy with dreadlocks who zigzagged through the thick grass in the middle of the median, like an idiot. She squeezed her hands so tight they paled. The light seemed to be broken because she was pretty sure she had sat there for at least five minutes while the guy came in and out of her vision.

Finally, she opened the window. "Hey!" The guy wasn't paying attention, so she yelled again.

He looked up, scanned the cars that were still stopped at the light. She waved him over. He looked perplexed.

"Yeah?" he asked.

"It's not here," she said. "The egg."

He sneered at her.

"You're looking in the wrong place," she said.

"How the fuck would you know?"

She was taken aback by his tone. "Because I've been hunting since before you were even born. Rod would never put the egg in the middle of a fucking intersection, you moron."

The guy flipped her off. The person behind her blared their horn. The light had turned green. Ada was steaming mad. She'd tried to help him!

"Suit yourself," she yelled and then stepped on the gas pedal. She couldn't think of what else to say and let whatever came to mind come out of her mouth. "Fucking Egghead!"

She'd been so focused on the Hunt that she'd not paid attention to where she was going and was on the wrong side of town.

"Dammit," she said and pulled into the lot of Sherman's Grocery instead of the Price Cutter, which was cheaper. Even though she had time to double back, she didn't have the energy to drive back through town and see all those people. She might end up in Oklahoma if she wasn't paying attention. Besides, it was a family business, a Black family business, not a chain. It felt wrong to leave and go to a chain store.

She parked the car and breathed in deeply before making her way to the entrance. The shopping carts inside the store vestibule were all stuck together, and people were waiting on her to extricate hers, which made her even more irritable. Finally, she gave up and found one out in the parking lot. The one she found had a faulty wheel and squeaked to high heaven, but she didn't want to deal with finding another one. Inside the grocery store, she fared no better. There were Easter egg decorations everywhere. Pastel pinks and purples and greens and yellows. She guessed it wasn't so bad that the Easter bunny made her think of gold and money. How many people could say those floppy ears and bow tie made them think of Jesus?

"No, we're going out hunting that day," a white woman said to someone on the phone she cradled between her ear and shoulder. "Simon! Stop it!" she said to a toddler she'd put in the shopping cart and who had proceeded to gnaw on a package of bread, plastic and all, he'd grabbed off a shelf. "Yes, all of us," she said into the phone once the kid's bread had been taken away. "You should join us! It'll be fun! Simon!" The boy screamed. "I gotta go."

Ada rolled her busted cart away from the woman and down the produce aisle. She didn't want to hear about other families and friends searching for the egg together and future tripping about the great time they were all going to have. She absentmindedly searched through her purse for her list. Her hand came up empty. She stopped to dig around inside her purse.

"Shit," she muttered. It'd take her even longer now.

She heard laughter behind her. Familiar laughter.

She swung around. Her heart beat too fast. Her mouth hung open, like a dog. She spun in place, looking for the source of the sound.

There were so many people out shopping. None she recognized. Only strangers swirling around her with their bodies and carts and conversation. But she'd heard that laughter before. Out in the woods. She was sure of it.

"Excuse me," someone said and tried to nudge her out of the way.

"Sorry," Ada replied and let the person get their iceberg lettuce unhindered by her body and cart and bafflement.

She tried to remember what she'd meant to buy, but she kept getting this feeling that someone was watching her or following her. She took a deep breath, exhaled it, and told herself to get a grip.

There's no one there, she muttered. *Don't be an idiot.*

Who even heard of the Hunter going into a grocery store to find his victim? That'd be a new one.

She walked down each aisle, forcing herself to take her time, pause, breathe, settle her nerves. By the time she got to the last aisle, she was mad again, at the prices of everything, at having forgotten her grocery list, at not finding the right kind of creamer she liked for her coffee. But she didn't want to be one of those people who asked the stocker if they had some in the back. She figured they endured more annoyance than Ada did. At least she didn't have to deal with the general public.

"Hi!"

Ada startled and then grumbled. She did have to deal with Maggie, though.

"What are you doing here?" Maggie asked.

Ada made a face. "Buying groceries."

"Gosh, we better double-check your pay stubs if you're able to shop here!" Maggie laughed like that was the funniest thing.

Ada raised her eyebrows, tightened her grip around the shopping cart handle.

"I mean, I can barely shop here," Maggie said. Then she reached out as if to touch Ada's arm before stopping. "I'm teasing." She cleared her throat, looked around. "I don't think I've seen you outside of work in years."

Ada reached for something off the shelf and dropped it in her cart. Didn't even look at the price. "I guess a lucky streak has to end eventually."

Ada pushed her cart down the aisle, away from Maggie. A bored Asian American teenage girl had been listening in, doing a poor job of pretending not to while on her phone. Ada passed her, and the girl offered a conspiratorial smirk. Ada's mood lifted briefly, but then Maggie was back at her side. Cart to cart.

Ada stopped to examine the back of a cereal box, hoping to ditch Maggie, but there she was. Right by Ada's side, with something on her mind she didn't have the courage to say.

"What is it, Maggie?" Ada finally asked, not looking up from the ingredients list.

Maggie fiddled with her hands, and then she pulled her cart out of the way. The bored teenager passed, following her mom. She flipped off Maggie behind her back and gave Ada a peace sign. Ada laughed. When Maggie smiled, Ada resumed her frown.

"I've been meaning to speak with you, but it never feels like the right time." Maggie complemented her whispered words with a creased brow.

"I don't like to talk about work outside of work."

"Well, it's not about work. Not exactly."

Ada waited. She didn't have time to rehash this again.

"I feel like there's still so much awkwardness between us. That was so long ago." Maggie motioned back and forth between them. Ada let her flounder. "I was hoping that maybe we could bury the hatchet." She held up a hand. "I don't expect us to hang out or go to the movies or what have you."

"Good. 'Cause that ain't happening." Ada wished the bored teenager were there to flip Maggie off again for Ada's amusement.

"I don't know how many times I can tell you how sorry I am." Maggie clutched her chest.

"You can say it however many times you like. Doesn't change the fact that you shared personal information with everyone at work, information I shared privately with you."

"I know," Maggie said. "I never meant to cause you harm."

"Doesn't matter what you meant. It matters what you did."

"And I'm deeply sorry for that."

Ada didn't respond.

Maggie's whole demeanor went from sorry and sweet to astonished. "How long are you gonna punish me?"

"Punish you?" Ada laughed. "The only thing I've done is stop trusting you. And for good reason."

Maggie looked like she was about to ugly cry. "You treat me like I'm some kind of monster."

"Well," Ada said.

A sound, something like a low growl, came from Maggie's throat. She pushed off her cart and then turned to face Ada again. "I have tried so hard with you. I've invited you to join—"

"I don't want to join your stupid Hunt team with your stupid T-shirts."

"I was only doing it because I felt sorry for you." Maggie smiled wicked-like. "I know you're too scared to go alone."

Ada's head fired with rage. "How—"

"Anthony told me," Maggie said. "I saw him at the Best Buy. He helped me out with my computer. It was all locked up."

Anthony knew how much she hated this woman! How dare he talk about her personal business?

"I'm not scared of shit," Ada said, all too aware of how much she sounded like her dad when he got his back up about something dumb. "But what makes you think I don't have friends? You think you're the only available option in this town?" She wanted to add *bitch!* to the end of the sentence but managed to keep her cool. Ada scanned Maggie and shook her head. "I wouldn't trust you to share the winnings, anyway."

Ada pushed her cart away from Maggie again, forcing herself to meander. Behind her Maggie said, "I guess we'll find out."

Ada grabbed a bottle of expensive ketchup to toss into her cart and yelled right back, "I guess we will!"

Ada had stopped hunting. Stopped puzzling out the clues. But when she closed her eyes and fell asleep, it's like her brain was hunting for her, running through woods and fields and down back alleys and in parking lots. Her eyes rapidly searching the ground. She'd woken up nauseous one morning. It had felt like the room was spinning.

In the week and a half since she'd gone hunting with Elijah, some white guy from Cedarville claimed to have found the egg. Had pictures and everything, posted them on Facebook and Instagram. The worst? He claimed to have found it near the water, where she'd gone with Elijah. Her heart sank when she heard. She'd lost her shot because she'd gotten scared that day. Had run up a damn tree! But days later, Rod revealed that the man had created a dupe of the real golden egg, hoping he could somehow trick Rod, even though everyone who'd ever hunted knew that Rod had a special stamp on the egg to ensure it was authentic.

Another chance to win? To show Maggie she was wrong? To beat her?

Ada scrambled for her phone out of her purse and texted Elijah: When can you go hunting again?

Slack message: Max McClure

TICKTOCK, IT'S TIME FOR THE KILL CLOCK!

It's Easter, bitches. You know what that means . . . SOMEONE'S GONNA DIE!

Who's it gonna be this year? So far, the office pool is swaying heavily in favor of Queen Ding-Dong, Maggie What's Her Face. God, she sucks! But there's a sucker born every minute, as they say, so Newbies are also in a close second.

Y'all best get your bets in now if you want in. The egg could be found any day now. $5 gets you in on the pool! Winner takes all!

Nine

Nell

Saturday, April 9
Afternoon
Eight days before Easter

Nell checked her phone again when she woke up from her nap. The same way she'd checked it just about every minute of every day all week long. A whole week. She hadn't meant for her and Tessa to stop talking altogether. She hadn't said, *We literally can't see each other. Or text.* But Tessa hadn't called her or texted her, so Nell did. Those little dots showed up, indicating that Tessa was typing. But then they disappeared. And appeared again and then disappeared. And Elijah hadn't said anything about Tessa calling or texting him. So what the fuck was the point of calling things off if Tessa was gonna disappear again?

Nell had called up Tessa after her talk with Elijah. They met in the clearing on Nell's night off. Tessa had a worried look on her face when she walked up and hugged herself tight against the cold night air.

"I been thinking . . ." Nell forced herself to sit still, not to run away. "I worry."

Nell could feel Tessa's body shake.

"Tessa," Nell said, hoping that she wouldn't have to say out loud what they both knew was coming.

Tessa frowned. "I don't like it when people call me by my name. It means something bad's about to come out of their mouth."

"I worry about what this"—she gestured to the two of them—"might make Elijah feel. He's graduating soon." Nell felt like she had when she'd played football with Garrett and his friends in the yard and they tackled her. Her own words knocked the wind right out of herself. "I'll help you with Elijah. I can't promise he'll want to talk to you or see you. But I'll do what I can." She paused for courage, reached for and held Tessa's hand in hers. "But I can't keep doing this. Not with him leaving. Things are going to be hard enough without adding this. Adding you . . ." She waited for a reaction that didn't come. "I don't want to put more on him. He can handle it. I know that. But he shouldn't have to. He's already shouldered enough." Emotion clogged Nell's throat; her eyes misted. "I don't want to lose him . . ."

"*Too*. That's what you were going to say, isn't it?" A fine line formed between Tessa's eyes. "You don't want to lose him too. Like me."

"You know I love you." Nell wanted to tell her how much she hated what she'd proposed about not seeing each other anymore, but that might lead to some sort of compromise or half measure. "But I don't feel right about it. I'm sorry."

Seemed like an hour passed between them without words.

"Okay," Tessa said at last. She eased her hand out of Nell's and hugged her knees close. "I know what you're saying." She stared at the ground and licked her lips, preparing them for speech, but stopped. A little sigh escaped her mouth, but she seemed to swallow her hurt. Finally, she nodded. Small and delicate. A whisper of understanding that pulled at Nell. "You don't have to explain," Tessa said. "I understand." She swiped at her eyes and nodded. Offered another smile. "You're a good aunt. You've been a good mother to him."

"You can be that too," Nell said, even though that description didn't feel like it applied to her, given their current circumstances.

Tessa squeezed her eyes against her tears and nodded.

"You needed some time for the other stuff," Nell said. She wanted so badly to hold her, grieve this together, but she kept her hands at her side. "And Elijah might need some time too. It's been hard. He's gonna have to come to a different understanding of you. But I know he can because he came from you."

Tessa shook her head, sniffled. "I'm not so sure about that."

"All you can do is try. That's why you reached out to me, right?"

Tessa seemed too upset to talk. Nell nudged her with her body.

"Or was your ongoing desire for me so overwhelming you couldn't stand it anymore?" Nell asked.

Tessa laughed. "You're ridiculous."

"Made you laugh, though."

Tessa shook her head and stared off into the distance. "You've always been able to do that." She sighed. "I'm gonna miss that."

"You don't have to miss me. I'm still gonna be here. Just with my pants on."

Tessa didn't laugh that time. They'd parted ways in their own cars shortly thereafter.

Nell hadn't slept much since that night, even though she had time now that she wasn't working all those extra days, so she could see Tessa without having to explain to Elijah where she went on her nights off. She stopped trying and took to lying on the couch to watch TV all day.

She tucked Grandma Holcomb's afghan blanket up under her chin. Her toes stuck through the holes, and the air chilled her skin. She had been thinking about calling in sick. Nell knew she was acting like some character in a Victorian novel, bound by circumstance, unable to be with the one she loved. Tortured and pining for a star-crossed lover.

At first, Nell had pretended that everything was right as rain, the lie coming so easy. Sometimes, pretending to be fine could work out to being fine, and that's what she needed to do for Elijah's sake. Take some deep breaths and say that everything was fine until it was.

"What's going on with you?" Elijah asked from where he sat in the glider chair—a hand-me-down from Grandma and Grandpa Holcomb, along with everything else on that five-acre plot of land—watching his shows. He liked to watch Korean zombie flicks at full volume, although he needed the captions to understand what was happening. But the TV was on mute. She hadn't even noticed him come into the room.

"Probably just a cold or something."

"Is it COVID?" he asked. She wasn't sure if he was genuinely concerned or if he was worried it might affect whatever plans he had that night. She told him no.

"Are you sure?" Suspicion tinged his voice. "There are new variants all the time."

"I'm sure." She sat up slowly, not wanting him to worry. Her head spun, and she saw stars. She hadn't moved from the couch since she'd eaten one of Elijah's granola bars for breakfast. Her mouth was dry. "I only needed to lie down."

"You're probably dehydrated," he said and downed a water bottle. He went into the kitchen, opened a cabinet, grabbed another water bottle, filled it, and handed it to her. "Do you need to stay home from work?"

"No," she said and held up the bottle. "I need to wake up." She downed the water and gave him a thumbs-up. "Thanks. Feeling better already."

Her answer seemed to satisfy him because he turned up the volume on the TV, which made her head pound.

She proceeded to her bedroom, where she changed out of the clothes she'd worn the night before and never removed.

Tessa's ringtone sang into the air from the living room.

Nell scrambled out the door and almost collided with Elijah.

"You forgot your phone," he said and handed it to her.

She waited to see if maybe he would ask who it was, but he didn't. "Thanks," she said and shut the door behind her.

They'd taken the lock off Grandma's bedroom door once she got dementia. Nell never bothered to put it back when she moved in. Out of caution, she took her phone to the bathroom and shut the door. No lock there either.

She tapped her phone screen, but there was nothing there. No text. No call notification.

She could've sworn she'd heard it go off but wondered if maybe she'd woken from a dream instead. Tessa hadn't texted or called, not for a week. Why would she now?

A thought interrupted: Maybe Tessa had gotten caught by the Hunter. Maybe she'd gone out to the clearing, hoping that Nell might show up. Maybe the Hunter had shown up instead?

Nell wasn't spiritual, and she didn't believe in the supernatural, but she did believe that if you thought about someone randomly, there was probably some reason why. Some cosmic string that held people together, and if something happened it was like the universe plucked that string to get your attention. Or maybe the universe cut that string between them, and Nell was still holding on tight, like Tessa dangled at the end of that rope. If she could just pull her up.

These were stupid thoughts. She was tired. Agitated. Sad. Her whole body jittered with not knowing what Tessa was thinking. She was not at all interested in spending twelve hours at work. Twelve hours of replaying their last meetup and wondering if she could've approached things differently. But she hated sitting in the house with Elijah looming, waiting with all his questions and accusations about Garrett even more. After their last conversation, Nell couldn't get the idea of Garrett being murdered out of her head. She'd thought about it before. But never seriously. She'd never believed it until now, and she wasn't even sure why. It's like she'd woken up from a slumber and everything and everyone she encountered said the world was flat when all along she'd been told it was round.

After showering and eating a bit to show Elijah she wasn't sick, she checked in with him on his schedule, something they'd done since he was old enough to stay home alone when she worked nights. Before then, a woman she'd gone on one date with before settling on being roommates to save money had kept an eye on him. Elijah mentioned he planned to be at the library a lot for a few days to work on a senior project due that week. Elijah had never been a dedicated student, but she'd seen his last report card and was happy he'd decided to take his last semester seriously, even if he wasn't planning on college.

"Okay," she said before leaving the house. "Be careful."

"It's the library," he said without looking away from the TV.

At work, she pulled into the parking lot, thinking she could get a head start on work and get caught up with Gunner, a white, middle-aged, hard-assed second-shift foreman, on any presses that might require attention. From the hallway, she heard the day crew bracing themselves for hour eleven of twelve. They usually hit the bathroom and the soda and candy, anything to keep them awake after a long shift. Nell stopped when she realized Janie was recounting a story about how her brother-in-law had gotten in trouble at work for having an office pool over who would die at the hands of the Hunter next.

"What kind of trouble?" Gunner asked.

Apparently, they'd withheld the brother-in-law's bonus, which led others in the room to express outrage because he wasn't doing anything wrong; he wasn't wrong about the deaths. Then Gunner asked if the brother-in-law usually won the pool, which Janie said he did. That led Sherry, the label-machine operator, to wonder if maybe the brother-in-law was actually the Hunter, given he won the pool most years. Janie objected to that, but the others laughed and played along while Nell's insides rumbled.

She walked into the break room and paused at the table where they all sat.

"Oh, Jesus, Nell. You scared us," Janie said and tried to laugh it off.

"You should be scared," Nell said, rage swarming.

Gunner acted affronted, smirking and turning away from her to mutter. "We're just blowing off some steam." He'd always been a son of a bitch, the kind of guy who talked big about hunting and kicking ass and being working class but didn't do shit but boss around a bunch of mostly marginalized women who did the actual work.

"By joking about people dying? You think that's funny?" she asked.

Gunner didn't respond, of course. He was one of those guys who liked to dish it out but couldn't take it when someone, especially a woman, had something to say back to him.

"Sorry, Nell," Janie said. "We didn't know you were there." They knew about Garrett. All of them did.

"You shouldn't need me in the room to be decent," Nell said and headed back the way she'd come, back to her truck, leaving the dumbstruck day crew behind her.

From the road, she called Maggie to let her know she was taking a sick day, even though Maggie would learn soon enough about what had happened in the break room. She hated that Maggie was the one she had to call. She asked Nell if it was serious. Probably not because she cared, but because she needed to know if they had to get a temp in to cover for Nell for an extended period of time. Maggie had been required to do that a lot during the past couple of years. She'd bitched and complained every time because apparently it was "a lot of work to find good help on such short notice." But then Joyce, who'd been there going on thirty years, died of COVID, and that put an end to those complaints. At least in public.

"I'm not quite feeling myself. Was up all night puking and came in to work just now but realized I should probably head home. Felt a little wobbly," Nell lied. Again. She didn't like how she kept doing that, but she couldn't seem to stop. Taking off work was self-care. If Maggie didn't act affronted by every time-off request, and the company gave them more time, then Nell wouldn't feel like she had to lie.

At the turnoff to the highway, Nell took a left instead of a right. She knew not to let herself go down this path again. But with Tessa's sudden appearance and now sudden absence, her head and her heart started fucking with her.

Twenty minutes later, after crossing from Arkansas into Oklahoma, she arrived at her destination and turned into the half-empty parking lot of the Cherokee Casino. She hadn't been here in years. She'd stopped going when Elijah moved in with her, even though the craving for the sounds and smells and escapism of the casino called to her every night until it was cut to the quick by the daily attentions of a child and time, until it was no bigger than a marble in her mind, still there, but not quite so present. She could walk away, but she didn't want to. That marble had become a fist, knocking at her insides, fighting to get out, saying time didn't matter. Elijah didn't need her attentions. He was at the library.

Self-care. That's what it was. A little self-care and soothing the ache of Tessa's absence and the realization that what everyone said might be true. Garrett had been murdered.

Tonight, only tonight. Then she would wake up, she'd talk to Elijah, she'd go down to the police station, maybe. Ask them to see the files. Something. She didn't know. Maybe she'd join Lloyd and Nancy and the Raleighs. Go all in. Join a protest. Demand answers. She'd figure it out tomorrow. But tonight? Tonight she would forget it all.

The neon sign of the casino glowed orange on her face before she took a step onto the curb from the parking lot asphalt. The lights and heater vents at the entrance warmed and welcomed her.

Upon opening the doors, she was assaulted by cigarette smoke. It felt like home. Inside, the ceilings were tall, the walls burnt orange; chandeliers made from antlers offered vague light. She bummed a cigarette from a Latino guy in a fringed leather jacket at a penny slot and wandered through the aisles of slot machines and card tables.

Nell had started visiting the casino after Garrett's death, soon after she turned eighteen. At first, she tried to use her fake ID to buy alcohol but got caught. Then she took to getting drunk in her truck before going in and kept the buzz going by knocking back the abandoned remains of what she found on various tables. She spent whatever time off she had from assorted jobs she'd acquired and lost pulling a lever, spending money she didn't have to spend, challenging God or whoever was up there or in charge of the universe to give her some good luck. She mostly lost, like all the others who sat on stools next to her. Sometimes, she'd sit in the casino restaurant for hours, stoned out of her mind on whatever someone had given her, watching the endless music videos that played on a loop on the oversize TVs while indulging herself in all-you-can-eat mashed potatoes and pot stickers. She lost jobs because she lost track of the days. She wasn't a high roller, so she couldn't get the free rooms. Most times, she sat there on a stool in front of a slot machine and dozed off until one of the waitresses nudged her or she almost fell off her stool. Then she'd drink coffee or an energy drink to try to perk up before giving in and sleeping in her truck.

The casino was the only place she could go where she felt anonymous.

That all had changed when Lloyd showed up. Every Tuesday, they'd chat, and then one day he'd offered her a job at Mayflower.

Elijah would be gone soon, out of the house. He didn't need her now. Not really. And with Tessa gone for what was probably forever, well . . . Nell was of a mind to get properly fucked.

An otherwise-attractive Indigenous woman in an ill-fitting maroon tuxedo came by with a tray of drinks. She stopped long enough to ask if she could get Nell something. She could, and she did. And she let five other women in similarly ill-fitting tuxedos bring her their glasses of Jack and Coke as she stationed herself at one of the slot machines and mindlessly fed quarters she couldn't afford to spend into the machine while time disappeared. She could've been sitting there for an hour. It could've been four. There were no windows. Just a warm honey glow from the alcohol and the orange-painted walls and wood trim and the candle-like light fixtures that made her feel like she was in a gigantic hunting lodge full of arcade games for adults. The skinny white woman in a slinky red dress next to her might've been there the whole time, or she might have come later that night. Maybe Nell wouldn't have talked to her if she hadn't had so many drinks, but she had. She looked like someone Nell had talked to before, so she asked. But the woman said no, she was from here in Oklahoma. She said the words shyly before laughing, taking a drink, and pulling her slot lever with her red-tipped fingernails. Eventually, at some point, at some time that Nell could not recall, those fingernails slid down Nell's arm and to her elbow.

The drinks had warmed and loosened Nell in a manner in which she had not felt warm or loose in a long time. Not even with Tessa. But like Tessa, and Ada on the picnic bench outside work, the woman's leg touched Nell's and ignited something within Nell. She let an alcoholic haze of fantasy overtake her about how she wished Tessa would walk through those doors, yank the woman's lovely dark-black locks so hard it pulled the smooth skin at her temples, which would create a high-pitched scream from between the stranger's plump red lips that Nell couldn't help but consider touching with hers. But given Nell had called it quits with Tessa, she and the woman entered an elevator.

Warm lights, the cigarette smoke, whiskey on their tongues.

I should go, Nell thought, but she couldn't make the words come out of her mouth. She'd had too much to drink. The problem with a casino. The drinks kept coming, and you couldn't keep count. Her brain countered: But then, why should she go?

The woman yanked every button off Nell's shirt. Each little piece of plastic pinged against a different surface of the hotel room they'd rented before slipping into the elevator—the wall, the floor, the side table, the TV. Nell collapsed in the middle of the hotel bed, nothing on but her socks, still feeling warm and fuzzy and good. And bad. So bad. Not because of what she was doing but knowing that Tessa probably wouldn't even care about the woman. She'd probably say it was good for Nell, that Nell was right, that she needed to move on. Maybe Tessa had only used Nell for sex and relief from her own horrible thoughts.

Yet Nell couldn't get a leash on her own guilt and badness. And when that woman slipped those pretty lips between Nell's legs and then covered her with her whole mouth, Nell's body buzzed with recollections of better days. The walls closed in around her like a cocoon, all soft and protective, and the woman's beautiful black strands of hair fell over Nell's torso. Her tongue ran the length of Nell, teasing her, reminding her of what goodness felt like.

Nell forced herself to let go of the fear of what might come. What could possibly come that hadn't happened already? Her brother was dead. Tessa was gone. Elijah was leaving. She didn't worry about being good to anyone or anything in that moment. She let those worries go. Let her mind buzz with the wild and weird of what was happening.

There was nothing harsh about the woman. She was so lovely. Her vowels and consonants so soft. Even when Nell clenched and her body rolled and released into an orgasm, the woman didn't buck or cuss. She caressed Nell as her body settled back into its normal rhythm. Nell lay there, doing nothing, unable to move, not even to stroke the woman's hair. She felt like maybe she had taken something other than alcohol, but she couldn't really remember.

The woman emptied another mini bottle of whiskey in one long pull and then put a can of Red Bull, of all things, to Nell's mouth, which she pried open with her fingers. The liquid coated her mouth in sweetness like cough syrup.

"Wake up." The woman gently slapped Nell on the face. Still stung, though. And kept her from dozing off.

The woman kissed Nell's lips then and moved down the bed. Her breasts were soft, her curves full, her nipples small, the triangle of hair that she locked into place on top of Nell so . . . she couldn't think of any other word. Nice. She looked too perfect, too sweet, too farm-girl innocent to be bucking against Nell for what felt like an age, the woman's fingers working on herself, that black hair flowing all around the soft skin of her shoulders and occasionally tickling Nell. Her mouth not made for the moans that escaped when she moved harder and harder, Nell gripping her hips tighter, until her body seized, and she released the most beautiful moan Nell had ever heard. Then, only then, did Nell start to cry.

She hadn't seen it coming, hadn't felt it. Hadn't known that she was the type of person that such a thing could happen to, so unawares. The most beautiful moan till now had come from Tessa. She wiped at the tears that streamed down her face.

"Aw," the woman whispered. "You're tender," she teased and gathered up her clothing.

"Where you going?" Nell wiped her eyes and stupidly wondered if it was possible that the woman had not seen her tears or heard her blubber. But her clothes were on so quickly. All that beautifulness, gone. "Don't leave," Nell said, worried that it had come out as a whimper. Her body had awakened at last, little by little, but every movement still took effort. She stretched out a hand to the woman.

The woman looked down at Nell. She didn't look so soft anymore, so pretty or sweet or shy. Tiny bits of mascara had smudged under her eyes. Her lipstick had smudged too. Her hair was a nest of black tangles. She twisted the cap to a bottle of vodka from the mini fridge, and the tiny metal top cracked. She emptied it and then placed it on the side table before grabbing her purse off the floor and heading to the door.

"Where're you going?" Nell asked again, and the woman chuckled in that way that said she didn't find what Nell had said all that funny.

"Home."

"Wait." Nell thought a bit and realized she couldn't recall the woman's name. She wasn't even sure she'd told her. Nell tried to prop herself up on her elbows. Her brain still had a time trying to catch her words, their meanings. "Don't go," she said, not even sure why. "Stay."

"No, thanks," the woman said and dug around in a purse for a cigarette and lighter. At the door, she paused with a hand on her hip and her purse slung from her wrist. She shook her head. "You're a mess."

Her tone hit Nell like a ton of bricks, and she plopped back down on the bed. "I'm sorry."

She opened the door. Anyone walking by would've seen Nell sprawled naked on the bed, but she was so low inside, and drunk, and what felt like something else, that she didn't even care. The woman hesitated and then spoke. "Y'all look so similar. You got different parts to you. But you look just like him."

Nell tried to work her brain around her meaning. "Elijah?" she asked, even though it couldn't be true. Not Elijah. Elijah wasn't like other boys. Elijah was like her.

"No." The woman looked shaken to the core. "Garrett."

When Nell sat up, the room spun. "What?" she asked, her words slurred. "Did you say 'Garrett'?"

The woman glanced out the door a moment, as if checking the hallway for someone, and then turned back to Nell. "You're not like the others, you know. I like you," she said. A flash of something like worry crossed her face before she lifted her chin, her whole countenance changed from sweet to sinister. "Shame Garrett had to die."

Shared Google Doc / The Hunt

VICTIM #10

On April 16, 2014, Henry Adams, white, sixty-nine, spent the evening with twin sisters Mary and Linda Harris, white, seventy, as he did most Saturday nights. The group had been meeting to play penny poker for several years, having grown up together. Henry had also dated both women at various times. Around 9:30 p.m., Henry excused himself to use the toilet. The women continued to play poker and talk for the next hour or so. They were not concerned by Henry's absence, they told police, because they knew Henry had "intestinal trouble." Around 10:30 p.m., Mary knocked on the bathroom door, as she needed to pee and there was only one bathroom in the sisters' home.

After some time, Linda joined her sister at the bathroom door. The two women eventually opened the door and found Henry dead on the toilet, with a magazine opened to a photo spread of the Kardashians on a beach vacation in Thailand. Asked why the women waited another thirty minutes to call the cops, Mary explained that she and Linda had broken into a "fit of giggles" and could not stop.

Henry's autopsy indicated that he had officially died of a fecal impaction on the toilet.

When we spoke to the sisters years later, they told us they "felt just terrible for laughing at Henry there on the toilet at first, as they had thought he'd had a heart attack from getting too excited by the photos." They were horrified to learn that the police had shared that tidbit with reporters and others around town that they had laughed at "poor Henry," which they thought was "insensitive."

Henry, Mary, and Linda were "die-hard" Eggheads since the inaugural Hunt and could often be seen out in Presley hunting, with Henry carrying the women's day bags full of snacks, beverages, and extra layers of clothing in case they "caught a chill."

On their last Hunt together, the day before he died, Henry had gone to the woods to "do his business." Upon his return, Henry put out their lunch things, including a bag of cookies the women didn't recognize. When asked where he got the cookies, Henry said that a "nice fellow" he'd met on the walk back from the woods gave them to him to "fuel his hunt." The women refused to eat something from a stranger and encouraged Henry to throw them away. They did not see Henry eat the cookies or throw them away. A few weeks after Henry's death, they called the police to tell them what they remembered but were "blown off" when they asked about an autopsy on Henry's stomach contents and if the police had found a bag of cookies at Henry's house.

Mary and Linda have not hunted since and rarely leave their home.

Ten

Ada

Sunday, April 10
Morning
Seven days before Easter

Nell's voice sounded distant, uncertain. "Ada . . . could you come down here to the casino?"

Maggie had made a big fuss the previous night about how Nell had called in sick and how she hoped it wasn't anything serious, even as her eyes seemed to sparkle with the potential of something exciting to talk about if it was.

Even though Elijah had confirmed that Nell had stayed home sick when Ada asked him about it, Ada suspected that Nell had called in to work for no good reason. Or maybe because she had broken up with that mystery woman. She'd been insufferably morose the past few days, at work and over the phone on their days off.

"What's wrong?" Ada asked. "Are you okay?"

"I don't think so."

"What's going on?" Ada covered the microphone with a hand so Elijah wouldn't hear her and Nell wouldn't hear Elijah if he started talking.

As embarrassed as she was about getting caught by Elijah with her pants down, she couldn't keep herself from the Hunt. Elijah had agreed, but only after he'd basically made Ada beg. And they'd been having a good morning. It had felt like a new beginning. But Nell's phone call had brought that to a pause.

Up ahead of her, Elijah slowly scanned the ground. He'd been quiet all morning. The good kind of quiet. Focused. Eyes on the prize that could be hidden somewhere in the park.

Nell made a stuttering noise that Ada couldn't interpret but that worried her.

"Nell?" No answer. Nothing but slot machines and background music. And then, the unmistakable sound of a walkie-talkie. "I'll be there soon," Ada said and ended the call.

She hurried over to Elijah. "We have to go. Something's come up," she said. "I'll drop you at home."

He raised his eyes from the ground and stared at her. "We're on a roll. We have it all mapped out."

"I know. I'm sorry." She sighed. Two Holcombs tied up in knots. And she was the one who had to hear it all. She checked her watch. "But I have to go."

He scrunched up his mouth. "What am I supposed to do?"

"I don't know. Play video games with Anthony," she said, walking off toward the car.

"He's probably working, or too busy."

"Well, find something else to do." She paused when she didn't hear him behind her. "Elijah. We have to go." She thought he might drop down to the ground and throw a fit the way he looked up to the sky and sulked.

"How long is your business gonna take?" he asked.

"I don't know." She had no idea what she was walking into. Considering Nell was at the casino, she wagered a guess. "I have to be at work tonight, though. So it can't last long."

"Why don't you call me when you're done? We had planned on being out here a while anyway." He sulked a bit more and then curled his lip in thought. "I can guard our spot. Keep looking until you return."

Tempting, but she couldn't leave him. "It's not safe."

"It's nine o'clock on a Sunday morning," he shot back. "No one murders people at nine a.m. My dad was murdered at night, and so was everyone else. I think I'm fine."

"There's no murderer," she said. She'd lied to herself so many times over the years, she knew she could at least fake that. "And if there was, which there is not, the victims could've been abducted during the day."

"Well, I'm safe, then. This is the one time in the history of the world that queer people haven't been the victim of the serial killer."

"As far as you know," Ada said. "Isn't that what you always tell me?"

"Touché." He paused for a minute, as if thinking through the details of a plan, and then planted a smile on his face. "You should go, though. I'll keep hunting." Before she could protest, he held up his hands. "There aren't even any trees here. Your biggest worry should be whether I die of starvation. Or heatstroke." He glanced at her pack. "You got anything to eat?"

The park had a few benches at the periphery, but it was mostly empty baseball and soccer fields. That didn't make her feel much better. She'd had her freak-out about hunting alone in an empty field, after all. But there were other people here, early-morning dog walkers and runners. More to come once the day got going. It was a park in a busy part of town, not some random clearing on the outskirts.

She rustled around in her backpack and gave him what she had. A handful of granola bars and a couple of apples. He'd brought his own water bottle. "Are you wearing sunscreen? It's supposed to get hot today." She couldn't help but ask. The boy was so white.

"I'm queer. Of course I'm wearing sunscreen!" He turned around and went back to staring at the ground. "Go! I'm fine!"

Nell had probably gotten drunk and needed a ride home. In that case, she should've called an Uber or a cab. But that walkie-talkie worried her. Ada didn't know what she was walking into, but it sounded like the kind of thing that would require a responsible adult.

She calculated the time it'd take to get to the casino, then Nell's house, and then back to meet up with Elijah before heading back to work after a bit more time to hunt.

"I'll call you after I pick—" She almost tripped up and mentioned Nell. "I'll call you as soon as I can. I don't think I'll be gone much longer than an hour or so."

Elijah waved a hand behind him, a lone, tall, skinny figure in the middle of a field that had begun to wake up with the sun.

Ada walked into the cold and smoke-soaked air of the casino. A fast-paced, party-rock REO Speedwagon song played from speakers hidden somewhere in the walls, which created an odd contrast with the mostly empty casino. There were a few people wandering about, but they were mostly employees. She rushed past the penny slots and the tables, beyond the closed-up nighttime bar and stage that welcomed small-town and once-big artists three times a week. In the vast cafeteria, fluorescent lights glared. A handful of tables were occupied by what looked like overnighters and breakfast-buffet lovers. She paused to take in their faces, looking for someone familiar. Off to the right, away from the others and tucked into a booth near the back, she found her.

Ada nearly gasped at the sight. Nell's hair was disheveled, the lines on her face chiseled in unflattering angles. Her shirt barely hung on her frame, like the buttons had been torn right off and tossed aside. Nell stared into a full cup of coffee that she'd wrapped her hands around, probably cold by now.

An Indigenous security guard stood off to the side, one arm tight across his chest, a hand across his nose and mouth. He had a dark ponytail down his back and kept a hand at his holster. A gun? Her heart tripped a beat, but no. Taser? She looked more closely. Nope.

Just a walkie-talkie. He must've been the person she'd heard in the background. She had to take a beat before she walked closer to Nell. She smelled of piss and alcohol and women's perfume, like she'd run through the beauty aisles of Dillard's after sleeping in the dumpster, all those sales folk firing at her like a gantlet to run. Those wild thoughts Ada'd had about Nell on her first hunt with Elijah came back to her. She hated herself for thinking Nell was anything but who she was: a dumbass. Nothing and no one to dream about. And then she felt stupid because what did it matter to her? They weren't dating, and she had no plans to start. For all Ada knew, Nell's secret lover was at the root of whatever Ada was looking at.

Nell didn't acknowledge Ada when she walked by. Didn't take her eyes off that coffee.

"Ma'am," the security officer, Homie, according to his name tag, said when she approached. "You know this woman?"

"Yeah. What happened?"

Homie swiped his hand across his head when she asked again. "I don't really know . . ." He lowered his voice and avoided her eyes. "She came running through the casino, naked, screaming about—"

She nudged him farther away from Nell, close to the hot and sour soup and wontons. "Naked?"

"Yeah," he said, casting a glance at Nell and then back to Ada, voice lowered. "Naked and screaming about some woman. At first, I thought she was another one of those folks from—"

"Another?"

"Yeah, another. Mostly white men."

"People come running through here naked all the time?"

"It's a casino. We sell alcohol. It happens. Thankfully, it was morning this time, not at night when it's packed." He shrugged. "But then I seen her. And I realized that it wasn't a man. And she didn't act like those men act when they get naked." He looked past her to where Nell sat. "She started yelling." He whispered it in the retelling, though. "'Where'd she go? That woman! That woman! She killed my brother!'"

Ada repeated the last line as a question, in case she hadn't heard properly. He nodded. She'd heard right. Lord, the Hunt had messed Nell up good this year.

He shook his head and returned to his normal voice. "It was strange. Stranger than usual. Most the time, they fall down drunk and laugh and stuff. Barely put up a fight when security tries to get ahold of them. But she was crying. Lashing out at them and screaming to let her go. That they needed to catch this other woman before she got away." He looked over at Nell. "She seemed really messed up. Like she was on drugs or something."

"She doesn't do drugs!" Ada whispered the words. Least not that Ada knew. Alcohol, sure. But with the Hunt in full swing, and everywhere—social media, the radio, highway billboards, posters, at work, Maggie's stupid T-shirts—perhaps drugs weren't out of the question.

Briefly, she'd let Elijah trip into her head, taking him out to hunt without Nell or Anthony knowing. And here Nell was, having some sort of psychotic break.

Elijah texted: When are you coming back?

Did you find the egg? she texted back. She'd told him only to text if he'd found it or it was in danger of being found by someone else. Or an actual emergency, not a hunger pang.

Ugh, he wrote.

She tucked her phone into her back pocket and put it on silent.

"What now?" Ada gestured at Nell, like she was some delicate or dangerous thing, someone that required hushed tones so as not to upset her balance. "Is there some kind of report or something? Some procedure to release her?"

"Oh, she's fine to go. We don't arrest people here."

She nodded and thanked the man. Assured him that she would get Nell home and that she'd be no more trouble, an assurance Ada couldn't guarantee. He nodded in return and then wandered into a row of blinking and dinging slot machines before he disappeared.

Ada eased toward Nell. Her nerves lit up a notch with each step. She'd never felt nervous around her. Or anxious. When Nell had first come on the factory, she'd looked at Ada with recognition, like she couldn't believe two young people had both ended up there. Ada ignored her for the longest time. Not wanting to speak to some white girl younger than her who'd been hired on as a night foreman when Ada had had to work her way up to running presses after two years on the label machine. Not wanting to waste her time with small talk. She didn't have time for friends.

But then Nell would come around, all cheerful, twirling a wrench or some other tool around her finger, asking if Ada needed something fixed. Ada swatted at her like a gnat. That never deterred Nell. If Nell had to work, she seemed to want to make it a good time, for everyone. Even after Maggie went and told everyone her brother had drowned and possibly been murdered by the Hunter, if rumors were to be believed, and how that must be so hard. Ada couldn't help herself after that. Nell played tough and jovial. But sometimes, Ada'd step outside the factory to get something in her car, and there Nell sat on the bench, looking up at the sky. Something like a haunted look on her face. But then again, Ada could've assumed that after what Maggie had said. When she'd seen Nell like that a few times, Ada'd had to go and fuss at her. Had to go and sit down. Poke at her.

Ada eased into the booth opposite Nell, who still didn't look up from her coffee.

Ada nodded her head at a girl in uniform, pointed at her coffee cup, and held up two fingers. When the server returned with their coffees, Ada thanked her and slid the fresh cup to Nell, not daring to touch the one she still cupped in her hands in case she had somehow gone feral since their phone call. She'd gone something like catatonic, that was for sure.

Ada busied herself with her sugar and creamer. She took her time fixing and sipping her coffee, hoping that Nell would finally say something. When she didn't, Ada drank and swallowed and readied her tongue for speech. But her phone buzzed again. She didn't need to look to know it was Elijah.

"You all right?" she asked Nell. Ada didn't know what else to say. It seemed too soon to ask about the particulars. Nell looked like a heathen and apparently had acted like one, too, so Ada assumed sex and a woman were involved. Ada couldn't help but feel sorry for Nell. If she was being honest, she recognized herself in Nell. Ada'd once been a young, dumb girl, drunk on the affections of someone who felt like love and tied her down.

Ada tried to think on what she could've heard then that might've helped her, might've gotten her across that particular finish line a little bit earlier with William, maybe a little less heartbroken. But nothing would've helped. The only thing that did was time and the distraction of a baby that needed every last bit of her.

They didn't speak for a while, so she asked again if Nell was all right.

Finally, Nell raised her head and looked at Ada. "I think I slept with the woman who killed my brother."

Shared Google Doc / The Hunt

VICTIM #2

On April 13, 2006, three days before Easter, Glen Olson, white, twenty-two, was found in a wooded area along Parker Lane. An autopsy was not conducted, as paraphernalia related to meth use was found on and near the body. The medical examiner listed overdose as the cause of death.

We spoke with Glen's family, who denied that he had a problem with drugs. We also spoke with his friends, who were never contacted by the police. They admitted that he enjoyed smoking weed and taking the occasional white pill, but they denied that he would be interested in meth, as it was a "fugly drug" and Glen had participated in several local modeling jobs. Asked why they didn't go to the police with this information, most of them shrugged and one added, "Maybe it's more that we're surprised. I guess you really can't know someone."

Glen was last seen on April 12, hunting for the egg with the friends we interviewed. In 2009, Glen's name was added to the list of victims of the Hunter due to the "suspicious" circumstances of his death.

Eleven

Nell

Sunday, April 10
Morning
Seven days before Easter

Nell couldn't find her sunglasses, though she could've sworn she'd come into the casino with them. She always had them on her, as well as her keys. And her wallet. All gone except, inexplicably, her phone. She tried to remember details but couldn't remember anything but the edges of a bad decision. A bad night. A woman. That woman. How would that woman know Garrett's name? Why had she said those things?

"Why would you think she killed your brother?" Ada asked.

Nell had known, clear as day, as soon as that woman had said Garrett's name, that she knew something. Maybe how Garrett ended up in Lee Creek a week after he'd been killed. She had to have known Nell before she even sat down next to her at the slots, before they entered the hotel room.

"She said his name," Nell said. "She knew him."

"She said his name?" Ada's tone sounded like an adult on *Sesame Street*. Or an after-school special about drug abuse. Calm, questioning. Concerned. "A lot of people know his name."

Nell didn't know how to explain and got irritated. "I know people know his name. But this woman, the way she said his name, other things . . ." Nell struggled to explain why she knew the woman had something to do with Garrett's death, but she knew. "She said things."

"What kind of things?"

Nell's brain felt fuzzed and off, like she was sitting in front of a test where she didn't understand the questions, let alone know the answers. "Things!"

"But what did—"

"She said she liked me. That I'm not like the others." Nell finally blurted out the words. "She said it was a shame Garrett had to die."

Ada blinked a lot and just sat there, upset, it seemed. Or confused. Maybe both. Finally, she said, "Maybe you misheard."

That's why Nell had torn out of the bed. She wanted to know what the woman had said: *Shame he died*, or *Shame he had to die*?

He died or *he* had *to die.*

They were two different things. By the time Nell had gotten to the hallway, the woman was gone. Nell rushed down the stairwell to the first floor, tripping and twisting her ankle in the process. But she scrambled to her feet and ran through the casino, yelling for the woman. Asking if anyone had seen her. Yelling that they had to have seen her. She was just there.

Then, someone gripped her arm, told her to calm down, to come with him. A satin jacket swished against her bare skin. Nell had jerked in the direction of the voice. It was the same security guard that Ada had talked to while Nell had stared into her coffee cup, trying to make sense of how she'd gone from being in a hotel bed with that woman to being surrounded by people pointing, laughing, holding hands over their mouths in shock.

"I didn't mishear." Nell wanted to cry. Maybe she was crying. She couldn't really pinpoint what was going on with her body, but something was decidedly not right. Her body seemed to move ten seconds after her brain. And she felt like bugs were crawling through her veins. Or what it might feel like if they were. Tickling and itching, with no way to scratch. "I know what she said." But did she?

He had to die.

The words wouldn't go away. Nor would the question that had begun to ping at her insides: What if the woman was the Hunter?

The lights of the cafeteria seemed to increase in brightness. Nell squeezed her eyes shut. The pings and whirly sounds of the slot machines agitated her. She wanted to tear off the top layer of her skin as well as her insides. Gut herself and be rid of that tickling, itching sensation that coursed through her. She couldn't even remember how she'd come to be in the cafeteria. When she'd returned to her room, gotten her clothes, and pulled them on. Her shirt pinned together with safety pins from someone she didn't remember seeing.

She glanced at her hands and placed the coffee to her lips, but it was cold.

Ada nudged another coffee toward her. Steam swirled above the brown liquid.

She pushed the cold coffee aside in favor of the hot one. She sipped it. It tasted good, like always. Maybe the coffee was what had kept her coming, not the gambling and booze, she thought, amused, because otherwise, she might have to keep thinking about how she'd ended up here, across from Ada, telling her what sounded increasingly like a bad trip. She'd know. She'd had them before.

"What time is it?" Nell asked. There were no clocks on the wall. It could be Sunday. Wednesday. Day or night.

Ada checked her phone. "A little after ten."

"At night?" Nell had left the factory at 5:00 p.m.

Ada laughed like people do when someone makes them uncomfortable but they don't know what to do with their discomfort. "Maybe I should call someone."

"No," Nell said. "No, don't call anyone. I just gotta get my bearings."

Ada sat back in her booth seat, lips pursed, eyes directed at the table, not moving. She wore her typical work outfit, jeans and a hoodie. No lipstick, though. She looked tired.

Everything felt jumbled in Nell's brain. What had happened felt like a blur. Maybe she'd been wrong about the woman. Maybe she had misheard, but why would the woman know his name? Had Nell misheard that as well in her drunken stupor?

"I need to get going," Ada finally said. "I have work tonight."

So it was morning. Nell patted her jeans again, thinking maybe she had somehow missed her keys the first time she'd checked. Nothing. "Could you give me a ride home?"

Ada drew in a long breath through her nose and out her mouth. She stood, her keys jangling in her hand. "Isn't that why you called?" Ada hauled up out of the booth seat and took off toward the casino doors.

Nell followed, like a kid in trouble with Mom. Confused by what had happened and why Ada was so angry.

The walk to the car felt like forever. Before Nell had a chance to open the passenger door, Ada had walked quickly to get there first. Nell had figured she wanted to get out of there as fast as possible. But Ada pulled a Texas A&M blanket out of the back seat and placed it on the passenger seat. Nell could've died of embarrassment right there.

Ada turned the radio up so loud Nell's ears rang from the impact. But she wasn't about to ask Ada to turn it down. She hated the silence between them more. Then her brain might try to find some way to explain to Ada or herself why she'd done what she'd done, even though she only remembered glimpses of it. But she remembered going willingly into that night, without hope and with a truckload of heartache, clinging to the first warm body she'd found that might replace Tessa.

Only that warm body knew about Garrett. Said he'd had to die. Nell didn't know what to do with the discomfort that clawed at her from the inside.

When they turned off the highway and onto the gravel road and then to the dirt road and came to Nell's mailbox, she said, "You can drop me off here."

Ada breathed in again, this time sharp and quick, and then brought the car to a jarring stop. Ada's jaw was set hard, like she'd been clenching it the whole time. Her lips still pursed tight, holding her thoughts in as she targeted her gaze through the windshield.

"Thanks for the ride," Nell said, knowing the words were no good, not fitting for the situation.

Ada squinted a bit, opened her mouth, and then shut it. She sucked her lips together tightly to shut down the words she probably wanted to say. Nell wanted to tell her the truth: that she'd been messing around with Tessa and they'd broken up because of Elijah. And then Nell had gotten fucked up and relapsed with gambling because she didn't have any other coping skills.

Nell couldn't say so, though. Not even to Ada, the closest thing she had to a friend. She didn't know for sure, but she guessed what Ada might say to all that.

Nell opened the passenger door and stepped out. The engine noise mingled with morning birdsong. Nell said one more word of thanks but didn't look at Ada after she headed toward the driveway.

Behind her, she heard Ada pull ahead and turn the car around up the road a piece, where the road forked to more distant dirt driveways than hers. Nell loitered at the mailbox. Opened it like any other morning, seeing what woes she might find in the form of bills and who knew what else. All the time thinking that she should have tried to tell Ada why she'd called in sick and ended up at the casino. Even though she didn't know why. Other than she was falling apart and she felt like maybe someone should know, for her own safety, and Elijah's, in case she didn't recognize herself come morning.

Ada's engine got louder after she had turned her car around and made to pass.

Ada brought the car to a pause. The window hummed as it lowered.

"Nell!"

Nell could barely stand how hopeful she felt at the sound of her name coming out of Ada's mouth. Among all the conflicting feelings and thoughts in her head, she couldn't understand why she felt almost as bad about losing Ada as she did about losing Tessa.

Ada glared at her through the passenger window. Her mouth had gone mad, it seemed, twitching with anger.

"You need to get your shit together. For Elijah." She rolled up the window and then left Nell standing in the dirt and dust she'd stirred up.

Shared Google Doc / The Hunt

VICTIM #8

Shawn Sartori, white, forty-eight, was found on Easter Sunday in 2012, by Eggheads searching for the golden egg. Not much is known about Shawn, as he lived alone and collected Social Security. Authorities officially listed his death as heatstroke and dehydration. With no known relatives, Shawn was cremated and buried in the city plot without ceremony. His belongings were collected and disposed of by the city.

Our conversations with neighbors revealed that though Shawn kept to himself, many noticed that he left the house every day at 5:00 a.m. and returned at 5:00 p.m. during the Hunt. A concerned neighbor called the police after she realized the feral cats he fed stopped coming around and the food bowl he usually left out was full of "nothing but rain."

Additionally, though Shawn's death is officially listed as heatstroke and dehydration, historical records indicate Presley's weather was mild and mostly cloudy in the three weeks leading up to the Hunt. Also, the police report noted that several unopened plastic bottles of water were also found in his backpack. No further information was available.

Twelve

Ada

Sunday, April 10
Midmorning
Seven days before Easter

Why did Ada feel so hurt by a woman who didn't even belong to her? She wanted to laugh at herself over such a stupid little crush that would never go anywhere—that was the whole point of a work crush! But she was also listening to Mariah Carey's "We Belong Together" on repeat, so all she felt was sad and mad and immature.

At first, she'd blamed Elijah for getting thoughts about Nell in her head. But he was a kid. She'd been weak and stupid enough to let the idea of someone finding her attractive—if it was even true!—infect her thinking and let her wander into delusions and daydreams. Nell was her friend. And coworker. And Nell was clearly a fool. How else could she explain what had happened at the casino?

Ada hated herself for being so disappointed in Nell. She hated herself even more for thinking that at least this way she wouldn't have to explain dating a woman to her parents or friends. Then she got mad at herself for thinking it.

Throughout the casino and then the car ride, her anger had only grown. By the time she'd dropped Nell off at the bottom of her driveway, Ada practically vibrated with it and couldn't control her mouth and said something mean. And there poor Nell had been, traumatized, walking up to the house all hangdog, tail tucked between her legs.

Damn fool, she muttered as she headed back to where she'd left Elijah, as fast as she thought she could get away with without being pulled over by a cop. She didn't want to deal with them today. She took it slow and easy and said a little prayer. At the stoplight, she rushed out a text to Elijah to let him know she was on her way—something she should've done in the first place, back at the casino, but she'd been too baffled. She cursed herself again for thinking any kind of something about Nell.

By the time she made it to the spot where she'd left Elijah, it was well past noon. She'd convinced him to get up early with her to beat anyone else who might've had the same idea about a location from the late-night clue. Ada had been gone more than three hours. She braced herself for the teenage tirade that was sure to come.

She parked the car in one of the small lots at the back of the park. She knew he wouldn't be where she'd left him, but it felt as good a starting point as any. Barely any bars out here, but her text to him finally went through. She shielded her eyes from the sun and glanced around to see if she might spot him. A Black man with a metal detector swung his equipment across the grass in the distance. A group of brown and white men kicked a soccer ball in one of the fields. Their whoops and laughter carried to a few white teenagers with too much time in front of a mirror with their black eyeliner pencils. They sat at a huddle of picnic tables smoking and drinking. By the looks of them, they fit that brand of young adults who came from good families but wanted to shirk responsibility and wealth and live in danger because their lives were too easy. They felt dead inside and needed something to excite them—at least that's what she imagined. If they only knew. She squinted, but none looked like Elijah, either at the picnic tables or on the field. His earlier texts that she'd ignored when she was with Nell included no indication of where he'd gone. They were only queries as to where she was.

She stared at her phone, hoping to see those three telltale dots that indicated Elijah was alive and well and pissed off.

My God, what would he think if he knew about Nell? She sure as hell wasn't gonna tell him.

She looked around some more and then drove her car around the one-way loop of the park to see if he might be somewhere among the dotted trees and public pavilions in the park, but it was to no avail.

The last time he'd disappeared, he'd gone to the 7-Eleven, so she drove to the convenience store across from the park to see if he might be there.

"Yeah," the cashier, an Asian American teenager with the name tag "Christa," said after Ada had shown her a photo of Elijah on her phone. "Saw him a couple hours ago."

Relief washed over Ada. At least he was alive. A dumb thought. Of course he was alive. Like Elijah had said, no one like him had been killed. "Did he say anything?"

"Like?" The cashier curled her lip and the vowel in irritation. A swath of months-old, once-red, now-faded pink hair covered one eye. Ada decided she was one of those filthy rich kids whose parents forced her to get a job after being caught smoking pot after school.

"Did he say he needed to use your phone or anything?"

The cashier expressed confusion and patted her back pockets. She pulled out her phone as if to confirm its presence. "Why would he use my phone?"

Ada clearly wouldn't get anywhere with this girl. "Never mind."

"Whatever," the girl said, a word that landed like nails on a chalkboard to Ada's ears. She'd warned Anthony she would wash his mouth out with soap if he didn't stop saying it.

Back in the car, she texted Anthony to see if he'd heard from Elijah that morning. He replied with one word: No. Anthony hated when she texted him while he was working—even though he'd texted her that morning to tell her he was going for dinner with friends that night.

Good! she'd replied hastily, the fire of irritation still raging and collecting everyone and everything in its path. More for me and Elijah!

He'd ignored her.

Finally, she texted Elijah one last time to tell him that she was waiting for him in the parking lot of the convenience store.

Even though it was spring, it was Arkansas. It'd been in the forties the day before, but it was running up to eighty at the moment. It was already stuffy in her car—at least outside, the breeze could catch you and provide relief. The smell of gas wafted to her. As the heat and day wore on, her anger subsided. While she waited, she replayed the scene from that morning in her mind. Her stomach dropped in embarrassment on Nell's behalf. Nell had had her fair share of empty-eye gazes over the years, but Ada'd never seen her like that. Nell looked shook to the bone. But all Ada could do at the time was feel angry and sorry for herself like some hormone-ravaged teen. Ridiculous. She was gonna get on some of those dating apps. Get something going with someone. Stop sniffing around her friend like she was in heat.

Other cars parked next to her, over and over. The sun beat down on her through the windshield. Her insides felt liked to boil. Plus, a mixed gaggle of teenagers had gathered near her car to eat chips and drink slushies, mindless chatter to Ada's ears until one of them mentioned that a girl in her homeroom had been chased by and barely gotten away from the Hunter a couple of years ago. They were so intense in their storytelling and listening that one of them even collapsed on the hood of Ada's car in play fear. Ada honked, and they moved down the sidewalk after flipping her off. She grumbled, rolled up the windows, and ran the AC a bit to cool herself down.

Nothing to do but wait. For a while, she contemplated going back to her hunt, given it was cut short that morning, even though she'd literally lost her hunting partner. But she abandoned the idea. Someone else might've found it already.

That's how low she felt. She didn't even want to hunt.

All she'd ever heard was how dumb she was for going out every year to hunt for a golden egg like some kid. This from people who regularly told her what they planned to buy when they won the lottery, the American Dream. Always dangling out of reach for people like her. So what if she hunted for a damn egg? What'd it matter to them? It didn't hurt them. But look at them: go into a store and buy a ticket and scratch it and then head home to wait for their fortunes to drop into their laps like magic. At least she got out and got some exercise. She moved her body and engaged her mind.

A bead of sweat eased its way down her chest and pooled in her bra. She swiped her forehead and then flicked through her Facebook posts before dozing off.

When she woke up, the sun had moved along in the sky, but not by much. Not enough to alarm her. Her bra was more soaked than before. And her mouth felt like someone had stuffed a dustrag in it. She grabbed her water bottle, but it was empty. She collected the loose change she kept in the console, locked up the car, and went inside the convenience store to get a Diet Coke.

The pink-haired cashier gave Ada her change and let her go without any acknowledgment of their earlier conversation. She'd be no use in finding Elijah.

When she turned on the car for a bit of AC, the clock indicated it was 4:00 p.m., about the time she'd normally get up and start getting supper on and cleaning herself up before heading to work. The original plan had been to hunt in the morning and then head home for some sleep before work. Now, if she got lucky, she'd make it home in ten or fifteen minutes and have ten to spare for changing into fresh clothing before taking off for her shift. She hadn't pulled an all-nighter with barely any sleep since Anthony was a baby. She wasn't looking forward to the reminder of how much that sucked.

She yawned, turned on the car, and made another loop around the park to see if Elijah happened to be there before heading home.

Nell had ruined the morning, and now Elijah had ruined her afternoon with his little tantrum.

That's all it was, she told herself, especially after the last time they'd gotten separated on a hunt.

Before turning out of the park and onto the highway, she texted him again. This time she told him she had to leave and to call her as soon as possible. Then, she navigated back to the convenience store, grabbed an energy drink, and sighed heavily at the prospect of the long night ahead.

KAOK News Report

Despite rising tension between fans and opponents, the Hunt for the Golden Egg is well underway, with so-called Eggheads out in full force today, eyes trained on the ground and heads full of hope for finding the golden egg, which comes with a $50,000 cash prize.

"Look. People are gonna say what they want. But people love the Hunt," Rod Halstrom, KCLS station owner, told us earlier today at a sales event at the Price Cutter. "It's a beautiful time of year, and families are excited to be out together, exploring our city and engaging in something besides the TV."

Local business owners share Rod's sentiments. Many report an increase of 40 percent in sales during the monthlong Hunt for the Golden Egg. "It's a boon to business, that's for sure," Kitty Corner Antiques owner Pearly Wood said. "You'd think that after all we've been through the past couple years, people would be pleased that everyone can get out and enjoy our town. But some people want to hold on to their conspiracies."

Local healthcare workers, however, are quick to add that despite conspiracies, the Hunt does present real problems. "I'd say, historically, we also see an increase in injuries," said Anita Donohue, an ER nurse at Mercy Medical. "Ankle sprains, cuts, head trauma . . . you name it. You've got kids running around without supervision and adults running around drinking and acting like fools. It's worse than lawnmower season."

Still, with only seven days left in the Hunt, Eggheads and new hunters alike are ramping up their efforts to find the egg.

"I been out here all day, every day, since the first day," said retiree Jesse Reindl. "For $50,000? [Beep] yeah, I'm gonna look. I don't care what anyone says. Hunting is guaranteed by the Second Amendment, ain't it?" Jesse added with a laugh.

Despite the general attitude of fun and festivities, Nancy Barker, unofficial spokesperson for the anti-Eggheads, vowed to continue her efforts to shut down the Hunt. "Someone's gonna get hurt," Nancy said. "Mark my words."

Aaron and Alice Raleigh, who spearheaded the effort to shut down the Hunt after their daughter Annalee died of a suspicious gunshot wound while hunting for the egg in 2013, were not available for comment.

"We're not gonna stop," Nancy said. "Wherever Rod goes, we're gonna be there. We're gonna remind him that the next death is on him."

Thirteen

Nell

Sunday, April 10
Midmorning
Seven days before Easter

Nell stepped up to the back door, which they used more than the front door, and was surprised when she found it locked. She'd been meaning to get a spare key and hide it somewhere, but like the lawn, she'd gotten too lazy. She could text Elijah, but she didn't want him coming home to see her like this. She knew she was a mess. She needed a shower and a lot of coffee and a lot of carbs. She felt wrung all out.

"Elijah?" she called out and waited.

The air was sticky, and the sun beat down. She banged on the door and called for him again. Finally, she walked around the trailer, checking to see if they'd left any windows open. Given the recent rain, she doubted it. If they had, she'd need to find some way to reach the windows. Her grandparents had situated the trailer high off the ground due to flooding, even though they were on a hill. But she guessed when floods were such a routine part of your life growing up in the river valley, you wanted assurances as a homeowner. The whole place looked a mess, inside and outside. She'd been so caught up with Tessa. Too tired to mow or clean anything unrelated to the places Tessa's hands and mouth roamed. Nell had hated girls like her in high school, girls who dropped everything for a boy. And now she'd practically become one of them.

She checked the front door, but it was locked too. That porch was closer to the living room windows, which didn't require a ladder. But none of the windows would budge either.

"To hell with it," she said and walked to the screened-in back porch, where she grabbed Grandpa's old rusty hammer that she kept on a ledge and then walked back to smash the front window. Needed to be fixed anyway. There was a crack in it from the '80s that had been taped over. Now she had an excuse to get a new one.

Once inside, she cleaned and vacuumed up the mess. Then she found some old boards and hammered those in place over the broken window. She didn't have any immediate neighbors in sight, so she wasn't worried about anyone calling the cops to say she was a burglar. When Elijah asked, she'd tell him she'd lost her keys. No lie there. Of course, now she had to figure out how to get her truck from the casino. And she'd have to dig up some spare keys somewhere.

Finally, she had a chance to take a shower. She stayed in there, scrubbing a lot and then standing there some more, until the water ran cold. She pulled on her sweatpants and a hoodie and opened the bedroom door slowly, dreading the sight of Elijah. But she was alone in the house.

On the kitchen table she found a note Elijah had written her to say he'd decided to stay over with a friend from school for a few nights to work on a school project because the library was a waste of time. Little shit didn't even ask first, just did it. Like he was an adult and responsible to no one but himself.

She texted him: Got your note. Good luck with your project. But next time, ask.

He replied right away with apologies and a smiley face emoji. She was too relieved to be alone to be mad at him too long. And part of her was relieved that he wasn't staying with Ada. Still, she wondered who this friend was. He almost always hung out with Anthony. Ada had said that they'd been in a fight and hadn't been hanging out much. Felt like a rite of passage to fall out with a friend in high school. She wondered how common it was to fall out twice, like she and Tessa had.

She felt like shit for sleeping with someone else right after she'd broken things off with Tessa. Now she felt like the high school boys she'd hated who had broken her girlfriends' hearts. A proper douchebag.

She typed out several messages to Tessa but backspaced on them all. For now, her focus was figuring out who the hell that woman from the casino was.

She pulled out a notebook and pen, sat down at the kitchen table, and wrote down everything she could remember about the woman. It wasn't much help. She didn't even remember her name. *Casino*, that's what she'd call her.

She woke up some time later, much later, after falling asleep on the notepad, grateful again that Elijah was at a friend's house and didn't have the opportunity to see her after one of her old-school ragers. Head like a concrete block, veins shriveled from dehydration, skin sticky with drinks and bodily fluids, hers and a stranger's. Sometimes, mostly when she was a little high to take the edge off a hard day, Elijah would ask her about the past, as if it were the good old days of fucking off with her friends instead of burying bad feelings brought on by Garrett's death.

Back then, she could call in to work and not worry about consequences, even if it meant losing her job. She'd get another shitty job somewhere else.

She picked up the phone again. "Caught something." Nell spoke low and tried to add a little gravel to her voice to sell it to Maggie.

"Is it COVID?" Nell was pretty sure Maggie wasn't allowed to ask that of employees.

"No," Nell said. "Bad cold." Too late, she realized she should have said she had the stomach flu to keep Maggie off her ass about it when she returned to work. COVID and stomach flu were one thing. A bad cold was no excuse to miss work.

She went to grab her keys off the microwave, where she usually kept them, and remembered why they weren't there.

She didn't want to ask Ada for another favor, so she broke down and got an Uber after finding her spare set of keys in a drawer. Elijah had put her credit card info in the app for her, even though she'd only used Uber once or twice. She figured it'd cost less in the middle of the day. But it cost her an arm and a leg to get to the casino.

Thankfully, the Uber driver wasn't chatty. He was too busy singing low along with the church music he played from a CD. Without a need to focus on the road, Nell stared out the back seat window and tried not to puke from waves of nausea. At the stoplights and stop signs and in fields and basically any spot that had green space, people wandered and stared at the ground. She'd never seen so many of them all at once. All types of people, young and old. Most in groups, some alone. If a tourist or random driver happened to wander through, they'd probably wonder who had gone missing.

"Welcome to Presley, Accident Capitol of the World," she mused. "All those people went missing, and they're just looking for an egg, not what happened to human beings," she added, mostly to herself.

The driver glanced at her in the rearview mirror but then went back to driving.

She closed her eyes and propped her head on the back of the seat for the remainder of the ride. Once they arrived at the parking lot, she nearly cried with relief that her truck hadn't been towed. It wouldn't be the first time from the casino either. Alone again, she sat inside it for a while with the window open, letting the breeze work its magic on her wooziness. She squirreled around in the glove box but couldn't find anything to eat. She couldn't stomach grabbing something from the casino buffet. Instead, she walked over to the separate casino convenience store–slash–gift shop building and grabbed a ginger ale, Gatorade, and saltines. She downed the ginger ale in one go.

Outside the convenience store, she sat on a bench and stared at the casino, which loomed nearby. It'd been like her second home. Or rather, like her first home after Garrett had died. Everyone walking around like ghosts while the world went on around them. Nobody talking to anyone but everyone aware they weren't alone.

She watched the parking lot, scanning all the people who came in and out, keeping an eye out for a white woman with long dark hair. But it was Sunday afternoon. There weren't many people there.

After a while, she shook out the last saltine from the bag and took off toward the casino.

The casino air and smell enveloped her like a baby blanket in which she could wrap herself and self-soothe all night. Out of habit, she wandered in the direction of the buffet. But someone grabbed her arm.

She spun around and found the security guy from earlier that morning. The one who had covered her with his satin security jacket and talked to Ada when she arrived. Poor guy's shift seemed longer than hers.

"Ma'am." The word hung heavy with exasperation, but his tone was warm and kind, and that made her want to crawl up inside the word and sit a while.

"I—"

"You really should go home." He reminded her of Lloyd when she'd first met him. Thoughtful eyes, like he really cared about her well-being. "Get yourself together."

She glanced at his name tag and held out her hands. "Homie, I know what you're thinking."

He tilted his head, frowned.

"I mean, maybe not. The thing is, I really need to know who that person was. The woman I was chasing, I think she might know something about my brother. He died a while back. Maybe you heard of him, Garrett Holcomb? Victim of the Hunter?"

He continued to stare at her with that tilt and that frown, like she was going to be trouble with a capital *T*.

"Look. I know my behavior was . . ." She paused to find a word that would make him believe that she was not going to be trouble. "Inappropriate."

He didn't change his stance.

"Concerning."

Nothing.

"Disturbing and unwelcome." The words didn't hurt. They were accurate. They were recitals about an old version of herself that had made a comeback. "Disrespectful to you, your coworkers, your patrons, the Cherokee Nation."

He rolled his eyes.

"Look. I'm embarrassed, and I'm deeply sorry for my actions." She cleared her throat. "I promise you I won't return after today. Put me on a list—"

"You're already on a list."

"Okay. That's fair. I get that." Hands out in supplication. "I just need to know who that woman was." He waited, so she continued, "Maybe there's video footage or something? A credit card slip with her name on it?"

His head tilt finally ended. He sighed. "You should go home. Get some rest. Think about things."

"I did! I will. Continue to get rest." She smiled, big. "See, the thing is, I can't really rest until I know who that woman is. So if I could—"

"Please don't make me escort you out of the building." He tilted his head again, raised his eyebrows.

She focused on the gold-and-red carpeting. Then the swirls moved, and the nausea returned. "Maybe tomorrow I could come back and take a look—"

"You need to go home, friend." Before she could add anything else, he repeated, "Go home."

She sighed heavily, but that didn't do anything. So she thanked the man and turned toward the door, leaving the comfort and warmth of what had once been her good place behind her and without any answers to show for it.

Shared Google Doc / The Hunt

VICTIM #16

On March 10, 2020, the Akhtars, Pakistani American, ages withheld, left for a weekend in Las Vegas "before things got shut down" while their twin teenage sons stayed with their grandparents in nearby Fort Smith. The twins, whose names have also been withheld by request, told their grandparents they were going to the Malco Cinema for a midnight showing of *The Rocky Horror Picture Show* and would not return until later that morning. The twins did not go to the movie but instead hosted a house party while their parents were away and invited their tenth-grade classmates.

One of the classmates in attendance was Elizabeth Ferrari, sixteen, Chinese American, who arrived with a group of friends. At the conclusion of the party, Elizabeth's friends were unable to locate her and assumed that she had caught a ride home with another classmate. Elizabeth was reported missing the next day by her parents. After an hourlong search of the Akhtar's property, Elizabeth's body was found in their barn, with a fentanyl "lollipop" in her mouth. Authorities confirmed that the house was "spotless" by the time the Akhtars arrived home, a result of the twins' thorough cleaning prior to their parents' return from Las Vegas. Police closed the case, citing accidental overdose as the cause of death.

Elizabeth's family publicly disputed the medical examiner and police's contention that their daughter was involved in drugs, having committed to a "straightedge" lifestyle.

We spoke with several of Elizabeth's friends, who confirmed that Elizabeth was "straightedge," as well as most of the tenth-grade class, in recognition of a classmate who had died of an overdose at the age of twelve. No one had seen fentanyl lollipops or any other illegal substances circulating at the party or at school. One of Elizabeth's friends mentioned that at one point in the evening, Elizabeth excused herself to go to the bathroom. Witnesses saw Elizabeth in line, but all indicated that she had left the line because she "could not wait." They expressed concern over her behavior, which they described as "erratic" and "confused."

None of Elizabeth's classmates mentioned the above information to police, claiming they were "afraid that no one would believe them" or worried that someone would call them "Eggheads" because Elizabeth and her classmates participated in the Hunt for the Golden Egg a few afternoons after school because Presley is "boring as shit." (Note: Egghead is considered a slur among the younger generation in Presley.) All the classmates were grounded by their parents after the event and were forbidden to "get involved in a family matter."

Fourteen

Ada

Sunday, April 10
Evening
Seven days before Easter

Elijah still hadn't returned Ada's text.

She chewed the inside of her bottom lip and considered the worst-case scenario as to his whereabouts, but then she stopped herself. No sense in thinking the worst. Elijah was fine. He had gotten annoyed that she'd been gone so long when she'd left to pick up Nell from the casino. Same as the first time they'd gone out. He was having a fit. That's all it was. Nothing more.

Still, while she waited for plastic caps to fill their boxes, she texted Anthony to see if he'd heard from Elijah.

Why do you keep asking me where he is? he texted back.

She had tried to keep her message loose and casual, but clearly, she had failed. 'Cause I need to know how much to buy at the grocery store. NOT THAT I MIND!!! But I need to know if he's planning on showing up!

Once those boys were gone, she was gonna eat takeout every night. It'd be cheaper than what she was doing now. Or at least, she'd eat it at least once a week. The rest of the time, she'd buy herself frozen dinners and wouldn't turn on anything but the microwave unless Anthony came home for the weekend or holidays. Then she'd cook. She loved to cook when she had time.

Her excuse seemed to satisfy Anthony because he wrote back quickly to say he didn't know. She guessed they still weren't talking.

She typed out another text to Elijah, this time telling him that he needed to quit playing games. He'd taken it too far. She lodged her phone in her back pocket. A radar sounded deep down inside her when she thought about where Elijah might be and told her that something was wrong, real wrong.

At least Nell wasn't at work that night.

"Nell called in two nights in a row?" Maggie had complained to Viv at the start of third shift. She'd been mad at Ada ever since they saw each other at the grocery store. "She must have a *real* nasty cold."

Ada was mostly grateful for the reprieve. She knew Nell would never want to talk about the casino, but Ada also didn't know how she was supposed to not talk about it and pretend like she hadn't had to pick Nell up that morning like a truant or a criminal. Ada also hadn't exactly been nice, letting her emotions overtake her. Emotions she didn't have any right to. She had about twenty-four hours to figure out what to say to her when the time came, and not just about the casino. She still didn't know where the hell Elijah was. She didn't want to have to deal with that on top of the awkwardness of seeing Nell again. She decided the best thing to do was to keep her mouth shut and pretend that she didn't know anything unless Nell asked her point blank about either.

Finally, she texted Nell, thinking that maybe it'd be best to rip off the bandage with first contact: Hey. Checking in. Hope Elijah's there to take care of you. She thought about adding a smile emoji but deleted it in case it looked like she was making fun of Nell.

Nell replied with a thumbs-up. Not helpful.

Ada checked her watch. Only two hours down and ten to go on her shift. She didn't know how she'd make it through the whole night after working the previous night, let alone hunting for an hour with Elijah, dealing with Nell at the casino, and then only a catnap here and there in the car while waiting for Elijah to show up that same day. Her eyes watered, and her mouth gaped with a yawn every few minutes. She yanked the neck of her hoodie to her eyes and held it there a while.

When Ada looked up from her texts, the cardboard box from press three was overflowing with plastic caps. She raced over to them and quickly replaced the full boxes with empties and then picked up all the ones from the floor and tossed them into the new box she'd set up for the press. Luckily, Gunner wasn't there to notice. Nell was easygoing about things, but if Gunner had seen her texting instead of working, and letting her boxes overflow, he would've screamed at her while also calling her a hothead and then written her up, like they were in high school. Not that Lloyd would do anything except give her a talking to or maybe ask if everything was okay at home and if she was interested in joining him and Nancy at church. She'd gone once, after she'd gotten caught before by Lloyd texting and ignoring her boxes. Lloyd and Nancy's church was way too extreme for Ada's taste. She wasn't into all that hellfire and brimstone shit. And she hated people who flung Bible verses out of their mouths for everything. She liked to cuss and drink and preferred uplifting sermons to those that tried to shame or terrify people. If Lloyd and Nancy's God was the right one, then she guessed she was going to Hell.

The noise from the machines nearly put Ada to sleep. She had to get some more coffee in her if she wanted to make it through the night.

She replaced a full box of milk caps from press six, the one closest to the break room, with an empty cardboard box, taped up the sides of the full box, and then placed it on the pallet. She stretched and yawned again but couldn't complete them because she heard a loud noise from behind press one, near the back wall, where the overhead lights didn't quite reach.

"Gunner?" she yelled out. He had reluctantly come in on his off day thanks to Nell's absenteeism. But he didn't respond.

She glanced around herself. Viv was nowhere to be seen, but she might've been in the bathroom or out having a smoke. The distinct beep of Kasey backing up the forklift came from behind the long plastic strips that separated the manufacturing from the shipping area.

Assured of other people's presence, Ada made her way to press one, where she'd heard the noise. Rather than peek around the corner, she made a wide curve to the back wall, so she could see someone hiding, if they were.

There on the floor was Nell's wrench. She knew it was Nell's because she preferred Milwaukee brand, with the red handle. Ada cursed herself for acting so foolish, believing there was something to be frightened of. But she also couldn't figure out what the wrench was doing back there. There was nothing on that side of the press for the wrench to have been used on, nothing to really set the wrench on and come back to it later. Almost like it fell from the ceiling. Nell wasn't one to lose or misplace her tools. She liked to keep things organized.

Before Ada could reach for it, she heard caps dropping to the floor and ran to clean up the latest mess she'd made by not paying attention.

Morning light broke through the small windows at the top of the building. As usual, the chatter among the crew had died down around 2:00 a.m., and the presses and label machines muffled everything but Gunner shouting out end-of-shift requests regarding cleanup and other nonsense Nell never bugged them about because she knew they were adults and didn't need to be reminded of their jobs. The final hour passed like the longest bout of insomnia. She was an odd mix of wired and tired, strung out and sour stomached from too much coffee to keep herself awake throughout her twelve-hour shift. She alternated between irritation with Elijah, and then Maggie, then Nell, and then back to Elijah and the spiraling fear that something terrible had happened to him and his body would be the one they found after the Hunt this year.

A bit before shift change at 6:00 a.m., Ada noticed that she'd missed a text. Elijah.

She released a whoop into the air and then exhaled long and hard before reading the message:

> SORRY. I didn't have service and then I sent a text, but it never went through I guess, but I'm fine. DON'T BE MAD! IT'S BAD FOR THE SKIN! Lol but also where were you?!? This is twice now?? Wtf? Jk, school deadline, at a friend's house to work on it, gotta go, xoxo.

She could've kissed the ground she was so thankful. She texted him back and apologized profusely, again, for leaving him and then somehow missing him when she returned. She also asked when he might be able to go hunting again, given that Easter was a week away. He replied that he didn't have time, which made her feel bad—she knew it was because she had left him again. And it meant she had no one else to go with. If she wanted to hunt, she had to go alone.

She followed up with other questions, like what time he'd left the park and if he'd heard from Anthony—just to be nosy while she had his attention—but he left those unanswered. At least he was safe. She hadn't lost him.

When she walked into the break room at shift change, Janie was in the middle of a complaint to Maggie, who had come in early, even though she'd probably only left the building at 9:00 p.m. the previous night. Janie was apparently fit to be tied after covering the new day shift label-operator's machine instead of her own presses for a second day. Ada couldn't blame her. Going from the presses to the label machine meant being tied to one spot all day, with no easy breaks. Your eyes glossing over from twelve hours of labels speeding past with only an occasional break when the box filled, the labels went askew, or the label roll ran out. Watching paint dry would be an improvement.

Ada didn't stick around for the usual chatter. Now that Elijah had turned up, she wanted one thing: sleep. She didn't even have the energy to think about hunting alone now. She grabbed her purse off the table where she'd left it before hitting the restroom and slung it on her shoulder. Before she could get to the door, she heard the KAOK morning anchorperson on the little break-room TV say the word *casino*.

Her stomach felt like it dropped ten floors. Everyone seemed to hush at the same moment. She slowed, turned, and inched toward the TV. Everyone else was looking up at it where it hung from the ceiling. The little banner at the bottom read: *Local woman causes a scene at casino.*

Shit.

On the screen, Nell ran naked through the casino on pixelated cell phone video, her body blurred but not her face The reporter relayed how the woman appeared to be screaming at onlookers to stop another person.

"She screamed something about the Hunter," one of the onlookers told the reporter. Her friend, who wore a similar outfit, an oversize Oklahoma Sooners sweatshirt, nodded her head and agreed that Nell had definitely mentioned the Hunter. The reporter stated that in an even more bizarre twist, Nell was identified by people on YouTube, where the video had gone viral, as the sister of the Hunter's alleged first victim, though the reporter stressed "alleged" and that there had been no evidence to support persistent rumors of a serial killer, which have plagued Presley for over a decade.

All hell broke loose in the break room, with people pointing and gasping and some laughing and others shaking their heads.

Maggie looked about to blow the top off her own head. "Well, I guess that means I'll need to find someone to take her place. Can't imagine she'll show her face here ever again." She glared at Ada with self-satisfaction, like she'd won a battle. "Nasty cold, huh?" she said and brushed past Ada on her way to her desk at the entrance to Lloyd's office.

"Fuck you," Ada muttered under her breath and took off before anyone decided to ask her, Nell's "work wife," if she knew what had happened.

The milky sunshine filtered through the clouds and provided some relief but not much. She rushed down the stairs, past the picnic table where she and Nell usually ate their midnight lunch, and toward her car. She didn't even care that the dew soaked her shoes, a usual grievance. Her bed awaited. That's all she cared about. Certainly not Nell. And not even Elijah, that little shit, who had worried the hell out of her for no good reason.

Twenty minutes until home, that's all she needed to stay awake for. Everything else could wait as she made her way to her car.

"Oh my God!" She clasped her chest at the sudden sight of Lloyd standing there. "You startled me!"

"Sorry about that," he said and held up his hands in apology.

"What are you doing here so early?" She added a smile after the question, even though she was tired as hell and didn't like people popping out of nowhere. He could've yelled out a hello. Unlike Maggie, Lloyd never came in early. She was used to seeing him at night, at the beginning of her shift, not the end.

Lloyd gave a quick smile in return and then proceeded to put on the worried face she'd seen on him time and again over the years, whether for layoffs or forced overtime or Hunt season. "I hate to bother you—"

Ada waved a hand in the air. "No bother. What's on your mind?"

"Has Nell called you?"

"No." If he hadn't already heard about Nell, he'd learn soon enough. And she'd rather he heard it from her instead of Maggie. "Is this about the news?"

He breathed in heavily through his nose and then pushed it out through his mouth in exasperation.

Lloyd was a God-fearing, churchgoing man. Lloyd treated them well and was easygoing compared to most managers. He'd always been nothing but nice to them both. He'd understood when they had to take time off because their kids were sick. And he'd even let it pass when Ada was in a bind and couldn't find a babysitter. Let Anthony hang out in the break room and even let him sleep on the couch in his office, as long as she promised he'd stay off the plant floor for liability reasons. Though Lloyd seemed to give Nell more rope than anyone else with which to pull herself up from whatever gutter she got herself into. There'd been many. But who knew what he'd do now that Nell had gone viral. One thing to feel bad for someone whose brother had disappeared and then been found dead years ago, with no absolute reason as to why, another excusing a video of their naked casino sprint, hollering about a killer on the morning news.

"Did you know?" He shook his head, with a bit of disgust. "Did she give any indication that things had gotten this bad?" Ada thought she also heard a tinge of admonishment toward Ada, as if she were responsible for Nell and her actions.

"I don't know what's going on with her," she said, her pulse ratcheting up in defense. "I guess the Hunt is really getting to her this year. But I hope you'll cut her some slack. Maggie mentioned—"

"No, no." Lloyd held out both hands as if to wave off trouble. "I wanted to check in to see if you knew how she's doing."

"Then you need to—"

"I'll talk to Maggie," he said, clearly anticipating what she was about to say.

Ada released some tension at his words and tone. "I haven't talked to Nell." Even though she trusted Lloyd, she didn't want it to slip that she'd picked up Nell at the casino and have it get back to Maggie.

"I guess it was bound to happen one day," Lloyd said. "That's got to be awful getting reminded every year of the bad thing you've done."

Ada furrowed her brow in confusion. "What are you t—"

He held out his hands to explain. "I mean, when I first met her, she was in a bad way. Didn't handle things so well. Which anyone could understand, given the circumstances. But I hoped she'd put some of that behavior behind her." He waited for Ada to say something, but anything she could say would feel like a betrayal of Nell. Still, he seemed to know a heck of a lot more about those days than Ada did.

He sucked in his lips and then released a little whistle. "I tell you what, though. The only person I blame is that Rod character. That man shouldn't have kept on with that Hunt all these years, what with knowing how many people it's harmed."

"I didn't know you believed in all that."

"What? The serial killer nonsense?"

She nodded.

"Of course not. But people end up getting hurt—"

"Dead," Ada corrected.

"I'm talking about the psychological aspect." He looked about to spit. "If nothing else, Rod should've called it off out of a moral and spiritual obligation to those who have been affected by these horrific events."

"The city's the one who lets it continue." Ada felt like she was on the defense again.

"Of course they do. Money talks," he said, a disgusted look on his face. "I'll check in with Nell. See if maybe me and Nancy can get her—"

Ada interrupted before Lloyd could mention church. "Don't worry. I'll check in with her, and I'll keep you posted. I think it's best if we give her some time."

Lloyd nodded but gave no indication that he agreed.

"Let me talk to her first." Ada rubbed her eyes. "Listen, I gotta get home and take a nap before I fall asleep on the road and kill someone."

He flinched.

"I'm just joking."

"You oughtn't joke about that." His tone reminded her of Pastor Crane, who preached at the church her parents attended. Like Pastor Crane, Lloyd had a side to him that veered toward the tragic. Loved Bible lessons that were horrifying and meant as a warning to others, if not the actual victim.

That's what Nell was, a victim. She'd never call herself that, and she'd be mortified to know that's how Ada viewed her. But Ada didn't see it as a bad thing. She saw it as an honest thing. Whoever took Garrett's life also took Nell's and her family's as well. They were never right after that.

KAOK News Twitter Update

"No comment."—Nora Holcomb when asked about the video featuring her daughter, Nell Holcomb, running naked and screaming through a casino. Nora is also the mother of Garrett Holcomb, the alleged—and unconfirmed—first victim of the Hunter.

Fifteen

Nell

Tuesday, April 12
Afternoon
Five days before Easter

Nell had been inside the stand-alone casino convenience store–slash–gift shop, tossing Combos into her mouth while fixing a large coffee to stay awake, when she first learned that she'd gone viral. She'd slept in her truck on Sunday and Monday night, hoping Casino, the woman, would return to the scene. The casino seemed as good a place as any to find her, unless Casino was the Hunter. Then maybe she was waiting in the parking lot, too, watching Nell, waiting for an opportunity to strike. At least Nell wasn't at home, and neither was Elijah. It turned out to be a blessing that he was staying with a friend for his school project. She had texted him again the previous day to tell him to stay away from the house. Roach infestation, she'd lied. The exterminators were there. But really, she'd been thinking about how she'd woken up that one day and thought she heard someone in the house. Maybe it was Casino. Or someone else. Maybe they were hunting her or Elijah.

Nonsense, she'd thought, but it hadn't stopped her from avoiding the house and ensuring Elijah did too.

At least in the parking lot, Nell was near people. Maybe they'd hear her scream if necessary. She had bought herself a pair of cheap binoculars, training them on everyone who pulled up in the parking lot and everyone who left the casino. She'd barely left the parking lot since the security guard had asked her to leave. The only time she left was to move the truck now and then in case she looked suspicious and to get something to eat from the convenience store. She was in the middle of tasting the cream-to-sugar ratio of her coffee when the midday news came on the TV behind the cashier. She was barely paying attention, blowing on the coffee and wondering if she'd ever find that woman again.

"Hey," the cashier, April, an Indigenous teenager, said. Nell had gotten to know her over the past twenty-four or forty-eight hours. She liked her. "Isn't that you?"

Nell looked up to see her pointing at the TV and then pointing at her. She edged closer to the counter and stared at the TV. It was like an out-of-body experience, watching a person who looked like Nell running through the casino in nothing but her socks, yelling unintelligible words. Over the past couple of days, she'd worked hard at repressing that memory while keeping the one regarding murder at hand. She'd been damn near close to getting her embarrassment mostly out of mind. But there she was on the TV. For all the world to see. Or at least Presley. But that was all the same to Nell.

She blinked and blinked, trying to reconcile the image on the screen with what she remembered. The news mentioned that several people had filmed and uploaded the incident to YouTube and Twitter and Facebook. Of course there had been video. There had been people there besides her and the security guard. Not many, but enough to see and take video.

She had planned to go hang out in the casino parking lot some more and wait for that woman. Instead, she tossed her coffee and sat at one of the little tables, not moving for hours, horrified at the prospect of showing her face, while April swept around her feet, her long braids swaying, and tried to convince her it wasn't so bad. Lots of folks got messed up at the casino. Mostly white people. Mostly men. All the while, daytime soaps came on the TV and then the courtroom shows and then talk shows until the news came on and there she was again.

About thirty minutes before she was supposed to either leave for work or call in sick again—yet had made no moves toward that endeavor—Lloyd called. He didn't say much about the particulars but let Nell know that he understood if she needed to take some time off, given it was almost Easter and he knew how difficult that was for her, what with the Hunt happening again. He left out the part about the news, but mentioned that the orders might get to piling up, and well . . . at some point he'd need to know when Nell was planning to return. If she was planning to return.

Lloyd's voice was thick with discomfort, and Nell hated to hear it. Lloyd had been good to her. He was fair, honest.

"I can get some temps in to cover you for a spell. It's no trouble, but, well . . . ," Lloyd said. "But you've called out a couple days already." He paused. "If you reckon you'd rather not show your face around here at all, I'd understand. Let me know, and I'll have Maggie reach out with some paperwork."

"No," Nell said. She wondered if maybe he'd hoped she would say okay and just leave. Maybe that would be easier for them all. But she couldn't do that. "I'm sorry. I'll be there tonight." She had wanted to call in again, so bad. She couldn't take another day off work, though. Not if she wanted to stay employed. "I was getting ready to leave."

"All right," he said. "But please let me know if you change your mind. I would understand." He paused again. "You know they hold GA meetings at our church."

"Oh?" Lloyd had started them. He'd tried to get her to join early on. Nell didn't want to go to some meeting and tell everyone her troubles. "I'll look into it."

He sighed. "I hope you do."

She told him she would, even though she wouldn't. The only thing she had in mind at that moment was figuring out what to say to Elijah and her parents when they found out. And Tessa.

That was a conversation she wasn't ready to have.

Until then, she had to brace herself for seeing her coworkers. She'd rather see her mom if she was being honest. Nell hated to return to work, to face Ada most of all, but what else could she do? There were bills to pay. A kid to get through high school. A secret breakup to navigate and ensure it didn't affect Elijah's relationship with his mom. Definitely pride to swallow and hide, but she couldn't do much about that. Everyone had seen the clip, either online or on the news. Nell could imagine her coworkers taking out their phones. Posting it all over their Facebook walls or their family group texts: You know that woman? The one whose brother was murdered? The naked one at the casino? Yeah, her. I work with her!!! Can you believe she showed her face at work?!?

"Good luck," April said when Nell finally stood and made her way to the exit. "You can always come back here to chill." Nell thanked her and waved goodbye, grateful for good wishes on what was shaping up to be a real shit show.

At work, as Nell had done years ago when she walked in after everyone learned from Maggie that Nell's brother had been murdered, Nell kept her head down and focused on the list of broken things to repair and tried to ignore the heat that bubbled and reddened her skin.

Barely disguised whispers trailed Nell as she made her way from the factory front door and through the break room, where she didn't make her usual stop to store her dinner, and then through the door to the factory floor and the comforting racket of the presses, muting the whispers.

She wondered if Tessa had seen the news. She hadn't texted or called. In case she hadn't, Nell wanted Tessa to hear it from her. She typed out a message, joking that she guessed their breakup had really done a number on her, ha ha, and that she would get her shit together and would explain everything to Elijah, who would probably laugh at her expense. The message had been received, that's all.

At work, there was always something to fix. Always. But not today. Today, every single machine seemed to be in good working order. So Nell had nothing to do but wander down the pathways of her mind. That's what had gotten her into such a bad way after Garrett had died. That's why she'd drowned in alcohol and slots for so long. If she hadn't, she would have been faced with her other destructive inclinations.

Her mind veered from her anxieties and embarrassment to fixate on a guy who had lived down the road. Paul, the only neighbor Nell ever spoke to on any regular basis. White guy. He'd inherited his land and house from his parents, like Nell had inherited hers from her grandparents. Paul was a sensitive type, liked to laugh and smile, and said polite things in a smooth tone of voice. He'd been married and divorced twice. No kids. No pets. Liked to read. He seemed happy. Nell had considered Paul a friend, someone to fill the ache and lonely hole left by Garrett's death. Ada was a friend, but Ada was almost too solution oriented for Nell some days. Some days Nell needed someone like Paul to talk to, someone who wouldn't ask her questions or offer solutions, just let Nell talk. For ten or so years, they'd made their small talk. And then one day bled into another, and Nell realized she hadn't seen Paul in a while. Once winter came and darkness took hold, the lights stayed off whether it was morning or night. Paul always kept the lawn cut, but the grass had grown between the cracks of stones that he'd used as a pathway.

He didn't answer anytime Nell knocked, so she stopped knocking, figuring he'd moved. One day, Nell had been checking the mail when Rachel, another one of Nell's neighbors, one of those traditional-looking but progressive white southern women, drove by and slowed her car. Said everybody was gonna pitch in to have the dirt road graded and wanted to see if Nell planned to put up a fight about it. Nell didn't like the idea of handing over her money, but she liked the idea of her truck getting torn up by the wide potholes that dotted the road even less. Before they parted ways, Nell asked Rachel if she'd heard anything about Paul. She was the kind of person who knew everything about other people without it seeming gossipy, like Maggie. More like, gathering information and needing to know in case of a problem.

"Paul?" Rachel asked, and then her expression shifted. Maybe because she knew—everybody knew—about Nell's history and didn't want to deliver bad news because she was considered fragile and one false move could send her to a straight razor, but Rachel did, in a kind but direct way. "He shot himself. I'm sorry. I thought you knew."

Nell thanked her and then went about her day. Nell then did a bit more digging online but couldn't find anything to elucidate what had led Paul to grab a shotgun and end it all. She wondered what she'd missed that would've let her know that Paul wasn't happy. Maybe they weren't even really friends. Just acquaintances. If they'd been friends, Nell would have Paul's phone number. She would've felt comfortable calling up his workplace to see if he was okay instead of letting the days bleed into one another and assuming that Paul was busy or had some family thing that kept him away, some reason that was none of her business for why she hadn't seen him.

Sometimes, during those long, long nights at the factory, wired physically but tired mentally, Nell thought about Paul. She couldn't stop thinking about him while she wandered the factory that night, trying to avoid people and trying to find things to keep herself busy and out of her head. But it was no use.

Sometimes, when life got hard or lonely after Garrett's death, Nell had considered the same choice as Paul. But as low as Nell ever got, she never could pull a trigger. She couldn't put her parents through more. Besides all that, Nell couldn't shake the embarrassment of someone finding her and having to see what she'd done to herself. The literal mess they'd have to clean up. Nell didn't want to do that to Elijah. She wouldn't do that, even if she wanted very much to disappear.

Nell walked the floor of the plant, hunting for an activity, trying to keep from circling morbid thoughts. If she accidentally came upon someone, the operator would find something to focus on and dash off away from her. She was grateful their mortification matched hers.

She wondered how long it'd take before the story died down. She knew it'd always be there under the surface, like the story of Garrett, something that new people would learn as soon as they came on at the factory, especially given Maggie seemed intent on retiring there. And she still had a long ways to go.

Nell could put the trailer up for sale after Elijah graduated. Or rent it. Take off. But where would she go? She didn't have savings. Barely enough in checking to cover the month's bills. A job like hers was hard to come by. Plenty of men were waiting in line, some from inside the factory, glaring at her like she'd stolen something from them they were entitled to. They all expected women to run the machines, not fix them. And she wasn't keen on starting all over again somewhere else. Starting back on the line, working her way back up to foreman. No, she'd stay exactly where she was. She was used to people looking at her, wondering what was wrong with her. To hell with them.

As Nell turned the corner, she bumped into Ada.

"Sorry," she said, automatically. She'd always been told by her grandma to be polite. To be sorry. To be deferential. Sometimes it made her feel like such a sucker.

Ada looked about as awkward as Nell felt. She cleared her throat and motioned for Nell to follow her.

Nell breathed in deep and slow. The machines were still making their usual racket. She was grateful for the noise. It'd keep whatever Ada had to say to her between the two of them.

As they walked closer to one of Ada's machines, the sixth and last press, way in the back of the factory and up against the wall, Nell noticed that the noise wasn't as loud as it usually was.

Finally, something to focus on. Nell gave a little nod to acknowledge she understood that she was now responsible for fixing Ada's press and opened the control panel, only there was nothing to fix. The machine had been turned off. She went to flip it back on, but Ada stopped her.

Nell could barely hear her above the surrounding noise, but she caught her words, like the loudest whisper.

"You doing okay?" Ada asked. Concern lined her face.

Nell nodded, gave Ada a thumbs-up, a smile. "Doing great!" Then she flipped the power switch. The press roared back to life.

Ada crossed her arms and shook her head at Nell. Maybe said other things, but Nell rushed away from her before she could ask any more questions. Their brief interaction had shaken Nell for reasons she couldn't explain. Ada hadn't run away or averted her eyes like everyone else or flat-out ignored Nell like that one time she got mad at Nell for some dumb thing Nell had said and still couldn't remember.

Nell had hoped that at least she and Ada could go back to normal. Sit on the picnic bench outside and shoot the shit without mentioning anything about what had happened, as if it hadn't. Their interaction felt like a good start. But that didn't mean Nell wanted to talk about it. The bandage was off. They had broached the subject, and now they could never talk about it again.

Still, Nell holed up in the front office for the rest of the night in case Ada decided their conversation required more discussion. Lloyd always locked his private office, but the exterior office space with Maggie's desk was nice and big. Comfy. Maggie had a desktop computer and photos of a dog and a candle whose smell reminded Nell of her grandma, a mixture of bacon and fabric softener. Odd, yet comforting. Enough that she could sit there most of the night and feel a little less bad all around. She even looked up the name of the company online to see how much the candle cost. More than she was willing to part with. Maggie must make a lot more than Nell did. She held the candle up to her nose and sniffed.

"What are you doing in here?" Maggie asked.

Nell dropped the candle. It hit the desk and then the floor with a thud. Nell thought for sure it'd break, but it didn't. This was that hard glass. The kind they'd find in the distant future and wonder at what had filled its interior.

"Oh." Nell picked up the candle and placed it back on Maggie's desk with a multitude of sorrys. "Uh. Sorry." She removed herself from Maggie's nice office chair. "I was looking for . . ." Nell scrambled for an excuse. "The number for that guy who fixed the loader a while back."

Maggie stared at her. Nell expected Maggie to yell at her or give her weird looks for sniffing her candle, as if Nell got off on sniffing all manner of things when panties were hard to procure.

But Maggie did something worse. She moved in close, closer than Nell had ever been to her, and laid her hand on Nell's arm. Then she whispered, "Oh, Nell. I'm so sorry." The words felt like a womb in which Nell could lie all day uninterrupted or tell all her secrets if she didn't know better.

"Sorry again," Nell said. She couldn't lift her gaze to meet Maggie's. "Like I said, just looking to see if you've got the number to the guy who fixed the loader a while back."

"Wait," Maggie said.

"I didn't find it, though, the number," Nell said and rushed toward the door.

What the hell was Maggie doing there so early? It was barely 4:00 a.m. But Nell had never asked anything about her, and she was too embarrassed by getting caught in her office to start. It felt disingenuous to ask after all these years of working together. Maggie would know that Nell was only asking because she was embarrassed, and that was too embarrassing itself. Nell told her to have a good day and closed the door behind her.

As 6:00 a.m. neared, Nell got antsy. She'd been able to avoid people on her own shift and had breezed past the first shift folks when they walked in around 5:30 a.m. The previous day, at the start of Nell's shift, they'd been tired at the end of a long twelve hours. Now they were fresh. Fully rested and probably full of questions or, at the very least, opinions. She

dreaded walking through the break room and decided instead to get lost in the shadows of the presses until her crew was gone and the first shift got settled into their machines, too busy to notice Nell. She walked fast, head down. She had it down to a near science at this point.

She'd not waited but fifteen minutes before she was able to sail clear of most people. She was sure someone had seen her, probably multiple people, but no one had stopped her, and the noise from the presses covered whatever cussing and taunts they might have sent her way when she passed. The door to the main office was closed, so she didn't have to see Maggie again or Lloyd at all. In the end, she was grateful to have seen Maggie. At least Maggie could tell Lloyd that Nell had shown up for work and there'd be no need for a temp or someone else to take her place. There'd not be a fight or another uncomfortable conversation. They could pretend like nothing had happened and everything was right as rain. Nell liked that about Lloyd, the desire to never talk about whatever we're embarrassed about again—after he tried to get her to church or a meeting.

Outside, Nell shielded her eyes from the sun and walked down the stairs, gratitude building with each step that brought her closer to her truck.

As Nell rounded the front of the truck, she jumped when she saw Ada standing there. She clutched her chest and shook her head.

"Jesus Christ," Nell said. "One of you is gonna give me a heart attack before the day is over."

"One of who? Lloyd jump out at you too?"

Nell swatted away the question with a hand. No need to tell her about the candle sniffing and Maggie.

Ada stood there with her arms crossed, glaring at her. "So?"

"So, what?" Nell fiddled with her keys.

"So you gonna avoid me now?"

Nell blew a long stream of air out of her mouth. "Look. I'm not really in the mood to rehash everything. The news pretty much covered it."

Ada mimicked Nell, breathing loud and long, but then she bit her lip, like she had something to say but had to force it to stay on her tongue. Kind of like when Maggie had been too startled to talk. If Nell wanted to, she could mention that to Ada, and then Ada would be mad at her, and Nell could get out of this conversation quickly.

Ada kept looking at Nell in a way that made Nell want to hide.

"I know I'm a piece of shit," Nell said. "So can we skip this part?"

"You are a piece of shit."

"Great. We're in agreement."

They stood without talking awhile. "I should get home," Nell said.

Before she could leave, Ada held out Nell's wrench. Nell puzzled at it.

"Figured you lost this," Ada said. "Found it behind press one the other night."

Nell took the wrench and stared at it before looking back at her truck.

"What?" Ada asked.

"This is my truck wrench."

Ada raised an eyebrow, like she didn't understand.

"I don't take it out of my truck. I use a different one for work, that I keep at work." She examined it. "Where'd you find it?"

Ada reiterated what she'd said before, but Nell couldn't remember ever taking it in with her. She never used her truck tools at work. She used her good work tools for work. And she kept them at work. So what the hell was her truck wrench doing at work?

"Is everything okay?" Ada asked.

Nell told her she was fine and took off toward her truck. She opened the tailgate and jumped in the back to examine her toolbox. The lock looked like it'd been toyed with, but that could have been Nell's fault. She'd lost the key once and had to jimmy it open. When she'd opened it, the wrench wasn't there; it was in her hand, right where Ada had placed it.

Nell's breath came quick and sharp. "Son of a bitch."

Shared Google Doc / The Hunt

VICTIM #11

On April 5, 2015, Michelle Shea, white, thirty-five, was found in a large field between the Price Cutter and the old railroad tracks. It is unknown how long Michelle was there, as the area is a haven for "vagrants and vultures," given its status as a dumping ground for both trash and human waste. The medical examiner estimates that her body had been there for at least a week before an unidentified individual reported the remains to the police. The official cause of death is considered suffocation, after Michelle allegedly choked on a granola bar while out hunting on her own.

Michelle's friends, who often went hunting with her but could not attend that day, disputed the cause of death, calling it "ludicrous" and questioning how an avid hiker and yoga fan could suddenly die from a granola bar. "They barely did an investigation. They found a granola bar in her throat and figured, well, that's what did it! It's sickening that they won't take her death seriously. That's what people do to women."

In response to the accusations, a spokesman for the Presley Police said, "If you don't like the facts, do your own autopsy."

Michelle was cremated and then buried in her hometown of St. Louis, Missouri.

Sixteen

Ada

Wednesday, April 13
Afternoon
Four days before Easter

Ada woke with a start and then screamed. She bolted up in bed and pulled the covers to her chin.

"It's me! It's just me," Anthony said as he stood over her, hand on her shoulder. "Sorry."

She put a hand toward her hair scarf. She must've slept like a stone. The room was still dark. The blackout curtains shut tight against the day. The clock radio blinked out 2:12 a.m.

"The electricity go out again?" she asked. Anthony nodded. He was dressed in the red basketball shorts and white Westside High Wolverines T-shirt he always wore around the house when he didn't have to work or go out, his day-off uniform. Her mouth felt dry and funky. She swiped her hand across it. "What time is it?"

"Four o'clock."

She groaned. Seemed like she'd just laid her head on the pillow, and now she had to get up and do it all again.

The lights had gone out enough over the years for him to know what time to wake her for work. She reached for his hand and squeezed it. "Thank you."

He didn't say anything, just nodded his head once and left the room, leaving a trail of cologne he'd put on for no reason other than his granddad did it, so he did too.

After showering and getting dressed, she walked out of the bedroom to prepare supper.

The house was quiet. Anthony's bedroom door was shut, but she knew he was in there. Probably had his headphones on, the volume up way too loud.

As soon as the burgers she was frying on the stove started to sizzle, she heard his door open. Teenage boys were like that, she'd told Nell once. *They don't want to talk. They want to sulk and play video games and eat.* That answer hadn't pleased her. But it was a fact. Anthony slumped onto the couch and began playing his video games. She glanced at the calendar she kept on the wall and then at the clock on the stove.

"Elijah coming for supper today?" she asked over her shoulder. During her shower, she'd finally woken up to the world and what had plagued her mind before she'd drifted into her stone sleep. Elijah. She'd gone from worrying about where he was to worrying about how he was doing, considering the news about Nell. At least that's what she told herself as her thoughts spun around to Nell every time. The video. How Nell had avoided her at work. How Nell had freaked out about the wrench and then taken off out of the parking lot before Ada could even ask what the hell was going on. She'd typed and deleted about ten texts since. Whatever it was, Nell didn't want Ada to know. That made Ada want to know even more. And it made her sad, knowing that there were things Nell kept from her. Or maybe she didn't trust her.

Anthony didn't reply to her query about Elijah, so she asked again.

"I said I don't know."

"You didn't say it."

"I shrugged it. Same thing." He didn't even look at her. She missed that bright-eyed, curious kid who used to go hunting for the golden egg with her.

"I can't cook your dinner and see you shrug."

She called him to eat. They made their plates up by the stove and then sat down at the table in silence. After their prayer, she ground some black pepper and salt onto her fries.

"Y'all still not talking?"

Anthony shrugged again.

She fussed with the tomato and lettuce on her bun, trying to hold back the shaking in her hands. She'd had a terrible dream that Elijah was running through the woods and someone was running after him. And there she sat in a tree, unable to move, mouth open but unable to make a sound. Dream dread clung to her like the slick of dish soap when the hand soap had run out.

"What happened between you two?" she asked, trying to extricate herself from the bad thoughts.

"Nothing," Anthony said, tearing into his burger, not lifting his eyes when he spoke. "I told you, he got annoyed that I got a job and can't do dumb shit with him anymore. Simple as that." He put a handful of fries in his mouth, the ends sticking out like he was some cartoon character.

"Slow down. You don't want to be like Michelle Shea, do you?" she asked. "Anthony!"

"Oh my God. Are you the Hunter? Are you going to force-feed this burger down my throat now?" He screamed like a teenager in a horror movie and then shoved the whole burger in his mouth.

She ignored him. Mayim Bialik made a funny comment about a contestant's backstory on the meet-the-contestant section of *Jeopardy!* Ada laughed, even though she felt bad about it, being a die-hard Alex Trebek fan. She'd watched episodes with her grandma as a kid and teenager. A commercial break came on, and she no longer had a distraction from the main thing on her mind. "Was Elijah at school today?"

"I don't know. We're not in the same classes." Anthony was in AP; Elijah was with the other kids. Anthony chewed and then swallowed before looking her dead in the eye. "Why are you asking so many questions about him?"

Ada took a drink of her iced tea. "Did you hear about Nell? The casino?"

He grimaced but didn't say more, just shrugged again. Underneath all that toughness, she could tell that something was bothering him.

"I was wondering if maybe he was at school, or skipped," she said.

"If that were you on the news, I'd definitely leave town." He pretended like he got a chill all up and down his body and shook. "Change my name. Create a whole new backstory."

"Oh, it's not that bad." She ate a couple of fries. Elijah's last text to her had come before she'd seen the video of Nell. He hadn't responded to any of her more recent texts about if they could go hunting one last time before Easter—a ruse so she could see how he was doing, see if he'd reply.

"Anybody say anything about it at school today?"

He tilted his head and raised an eyebrow. Of course they would. They were teenagers.

"Did you text him?" she asked.

He nodded.

She knew that no matter what, Anthony wouldn't bail on Elijah. "What'd you say?"

He had slowed his pace and now made ketchup circles with a fry. "Nothing, really. Just *hey, what's up*. It's weird. What am I supposed to write? Ask if he saw the video of his aunt naked on the news?" he asked. "Was Nell at work last night?"

She nodded. Anthony looked worried.

"What was wrong with her? Was she on something?"

"I don't know," she said. "This is a strange situation. But everything's gonna be all right. I saw Nell. I talked to her. She's fine. I just want to make sure Elijah's okay too."

"Okay." He chewed his last fry slowly. When he finished, he asked, "Do you think it's true what everyone's been saying?" She raised her eyebrows, questioning. "Everyone online is saying that Nell was chasing after some woman and screaming that she was the Hunter."

She had to think hard on that one. The whole thing sounded ludicrous. Nell had been certain, absolutely certain, that the woman had meant her harm. Had done Garrett harm. Maybe with a wrench? Did that have something to do with the way she was acting?

Ada knew how grief had a way of tearing up your head. How reality got a little fuzzed. How an accident could turn into something sinister. All one needed to do was look at the Raleighs and Nancy and Lloyd.

"I don't know what to believe, to be honest," she told him, and it was the truth. But something else tugged at her. All through her shift the previous night and then through her shower before supper, she'd thought about it and weighed whether to tell Anthony. She'd never lied to him. They'd always been friends. The best. So much that her dad had told her it was unnatural to be that close to your son. That made Ada feel weird, like her dad thought she was doing something untoward with Anthony. The thought made her skin crawl. She was horrified and told her dad that plenty of single mothers and sons were close because they had to tough it out together. He laughed in that cynical way that cast an ugly film over everything and mentioned that she had done nothing alone. She'd had the help of her father and her mother. Had everything handed to her. They hadn't talked for three months after that. And then Christmas had come, and they'd hugged and pretended like nothing had been wrong and no time had passed at all.

"I went hunting with Elijah," Ada said. "A few times."

Anthony's brow furrowed. "Seriously?"

He sounded so much like her dad at times, she wanted to slap it right out of him, even though she never once hit him. Not ever. Still, her dad's tone coming through him sounded like an evil spirit. Something that had to be exorcised.

"It's not weird," she said, anticipating what he'd say next.

He rolled his eyes again. It'd become an irritating habit lately. "What are you gonna do when I'm not here?"

"One more year. That's all I was asking." She took their plates to the counter and then placed them in the sink. He had no idea how he hurt her sometimes. She wondered if it ever occurred to him how his leaving for college would affect her, how his offhand remarks about not being able to wait to "get out of here" felt like a hundred tiny knives stabbing her heart. As if *here* was the worst place one could be.

The trailer only had two bedrooms and one bath, but it was clean and smelled nice. Not used. Contemporary. No ratty furniture. No chipped plates. No rust running down the siding. Fresh paint on the walls and front porch. Crocuses coming up along the edges. Off-white carpet in the living room and bedrooms. Flooring that looked like real wood in the kitchen and their shared bathroom—not that log cabin shit either. Bright, yet warm. A silver wall mirror to offer more light into the room and onto the paintings, and curtains that when closed could be shut to remove any reminders that they lived in a trailer park, not a subdivision, like Ada's parents, apparently. All those dreams they'd had for her had gone to dust with Anthony's arrival. But it was a nice trailer in a nice trailer park in the nicest school district in town.

But maybe *here* meant her.

"I know you're gonna be gone soon. I wanted to spend more time with you."

He slumped next to her, but at least he was there, his way of showing that he understood—even if he wouldn't say it. He took the dishes she'd rinsed and placed them in the dishwasher for her. He was good at it. Knew all the right spots and angles to get everything to fit.

"It's not like I'm leaving the country," he said.

"Texas might as well be another country," she grumbled.

"What I mean is, I'll be back."

"I know." She wanted to cry, but she knew it'd make him feel like he had to comfort her or something. She didn't need that. She needed the release. And she didn't want him to feel bad. It was normal to cry for someone you love, she'd always told him. He had always been so sweet, snuggled up next to her and let her pet his head. "But things will be different for me. You know that, right? It'll be an adjustment, being alone." Before he could speak, she held up a hand. "I love to be alone. I'm not complaining. But it's not just a change for you. It's a change for me too. My whole routine is going to be different now. And I'm looking forward to it the same way you're looking forward to college." She paused. "Not looking forward to you being gone. That's not what I'm saying. But a change. It's a new chapter in my life too." His eyes focused on her. He was so good at active listening. She'd raised him right. "But it's still a change. A big one. I know you'll be back. But I'm still gonna miss you something fierce."

"I'm gonna miss you too," he said. He wiped his hands on a towel and then leaned against the counter. After a moment to think, he said, "I'll go with you if you want. Hunting." He looked up at her. "If you'll still have me."

She smiled and pulled him in for a hug. He felt so strong and adult in her arms it almost took her breath away. "I'll always have you." She turned to clean up the stove before heading to her bedroom to get ready for work.

"Wanna go tomorrow?" he asked before she left the living room.

"Hmm?" Her mind had moved on to work anxiety and dread as she cleaned, future tripping about another long night in a sea of endless nights that seemed to have no end. Only this night would be filled with questions about Elijah and Nell.

"Hunting," he said, giving her a look. "The thing we just talked about?"

She shook her head to clear the ugh and refocus. "Right. Sure. Yeah, tomorrow works. As long as you can go early."

He nodded as his fingers danced across the face of his phone. "You want Elijah to come too? Maybe he'll answer if it's about this and not Nell or how he's doing. We could go to breakfast after," he said. "As long as you promise not to make it a thing if he says yes. No asking him how he's doing."

"If you want him there and don't mind," she said. "But I'm happy if it's just us too."

"Okay," he said, without indicating which choice he preferred.

She smiled, tight. "I gotta get ready for work," she said and left a trail of anxiety behind her as she walked to her bedroom.

KAOK News Report

A local woman is reporting a close encounter with the Hunter, the alleged serial killer whose story has gripped Presley in recent days due to the return of the controversial Hunt for the Golden Egg.

Robyn Robertson, thirty-eight, said she was walking her dog near the Belle Pointe Golf Club in the foggy early-morning hours when she said her dog "went absolutely wild, chasing after something in the middle of the course."

"I figured it was a squirrel. Romeo has a strong attraction to them," Robyn said. "I don't know what it is about them, but he starts spinning and yelping and, well, getting excited, I guess you'd call it. He doesn't want to hurt them. He just wants to play. So as soon as he saw what I thought was a squirrel, he took off." Robyn said she lost control of Romeo, a purebred Maltese, and raced after him. Shortly thereafter, she said she got lost, despite being on an open golf course. "It was so foggy that morning. And the course is so big. I wasn't worried for myself. I was worried for Romeo! He's an adult, but he's so little. There's no telling what might happen to him. Someone could shoot him or hit him with their golf cart. I don't know!" she said, laughing at her ordeal.

Unbeknownst to Robyn, she would be worried about more than her little white Lothario.

"I looked for what felt like forever. And I broke down crying right there in the middle of the grass," Robyn said, gripping Romeo tight and kissing his head when we spoke outside her home. "But that's when I heard someone walking toward me, like the crunching of grass, which I know sounds weird because there was dew. For a moment, I thought it was Romeo. So I walked toward the noise, cooing his name in case he was scared too." Robyn said that as soon as she got closer, she heard the sound of someone running toward her. "I knew it wasn't Romeo. I knew it. It was too heavy. He's just a baby!"

Robyn said she took off running across the course, but at that point, it was so foggy, she didn't know where she was going. It was only a stroke of luck that prevented her from being hit by Barry Head, forty-two, as he was driving home from Target.

"Oh my God, I thought I was gonna have a heart attack right then and there! She came barreling into the street like a banshee!"

Lucky for Robyn, Barry was quick on the brakes and barely missed hitting her with his car. And lucky for Robyn, Aaron Raleigh pulled up behind Barry holding a scared and tired Romeo in his arms. Aaron, forty-eight, the father of Annalee Raleigh, one of the alleged victims of the Hunter, declined to be interviewed on video but said he was on his way home from the gym when he noticed Romeo on the side of the road.

"I'm grateful to Barry for not hitting me, obviously," Robyn laughed. "But I'm more grateful to Aaron for not only seeing Romeo on the side of the road but stopping to help him. There aren't many people like that, people who would stop and help an animal, let alone a person." Robyn wiped away tears. "I can't help but think about all the bad things that could've happened to him if he'd gotten lost."

Asked of her own frightful encounter on the course, with someone she now believes could be the Hunter, she said, "I'm shaken up. Of course. But I was so focused on finding Romeo, I'm not sure it really hit me yet that I was in real danger." But after talking with friends and family, Robyn is coming to terms with the fact that she may have come face-to-face with a killer.

"I'm gonna be haunted by all this for a long time," Robyn said, hugging Romeo close. "And we're certainly not going out in the fog again. At least not until after Easter."

Despite this latest encounter, the Hunt continues.

Seventeen

Nell

Wednesday, April 13
Afternoon
Four days before Easter

Nell rushed through the doors of the casino. This time, she didn't head for the cafeteria or the slots. She headed right for Homie, the security guy who had thrown her out.

As soon as he came close, he recognized her and tilted his head back into a giant sigh.

"I need to see the video," she said.

"Ay-yi-yi." He shook his head at her. "You are really a sucker for punishment, aren't you, sis?"

She pulled the wrench from her back pocket, which startled him. He backed away and drew his Taser out of its holster.

"Shit, sorry," she said and held up her hands in surrender. "It's a wrench."

He clutched a hand to his chest and holstered the Taser. "You can't be going around pulling out weapons like that."

"It's not a weapon—"

"If it can kill a man, it's a weapon."

She had a mind to ask if that also applied to nonmen, but she needed his help. "I need to see the videotape of the parking lot. That's all I'm trying to do. I don't want to cause a scene or anything."

He eyed her. "Last time you were in here, you asked for video of the casino. Now the parking lot? You know we can't give you that. Probably not even with a warrant. You're on sovereign land."

She returned the wrench to her back pocket, held out her hands, pleading. "I know. Here's the thing, I think that maybe someone broke into my truck and stole my wrench."

He screwed up his face in confusion.

"Yes," she said, anticipating what he'd say. "Yes, I know that I'm holding the wrench, but someone stole it from my truck and then put it behind a press at work. Probably on the same night that that woman seduced me."

He tilted his head again, lifted an eyebrow while closing one eye. "Seduced, eh?"

She breathed in and gave it one last go. "Someone's fucking with me. They broke into my truck." She hadn't confirmed this, but she believed it could be true. "They stole my wrench and then left it where it shouldn't be just to scare me. Maybe it was that woman."

Homie considered. "So you think someone is messing with you? Trying to get in your head?" She nodded. "And you think that lady could be the Hunter?"

She hadn't mentioned the Hunter to him, but of course he'd know. Everyone knew. "I don't know if it's her. Maybe. Maybe she's working with the Hunter."

He took a while to think about it, but then he sighed and shook his head. "I think maybe you need to go home, get some rest." He eyed her suspiciously. "Have you slept? You don't look like you've slept."

"If I could—" Before she could release the words, two more security guards appeared between a row of slot machines. "Oh, come on. I'm—"

"I told you what would happen if you came back here."

"Yes, but—" The new guards stood next to Homie and lodged their hands on their hips. "Fine. Fine," she said. "But I'm not giving up!" she yelled on her way out of the casino.

Shared Google Doc / The Hunt

VICTIM #3

Dave and Mike Dryden, brothers, white, aged fourteen and sixteen, respectively, spent two hours hunting on April 3, 2007. They had not participated in the Hunt in prior years but heard that it could be "scary." Dave told police they headed out but "got bored" sometime later and decided to hide and jump out at one another. After about thirty minutes, Dave came out of hiding and called for his brother out of worry that he had left him there alone.

After looking for Mike for another ten minutes or so, Dave said Mike jumped from a medium-size tree to scare Dave. However, the strings of the hoodie Mike wore got hung on the limb. While Mike struggled, Dave scrambled up the tree, but before he could get to Mike, Mike fell to the ground and was unresponsive. After a week in a coma, Mike passed from suffocation and his injuries upon falling from the tree.

We contacted Dave through social media direct messages. When asked about what happened, we noted a discrepancy between what appeared in the police report and what he told us. The police report indicates that "Mike jumped." In our conversations, Dave insisted that "Mike appeared to jump. But it was almost as if he slipped on the bark of the wet branch and got caught." When we asked if he thought Mike jumped or fell, Dave paused and said, "Everything happened fast. I wasn't really thinking. I was trying to save my brother. But I didn't tell them Mike jumped. I told them Mike fell. But thinking back, it's almost like he was pushed."

The Drydens moved from Presley shortly after Mike's funeral.

Eighteen

Ada

Thursday, April 14
12:30 a.m.
Three days before Easter

The air was warm, the night sky clear, and the moon almost full, and Ada could've cursed Mother Nature for being so nice and visible on that one night. She wanted to bury herself in darkness and cold, with a scarf to cover her face.

She walked toward the picnic bench where Nell sat. She took in a deep breath when she approached. Nell had come in to work that evening like a bat out of hell. Everyone in the break room had been startled. No one had ever seen her that way. After Nell slammed the door to the plant behind her, they all made guesses as to the specificity of her anger, though the general subject wasn't hard to guess.

They all gave Nell a wide berth all night as she barreled across the floor. Ada hadn't even had the nerve to interrupt her while they were working. But she figured their lunch break was the best time to try. Something else had begun to claw at Ada.

Ada hadn't heard back from Elijah since Sunday, and she was worried. All night, she'd told herself not to be, that he probably didn't want to talk to her because she was friends with Nell, whom he was probably mortified by right now and not talking to, if Anthony's reaction to the hypothetical of Ada in that scenario was any indication. But mostly, she missed her friend. She missed knowing what was going on with Nell. She missed the silly back-and-forth and laughter.

"Mind if I sit?" she asked.

"You've never asked before," Nell said. "Why would you start now?"

Nell's face looked haggard. Skin, sallow. Hair limp and oily looking. She didn't style her hair in the way she usually did, ensuring every piece was in place just so, or even cover it with one of those hipster knit caps. William used to wear them too.

Nell didn't say anything more, so Ada sat down next to her at the table.

"Got any leads on why my press has been acting up?" Ada asked, not sure what else to say.

"Leads?" Nell ran her tongue along her gums. "You sound like those true-crime people, the citizen detectives."

Ada allowed herself a moment so she wouldn't inadvertently snap at Nell. Nell was obviously wounded from what had happened, not to mention how bitchy Ada had been to her after she'd picked her up from the casino.

Ada let the subject drop, and they sat there in silence. The first time it'd ever felt that excruciating.

They'd spent so much time out here over the years. After Ada had decided she'd allow a friendship with Nell, and especially after Elijah had come into the picture, Ada used to visit Nell's house. Nell never had parties, but she had people over for the nonreligious holidays, the ones where you didn't really have to make a fuss. Ada and Anthony would come by after they'd already made the rounds to the family church and then to her parents' house, where cousins and aunts and uncles and other people she'd known all her life so they might as well have been family congregated. She supposed Nell wanted to create some sort of normalcy for Elijah. Some sort of family out of the ragtag band of loose friends and acquaintances Nell had acquired over the years. Many of them former coworkers who'd moved on to do other things. As long as she'd known Nell, she'd never spent much time with her family, even on holidays, even though they all lived within Presley and were all still alive, excepting Garrett, of course. Ada couldn't imagine what that'd be like, to have been the last person to see someone alive. Even though Nell would crack jokes and smile and make people laugh, there'd always been a haunted look in her eyes.

Was Ada the last to see Elijah alive? The thought had popped into her mind earlier in her shift and hovered there since, even though he'd said he was staying with a friend. She'd looked at his last text what felt like a thousand times to confirm. Something about it didn't seem right.

Ada's heart raced at speaking to Nell, despite them speaking so many times over so many years. "Elijah still staying with friends?"

Nell wiped her face, not once looking at Ada. "Yeah."

She didn't like Nell's answer. "Who's he staying with so long?" Nell had always been particular about Elijah, protective in a loose and easy-going way. But she knew where Elijah was and who he was with. This was new and different and alarming.

Nell stood, but Ada was quick and caught Nell's hand before she could leave.

"You know you can talk to me, right?" Ada asked. "What you tell me is private. I don't go talking about it with anyone."

Nell didn't say anything, but she didn't leave. Nell's hand felt warm in hers. Ada couldn't recall them ever touching hands like this.

"And if you can't talk to me, I hope you'll talk to someone," Ada said. Nell's jaw tensed. "There are people who could help." She stopped short of mentioning how Prozac had helped her.

Nell let go of Ada's hand. But she sat back down.

After a stretch of silence between them, Ada asked, "Is Elijah doing okay?"

"Fine. I guess. Why?" But then Ada's question seemed to click for Nell. "Right."

“I don’t know if he knows. About, you know.”

“Has Anthony said anything?” Nell asked. Before Ada could respond, she added, “About Elijah. And if he’s okay?”

“No. He said they haven’t been talking much. That’s why I was wondering.”

“Oh,” Nell muttered. “I didn’t know that.” She looked out across the parking lot. “You want a pull?”

Ada nodded and Nell handed over her vape pen. That little tug and the accompanying cloud of mango and peach fumes felt like some kind of relief. A reminder of good days, a promise of better ones to come. She hoped. She prayed. She’d actually gotten on her knees the previous night and asked for God to forgive her for keeping Nell in the dark about going hunting with Elijah, for creating any trouble at home. It felt silly to worry about, given Nell’s other trouble. But like hard-water stains on a tub, it still clung to Ada’s mind that she had done something wrong.

“Anthony said he didn’t see Elijah at school today. And he hasn’t heard from him,” Ada added. “I haven’t either. Sorry. It’s probably nothing.”

Nell knit her eyebrows in confusion. She pulled out her phone and scrolled through texts, presumably to check what Elijah had said. Apparently, she didn’t find anything because she tossed her phone to the picnic table. Nell’s face went ashen, and then it got red. Ada had read similar descriptions of characters in books and always wondered about it, but now she knew it was true.

Ada took another long pull on the vape pen and then handed it back to Nell. Ada had practiced this conversation. “When’s he supposed to come home?” She watched Nell’s face to see if there was any reason for her to run or take cover. She didn’t know what this kind of information might do to her. Would it be better for Nell if Ada stayed silent? Or if she came clean?

“Jesus, Ada.” Nell’s words cut but her tone was even. “Why do you care?” Ada must’ve done a poor job cloaking the are-you-fucking-kidding-me? look on her face because Nell shut her mouth and turned away to stare in front of herself.

Ada swallowed and finally got the courage to say the thing she'd needed to say despite her irritation with Nell. "I haven't seen Elijah all week. And neither has Anthony. He hasn't been over for dinner. And he hasn't responded to our texts."

"Well," Nell said and sighed. "I mean, he probably saw the news and decided to stay with his friend. He knows we work together. Anthony knows me. Would you want to come around if you were him?"

Everything about Nell seemed weighed down and angry, which made sense, given her recent circumstances. But alarms went off in Ada at how unconcerned she seemed as to Elijah's whereabouts. He'd been gone all week at some friend's house, and Nell couldn't even tell Ada who that friend was.

"I want to make sure he's okay," Ada said.

"I mean, probably not. Considering." Nell laughed, self-deprecating and unfunny.

Ada paused. "I'm a little worried." And not just about Elijah. Not for the first time, Ada wondered if Nell was like that guy she'd told Ada about the previous year, the neighbor who had shot himself. She worried what kind of bad news could send Nell the same way.

"I'm sure he's fine." Nell checked her phone again. Typed out a message. She sat a little straighter. Her malaise seemed to clear to make room for concern, the realization that she should probably pay attention to something besides herself. "I guess I . . . with everything happening, I . . . I don't know. I forgot about him, I guess." She glanced at Ada. "That sounds so bad."

"No—"

"It's bad." Nell nodded, mostly to herself. "I know that makes me sound like a piece of shit, which we've already established I am," she said. "I have no clue where Elijah is because I've been so focused on trying to find that woman from the casino." She scratched at her head and looked confused. "But I guess it's also that he always kind of does his own thing. He doesn't really need me."

Ada wanted to know more about this woman from the casino, but she thought it best to focus on one thing at a time. "That's not true. You've always made sure you know where he is and that he's safe."

"It is true." Nell stared at Ada. "You know it is. You take care of him more than I do."

"I let him come over for dinner. But that's not about you. Teenagers never want to be home with their parents. Guardians," she corrected. Nell had always been firm in not being called his parent. "You know that," Ada said. "He's got a fine life, a great life, considering how it started. He's not neglected. He's independent, is all. But I . . . well, I haven't heard from him. I've been texting, and he's not been at school."

Nell chewed on her top lip and shook her head. "When did you say you last saw him?"

Ada paused. "Sunday."

Nell seemed to calculate the days, but then pulled out her phone to check. "It's Thursday."

"I know," Ada said, ashamed it'd taken her that long to mention it.

"Where'd you see him last? At your house?"

"I left him at Chaffin Park."

Nell furrowed her eyebrows in confusion.

"We went hunting together." Ada's insides trembled along with her voice. "Anthony didn't want to go this year. So Elijah offered. I told him no, but . . ." Words failed her.

"You didn't want to go alone because of the rumors." Nell glanced to the side. "I thought you didn't believe in all that."

"I'm sorry." Ada's breathing felt labored, like she couldn't get enough air. She thought she might have to drop her head between her knees. "I fucked up."

There was no anguish on Nell's face. Everything was blank. "Neither one of you said a thing to me."

"Elijah knew you'd be mad." Ada shrank at Nell's glare. "And me. I knew you'd be mad at me."

"I am mad. You should've told me he was going hunting with you. He should have."

Ada wanted to get away from this feeling, from Nell's admonishment. "I know."

"You know, but you didn't. I get him, but not you. You're an adult. And sneaking out like some teenager who's been grounded and afraid of getting caught. You should've told me." Nell looked pure disgusted. "And it's not like I'd forbid him from going hunting. He's nearly a grown man. He's almost eighteen. He can do what he wants, despite what I want."

"You're right," Ada said, hands up in surrender. "I should've told you. We were . . . I," Ada corrected. "I was nervous about what you'd say. Given everything."

"Well, I'm not fucking pleased. That's for damn sure. But like I said, I can't forbid him from doing something just because it makes me uncomfortable." Nell stopped talking and eventually she stopped looking like she wanted to bite Ada's head off. Finally, she seemed to settle before some thought crinkled her brow. "Why'd you leave Elijah at the park?"

Ada felt like she was shaking all over, so she sat on her hands. "Because you called me from the casino."

The anger that had spread across Nell's face now turned to ash. Her eyes welled with tears. She closed them and shook her head. "Fuck."

"I tried to get him to go home, but he wanted to stay. I said I'd be right back." Ada focused on Nell, as if she could gauge whether she'd gone too far, told Nell more than she could handle. "When I got back, he wasn't there. I waited all day. Texted him. Called," she said. "He responded that night—"

"So you *have* heard from him?"

"Yes, but . . ." Ada paused. "Something doesn't feel right. I haven't seen him since Sunday. And the only thing he sent was this text where he's like, 'I'm staying with a friend. Don't worry.' And then he made this joke about how worrying is bad for my face."

Nell was quiet for a long time. Finally, "I found a note on Sunday after you dropped me off. And I texted him again on Monday," Nell said, a haunted look on her face. "That's the last I've heard from him."

Text Messages between Fernando Colón and Saba Abdul

Saba: I don't know. Should we go??

Fernando: I'm sure it's fine. Right?

Saba: If there were really a killer, we would know. Like, *know know* right? RIGHT?!

Fernando: That would require the cops to do something other than bust teenagers for a little pot. Like I can't even. It's so lame. It's legal practically everywhere else.

Saba: FERNANDO. FOCUS.

Fernando: Fine. Fine. I don't know. I say fuck it. Let's go.

Saba: Yeah? You sure?

Fernando: What the fuck else are we gonna do in this town? Might as well try to win some dough. And if we don't, maybe we'll get sorta famous as his next victims. Lol.

Saba: You're sick. And I LOVE THAT ABOUT YOU. Let's do it. See you in thirty. Xoxo.

Fernando: Xoxo!

Nineteen

Nell

Thursday, April 14
Morning
Three days before Easter

Nell stopped at the Walmart to use the restroom and grab a coffee to help her survive on the four or so hours of sleep she'd gotten in the past forty-eight hours. She had been wandering around all night and morning. She'd taken off from work, right after her conversation with Ada. Everything else, all those other worries, fell away. She only cared about finding Elijah and ensuring he was okay.

Back in her truck, she called Ada again around 11:00 a.m., even though she knew she'd wake her up. Ada said she couldn't sleep anyway. And she hadn't heard from Elijah since she and Nell spoke on their break. Nor had Anthony, who was now at school and texting that Elijah hadn't shown up for homeroom again. Nell asked Ada to repeat everything, starting with the last time either had seen Elijah.

"We can call the cops," Ada said. "They might help."

"They won't do shit," Nell said, surprised that Ada would even suggest it.

"You don't know that. You could go down there right now—"

"They don't give a shit about a gay kid, Ada." Irritation edged her every word, but she couldn't stop it coming. She was mad at Ada. At herself mostly. "We're better off dead to people like that. You should know." Nell sputtered with rage. She didn't know what to do. Where to go.

Ada finally sighed and said, "We could put up some posters."

"No. He's just getting something out of his system," Nell said. The words came out like a recital, one she had been telling herself for days, even as her subconscious had known that something was off. But she was too busy feeling stupid to give it any attention.

"We could—"

"He's not missing." Nell scraped her cracked, dry hands along her face.

"Nell," Ada said, her voice sounding gentle and soft. "He is." After Nell didn't say anything, Ada continued: "Maggie's here. If you were wanting to talk to her."

Nell had almost forgotten about her, given all her panic over Elijah. "No, I'll deal with her later."

"I could give her a message." Nell knew that Ada was legitimately worried because she was willing to talk to Maggie on purpose.

In the distance, Nell spotted two people staring at the ground. Ada said something else, but Nell was too focused on what they were doing to hear. They stopped, bent down. Then they carried on, looking at another spot. The fucking Hunt, she realized.

"Sorry, Ada. I gotta go. Call me if you hear from him," Nell said and hung up the phone.

Nell opened the window and propped her arm there.

Not knowing what else to do or where to go—sleep was impossible—Nell headed to the high school. Cardboard rabbits and cutouts of Easter eggs had been taped to the front doors like the building housed an elementary school instead of a high school. The secretary looked like she'd stepped right out of a reality show about a bunch of bitchy white women and addressed Nell with indifference that soon shifted to recognition and then disgust when she apparently recognized Nell from the news. No, she said, Elijah hadn't come to school that day or the day before. Or the day before that. Apparently, he had called in sick, pretending to be Nell, which wasn't that hard, with his more femme voice and hers sounding more butch.

"I guess he lied," the secretary said. "But who could blame him?" She didn't even bother to mutter this under her breath.

Any other day Nell would've asked if she really meant to say what she'd said because that kind of shit could get someone knocked in the teeth, but the woman was right. Nell's viral moment was likely the reason he'd gone MIA. High school was bad enough without adding your family's mortifying behavior on top.

The woman shook her head and glared. "You should keep track of—"

Nell walked out of the office without hearing the rest of her sentence. She assumed it was nothing good.

Outside the high school, the day was near warm, but the wind came by and bit at Nell's cheeks. She pulled the collar of her jacket up and walked the perimeter of the building, reasoning Elijah was hiding out somewhere around there. She'd checked everywhere else she could think he'd be and had come up empty, so it seemed like as good a plan as any. Nell had gone here herself, back in high school. And all her cousins. Her parents. Her brother.

Garrett had died Nell's senior year, with prom around the corner. Nell had daydreamed about pinning a corsage on Tessa's gown. But then they'd found his body and Nell never went back again, even though everyone who wasn't her family said she should, that she was college material. She probably could've gotten a scholarship. Her own family's interest in her future had died the day Garrett was found.

Nell headed toward the outer building that held the FFA. Elijah wouldn't be caught dead in there unless there was some emergency, like a tornado warning or a band of rednecks on his tail, but she checked it anyway because it was a building, and a building could hold a kid who was mad at his guardian. A bunch of kids and cows turned at the interruption and then went back to what they were doing after Nell glanced around and found no sign of Elijah. No matter where she looked, Elijah was nowhere to be found.

After checking out the school, she drove to all the drive-through restaurants and walked inside to take a look. She wandered through three gas stations and checked all the men's bathrooms when she was sure they were empty and no men would walk in on her. She could pass with her hat on even if they did, but she wasn't in the mood for a potential altercation. At the last gas station, she filled the tank and tried to think of where Elijah might go, but she kept drawing a blank. Elijah didn't work because he got money from Tessa every month. Nell figured maybe he deserved not to worry about a job until he was older. He only went out of town when he went somewhere with Anthony. He only had his dirt bike.

Nell hadn't asked Elijah where he was going when he went out at night recently. Nell had let him go because she trusted him. She figured he'd be at Anthony's house. She hadn't needed anyone's phone number, because of course Elijah would come home. He always came home. There was no reason not to. She knew Elijah had other friends. But there hadn't ever been any reason for Nell to know the specific details of where they lived or who they were, and a fresh bout of worry and guilt streamed through her. What kind of fucking guardian doesn't even know who their kid is staying with for several days?

Then, the thing she didn't want to think and had tried to push away barreled into her brain: It couldn't happen twice. Could it? She couldn't lose Elijah after she'd already lost her brother, could she?

The idea that it could swirled until finally Nell turned into the mostly empty parking lot of Sherman's Grocery to rummage through her center console for some ibuprofen, which she found and swallowed dry. She turned off the ignition and sat there, head propped on the steering wheel, unsure what to do and unclear about when the current iteration of her life had started going downhill.

Anxiety crackled in her veins. As much as she didn't want to think about Garrett and how they'd found him, her mind kept turning its attention toward unsettling ideas about the Hunter and Elijah being the next, maybe the last, in a long line of victims. A bookend to where it had all begun with Garrett.

No, she told herself. Don't go thinking wild thoughts. Elijah was loud and outrageous at times. But he was also sensitive, especially to other people's opinions of him.

The school secretary had all but confirmed Nell's fear. Elijah had seen the video of Nell at the casino and had run away, going so far as to call in sick.

Nell kept telling herself that because it was more comforting than the other possibility. Elijah would be fine. He'd come home after the embarrassment Nell had caused had died down. Nell would let Elijah quit school, get his GED if he wanted. He didn't want to go to college anyway. Always talked about going to New York City. Nell remembered that. New York sounded a lot safer for someone like Elijah than Presley anyway.

She texted him to let him know about the GED but didn't mention anything about the video. Only added, Sorry about everything. I fucked up. Please text me back, she wrote. I'm freaking out.

The sounds of life in the grocery store parking lot greeted her once she hit send and her focus was no longer on her phone.

The sun had gone down, and Nell's shift was already well underway. She'd forgotten to call after getting so wrapped up in finding Elijah. She checked her phone and saw the text from Lloyd, asking if she planned to come in to work or not. No exclamation points or emojis this time. His patience with her was wearing thin, she knew. She tapped out a reply that she'd text him later.

She was tired, mentally and physically, but she couldn't go home and sleep. She couldn't sleep in the truck either. Even though it was dark except for the parking lot lights and the cars pausing at the stoplight. Everyone coming and going like always, like normal. Elijah could be out there somewhere. She'd left him a note on the kitchen table, telling him to call her as soon as he came home. And she'd called him and left voice mails too.

She hopped out of the truck, went inside the grocery store, and grabbed herself a soda, a premade ham and cheese sandwich, and some chips to eat in the truck.

She sat there for a long while, letting all her bad thoughts consume her, thinking that maybe that was a good thing, like a purge. If she let them come, maybe she could start empty again. She turned on the radio to the country station she liked. But then she turned the dial to KCLS. She hadn't listened to it since high school, since even before everyone else started talking about KCLS's Hunt for the Golden Egg being a hunting ground for a serial killer. Rod voiced all the Hunt clues and most of the commercials and still DJ'd. His voice would always remind her of the worst day of her life.

As if on cue, Rod's voice rumbled low amid the tinkling gothic background music that felt more fitting for Halloween than Easter:

Walk along the leaves instead of the road.
But don't walk too far or the trail is sure to grow cold.

"Oh, shut up," she said.

Nell listened for a while anyway. Part of her purge. But mostly she stared out the window and back at the store through her rearview mirror.

A few older ladies, white and Black, went in and out of the store, wielding shopping carts whose wheels were intent on going the opposite direction of where the women wanted to go. One abandoned her cart after struggling with it, unwilling to continue to the corral.

Nell rummaged around in the glove box and found her vape pen. She kept an extra in there because Ada had a bad habit of taking Nell's. She hopped out of the truck and unlocked the toolbox at the back of the truck to find the WD-40 that'd been rattling around in there for months. After a customer had pushed her cart into the corral, Nell went to work on the wheels, starting from the back to the front of the long cart line. She crouched down for a while and pushed past the point of prudency until her knees ached and her feet needled. Then, she took to going down the line on one knee, using her work grease towel as a cushion, switching here and there. She was over halfway through the line of carts by the time a cart pusher, a young Black man, headed her way.

He wore the standard white button-down T-shirt, tie, and grocery apron required of his role. Nell recognized him even without his jersey on. He played over at Eastside. Running back. Nell hadn't been to any games, but she'd seen the local news and read the newspapers during breaks at work enough to recognize this kid. A senior. Lightning fast. People talked about college scouts. The SEC. Everybody wanted him to stay in Arkansas, go to U of A, and become a Razorback, although he was smart enough to get an academic scholarship out of state, at a top school.

Nell remembered Garrett talking about similar dreams he had, even though their school rarely won a game. He'd been okay on the field, nothing spectacular. Nothing to get in the local paper. But that never stopped anyone from their small town from filling Garrett's or his friends' heads full of fantasies of how talented they were, how they could go to college, play football, be great someday. Be somebody.

"Evening," Nell said to the cart pusher when he wandered up to her, suspicious.

The kid—Matt was his name—lifted his head, gave her barely a nod. His sleeves were pushed up, and Nell could see the muscles of his forearm, tight and firm, like they gathered strength as they went up his arms. His high school probably had a good weight room on account of all them boosters and just plain more people to care about things like winning.

"Don't you play for Eastside?" she asked.

"Yeah," he said. "My pops owns this." He gestured toward the store. "Better than fast food."

"I hear that," she said. She'd worked at the Sonic in high school. It wasn't all that bad.

Matt gathered a rogue cart off to the side of the corral, bundled his rope, and looked at Nell, waiting for something, she supposed.

"You need these?" Nell asked and motioned toward the carts.

"Yeah."

"All right." Nell lifted herself off the hard asphalt and felt older than she ought in the process, wondering when she'd gotten to feeling middle aged even though she was in her midthirties. "Shit," she said, more to herself than the kid, and gripped her lower back.

Matt chuckled and threaded the rope through the carts. "What are you doing anyway?"

"Fixing your wheels." Nell gripped the WD-40 can and shook it. "About out."

Matt lifted an eyebrow and quietly laughed, like you do at someone who you're not sure about. "Yeah. But why?"

"They needed fixing," Nell said. "Been watching people struggle with the carts a while now. They're going all over the place. Making a racket. So I fixed them."

Matt shook his head and muttered under his breath, but Nell could hear him. Nell knew she looked off. She couldn't fault the kid for thinking she was.

"Don't you ever just do something because it needs doing?" Nell asked.

Matt jerked the line of carts out of the corral and eyed Nell without speaking.

"I'm good at fixing things," Nell said softly. Then she fell silent against the rattle of the carts as Matt teased them out of their metal cage.

She watched him until he stopped and made a motion like he was ready to pull the line of twenty carts out and push them back inside the store for the night. Nell hadn't noticed that the exterior lights had flicked off and that the parking lot was now empty, save for her truck and the employee cars parked at the outer edges.

Matt was now easing into a curve toward the entrance of the store.

Nell wondered at herself, at the empty can of WD-40, the kid.

"Hey," Nell said and walked a bit closer so Matt could hear.

His body seemed to tighten and prepare for a fight.

"I'm looking for someone," she explained, and his shoulders settled back down from his ears. She pulled out her phone and unlocked the screen. Nell held up the phone and showed Matt a picture of Elijah.

Matt's eyes glanced at the screen and then back at Nell. Recognition washed over him. "No. But you're that woman from the casino, aren't you?"

Nell didn't nod, but something on her face must've told Matt he was correct.

"Sorry about your brother," he said.

"Thanks." Nobody really ever said that anymore. It'd been so long ago. The words cut closer than Nell had felt in a while.

"I haven't seen him," Matt said. "Sorry."

There wasn't much else to say, so Matt pushed the carts forward. "You should check Rumors. Over in Fort Smith," he offered over his shoulder. Fort Smith was twenty miles away. Nearest town one could get lost in. "That's where a lot of the queer kids hang out."

She gave him a little nod. The carts rumbled and dissipated as Matt neared and then entered the grocery store. By the time Nell returned to her truck, the interior lights of the store had dimmed and the wind had picked up and cast a chill on everything. She let the truck warm up a bit. While doing so, a handful of employees, including Matt, trekked from the store entrance to their cars. He wore his Eastside hoodie, hands shoved into the front pocket. When he passed by Nell's truck, he removed his hand from his pocket and lifted it in a quick wave. Nell nodded and also managed to smile before putting the truck into drive and heading out of the parking lot.

Nell pushed away memories of a similar day that had run into night, running around town, looking in dark corners, fearing the worst.

Shared Google Doc / The Hunt

VICTIM #5

On March 15, 2009, Philip Tomlinson (nicknamed Big Phil despite his small stature), white, fifty-nine, invited his friends over to shoot guns. They shot in the direction of a homemade hay berm located at the back of Big Phil's property and at the panhandle of Walter (Wally) McAuley's lot. Wally, white, sixty-seven, reported the gunshots to authorities. Big Phil received a warning, though they could not say that Big Phil was not within his rights to shoot guns on his property—especially given that Wally's dwellings were north and at least two hundred feet from the site of the firearms being discharged.

Following the initial incident, the authorities were called to the property a total of thirteen times, primarily complaints from Wally about noise, alleged property damage, and discharge of weapons near his dogs.

On April 10, the rural route carrier called 911 and advised that he found Wally "slumped" against his trailer siding, looking like a "bloody mess."

Based on evidence found on the scene, they determined that Big Phil and Wally had an in-person altercation across the barbed wire fence that separated their properties. Wally was alleged to have grabbed Big Phil by the collar and attempted to pull him through the barbed wire fence, at which point the wire sliced Big Phil's neck and he bled out on the scene. The cause of death was officially determined to be a homicide.

Speaking with Wally, where he currently resides at the Tucker Unit, which is managed by the Arkansas Department of Corrections, we learned that Wally has little to no recollection of the day he was alleged to have murdered Big Phil. According to police records, a tox screen was completed on Wally. They found large amounts of THC in Wally's system. Notably, they also found large tracts of marijuana on his property, a rumored source of contention between the two men. However, Wally denies that he ingested anything but his usual dose to calm down, though he admits that perhaps the weed and his blood thinners affected him adversely that day, as he does remember "waking up anxious." Though he did not like Big Phil "in any way, shape, or form" and had "threatened to kill Big Phil on occasion," he insists that he was only "mouthing" and had no true desire for violence. But, Wally added, "I can't remember shit about that day, so who knows."

Neither Big Phil nor Wally was involved in the Hunt for the Golden Egg at any point according to friends and family. However, records indicate that both Big Phil and Wally had made trespassing complaints that year regarding participants in the Hunt for the Golden Egg, self-described Eggheads.

Twenty

Ada

Thursday, April 14
Evening
Three days before Easter

Ada should've come clean. Of course she should've come clean to Nell about Elijah!

But she'd not, and now Nell knew the truth, so now Nell wasn't talking to Ada, and everyone at work talked about how Nell and Ada were going through a "divorce" and cackled like it was some kind of reality TV show. She guessed she deserved that.

Nell hadn't come in to work again, and Ada had tried to smooth it over the best she knew how. But Lloyd wasn't about to hear it. He stood between his giant oak desk and the paneled wood walls, his face red and puffy.

"I've got Maggie screaming in my ear because Gunner is screaming in her ear. And Nancy is also screaming in my ear because I should be home right now, eating supper and spending time with my family, instead of listening to you excuse Nell's behavior. Again!"

"Lloyd—"

"Don't!" He paused to take a breath; he'd gone so heavy on the rant. "I understand that Nell is your friend. She's my friend too. But I can't be letting her get away with not showing up to work. How am I supposed to explain that to everyone else? Now I've got Janie and Viv and Marcy coming in to complain that if Nell's got that much vacation and sick time, then the rest of them should have it too. I can't afford to give everyone all that time off!"

"I know," Ada said and held up her hands as if to tell him to settle. "I know, Lloyd. I'm just saying—"

"I'm tired of this!"

She'd never seen him so mad. Never ever heard him yell. "But—"

"No!" Lloyd didn't let her finish. "This is why I hate that damn Hunt." She'd definitely never heard Lloyd cuss. "Every single year it's the same thing. We have to relive it over and over."

She hadn't realized how much Lloyd had taken it personally. Sweat broke out on his forehead. His shirt was already soaked at the armpits. "Maybe you should sit down." She worried he might collapse and die of a heart attack right there.

"Don't tell me to sit down!"

She jumped back at his tone. He didn't seem to notice or care.

"I'm the boss here. Yet you two treat me like your friend—"

"You just said we were fri—"

"Like you can skip work and come back and everything's fine!" He didn't even let her finish. "Like I won't notice. Or you come in here and you make excuses for this bad behavior, thinking that you can smooth me over. Well, I'm done, you hear me? Done!"

Ada wept. She couldn't help herself. All that adrenaline toppled her when things got tense.

"Don't you start crying!" He'd gone full meltdown. "Don't you try to sway me with your tears!"

She backed into the small, pale-yellow couch he kept in his office and plopped onto it. She couldn't stop crying even if she wanted to, which she did. Very much.

"Ada!" he yelled, but his tone also indicated a level of worry. "I mean it!"

That made her cry harder. She hated crying. Especially at work. That was so embarrassing. And after him accusing her of coming in there, trying to smooth him over, as he called it. Well, that was about as mortified as she'd ever been outside of getting caught by Elijah with her pants down, especially because she knew—she just knew!—that Maggie was probably right outside Lloyd's office, ear to the door, listening to every word. Probably taking notes. Or even worse, recording it.

"Elijah's missing!" she yelled. "That's why Nell's not at work."

Lloyd came out from behind his desk and stood in the middle of the room, blinking rapidly. "What do you mean he's missing?"

"He's missing." She swiped her eyes and blew her nose on her pocket tissue. "We haven't seen him since Sunday."

"Sunday? But that's before we even saw the news with Nell!"

"I know. That's why I'm worried. This is before all that." She sniffled and wiped her nose again. "He basically told us the same thing: *I'm okay. Don't worry.* But that was Sunday, and we haven't heard from him since."

Lloyd sat back on his desk, as if the wind had been knocked clear out of him. "Is he okay?"

"I don't know, Lloyd! That's what I'm trying to tell you!"

Before she knew what was happening, he'd dropped his head in a hand and started bawling.

"Shit. Shit!" She rushed to stand and saw stars. "Don't cry." Jesus, why was *he* crying?

"This is all my fault," he said.

"What?" She felt disoriented by the change in his mood. She knew he was fond of Elijah, but she had no idea why he'd be this upset.

He rubbed at his face and collected himself. Cleared his throat. "We should've shut that thing down. For good. Last year, when we had the chance." He banged his fist on the desk. "But the city didn't want to. And Rod certainly didn't want to miss out on all that—"

A small knock came at the door, and then a whisper of words: "Is everything okay in there?"

"Go away!" Lloyd yelled. Ada could only imagine how upsetting that would be to Maggie. But then the two of them were in proximity to each other every day, so who knew what kind of irritations and altercations happened when no one else was around.

Ada waited for Lloyd to say something else, but he stared at the floor. She wasn't sure what she was supposed to do now. She'd asked Phonesavanh to cover her presses for her, though. And that'd been at least half an hour ago. She was nice, but even she could get irritable sometimes.

"I should get back out to the floor," Ada said.

Lloyd didn't move, but he raised his eyes to her in a way that mildly disturbed her.

"I'm sorry for bringing this up. I . . ." She sighed. "I thought you should know what's really going on."

He nodded and stood, hiked his pants, and smoothed his blue button-down where it was tucked in. "I'm glad you told me. I needed to know." He lodged his hands on his hips. He seemed normal again. Less Hulk-like. "It's a good reminder of something I've been meaning to do. Something that's long overdue."

Ada had no idea what he had in mind, given he and Nancy had been at it for years to no avail. But she didn't want to rile him up again. She hadn't enjoyed the experience the first time.

"You let me know if you hear from Elijah," he said as she made her way to the door. "Or Nell."

"I will," Ada said and opened the door.

Maggie sat at her desk, lips in a tight line, chin up but eyes down, looking at her computer screen. Ada had expected her fingers to be typing ninety miles an hour, but she quietly scrolled, her mouse emitting little clicks every now and then. Not once did she look up at Ada.

Ada knew that this moment would come back to bite her. She didn't know how. But she knew that Maggie wouldn't be pleased about the way Lloyd had yelled at her, not with Ada there to witness it. Maggie wouldn't be pleased at all. She'd find some way to make Ada pay for what she'd elicited from Lloyd and what had come out as fire toward Maggie.

Shared Google Doc / The Hunt

VICTIM #7

On April 23, 2011, Nikki Mancini, white, forty-four, was found behind a dumpster on Sixth Street. The records state that she was "murdered" but include no further details. When we requested more information on Nikki, we were told that the case had gone cold. We were asked not to call back.

Nikki was born and raised in Presley and was an active member of her church choir. She worked as a home health aide for primarily elderly patients and "held many hands as they passed." Patient families knew her as "Miss Nikki" and spoke of her soft and sweet demeanor.

Nikki had allegedly fallen on hard times after her parents passed away in a car accident. She lost her home and was rumored to have been seen on Sixth Street on occasion. "She did what she had to do," said an unidentified woman, who did not want to be named. "She was the nicest. And they didn't do jack shit when they found her. Just let her rot behind that dumpster and tossed her in with the others in the city grave."

When asked about Nikki's involvement in the Hunt, she said that she and some of the others would occasionally go hunting, "searching for riches among the trash" and "dreaming about the vacations they'd take down to the Gulf if they found the egg."

Twenty-One

Nell

Friday, April 15
1:00 a.m.
Two days before Easter

The music inside Rumors thumped and played some god-awful racket that made Nell feel like a boomer. The dance floor was packed with a diverse crowd of queer couples and a handful of people whom she suspected were straight girls. They bounced and jumped up and down, jumbling Nell's eyes with the rainbow-colored lights that pinged around the small room. Someone grabbed her ass as soon as she became ensconced in the crowd. She navigated to the less populated sections in the areas around the nonalcoholic bar. Guys in tight muscle shirts and femmes with sleek styled hair stared at Nell and whispered. For a moment she felt like some kind of alien, the way she had sometimes felt when they went to away games or visited places outside Presley, where she felt more at ease. Where people knew her.

She wished a club like this had existed back when she was in high school. Maybe then she could've found some other girl to obsess over, a girl who would return some of the affection Nell had been bursting to give Tessa. Maybe then she wouldn't have cared about Tessa and

Garrett. They could've kept on driving that night, and everything would be different. Garrett and Tessa would be married. Elijah would live with them. And Nell? Shit. She had no idea. Garrett's death had struck in the middle of her teenage angst, and she'd not had time to even think or care about something so broad and uncertain as the Future.

She wanted to walk right out the door, get back in her truck, and start driving—away from everything. But she couldn't leave Elijah. He was the one thing she felt like she'd done right. She may not have been a stellar cook or great at paying attention to the details, but she'd given him a home. She'd raised him not to care about what others thought of him but to be thoughtful toward others. Elijah was a good kid. He never gave Nell any real trouble. Maybe somehow, someway, Nell had made it possible for Elijah to be who he was. She hoped she'd also helped him figure out how to survive.

Nell fingered the corner of the phone in her pocket, inhaled, and walked up to each kid, even the ones who'd initially turned their backs on her when she'd started their way, as if she were some creepy older woman cruising for teenage girls. But then they squealed, called her an "ICON." The way they said the word felt like an all-caps assault. As if literally showing your ass on TV was something to celebrate. But she was a queer woman on the local news. That didn't happen often in Arkansas, with or without a crime or embarrassing life moment attached. Though there was that meth stuff that had happened up in Drear's Bluff. And she'd heard something about a woman who'd confessed to killing her stepdad over in Maud years ago. Still.

She shook off her discomfort and showed everyone a picture of Elijah. Lots of them had seen Elijah in the past. No one had seen Elijah recently.

Outside the club, she took a great gasp of air and blew her nose, trying to get the smell of a hundred different brands of cologne and perfume out of her nose.

Finally, she made her way back to Presley and the last place she wanted to go. The place she was pretty sure wouldn't do shit. But she had to try.

The cop at the counter looked at the photo of Elijah, made a face. He was one of those "tough guys." All tattoos and swagger. Itching for their trigger, waiting for "contempt of cop" or a Popsicle stick in a pocket. She hoped he knew what she thought of him and the rest of them: a bunch of pasty-white men who got off on playing cops and robbers but didn't do shit for anyone but their own kind. And only if they fit the right criteria, which she and Elijah certainly did not.

"You check Sex—" He stopped himself from using the slang term for that road, but not out of any kind of sensitivity. "Sixth Street?" the cop asked with a smirk.

"He's not a sex worker." Nell could've slammed her fist right through the guy's face. "And if he was, who cares. He's still missing."

"Sex worker," he repeated, in what Nell's grandmother would call a highfalutin manner. The cop chuckled and turned in his seat toward the other cops who sat behind him doing nothing. He hooked his thumb at Nell, like he was saying, *Get a load of this one with her wokeness.*

She ignored him and instead recited information about Elijah's height and weight and when Nell had last seen him or heard from him until she confirmed he'd written it down.

"He sent you a text?"

"Yeah, but it's been days. He hasn't been at school."

"So go to the friend's house."

"He's not at the friend's house," she said, even though she couldn't be sure.

"You checked with the friend's parents?"

Nell rubbed her forehead. There was no point telling him that she didn't even know the friend's name. Instead, she asked if they could keep an eye out and give her a call if anyone who looked like Elijah showed up.

The cop waved a hand when Nell started to tell him her name. The guy already knew. Everyone knew Nell. If they didn't before, they did now.

"What am I supposed to do?" Nell asked him. She wondered if that report was all for show, some small CYA the cops could pull out if anything happened later and they got questioned about it. "Am I just supposed to go home and wait for him to show up?"

"Yes, *sir*," the cop said, without looking up from some piece of paper he was reading.

That grated Nell, but she didn't have the energy to fight. "That's all you can do?"

The cop leaned one arm on the counter. He sighed and looked at his nails like he had nothing better to do but still hated to be bothered by something as trivial as someone's kid who'd gone missing. "We'll put him down as missing. But that's about the limit of our capabilities in such matters."

"Even though there's a serial killer out there?"

"Oh Jesus. We got ourselves a live one, guys." The cop chuckled again. This time he was joined by the others behind him who sat in their chairs or on their desks, holding chipped coffee mugs, a copy and paste from TV shows. Finally, after a good long laugh, he turned back to Nell. "Look, the kid's almost eighteen. Ain't nothing we could do even if there *was* a killer. You know how many folks call in here every Easter, asking us to go out and find their friends who went missing? The number of prank calls we get?" Nell hadn't noticed any phones ringing since she'd walked inside, and Easter was around the corner. "Shit, we had this guy up and die in a bona fide, actual car accident because we had everybody out looking for someone who was reported missing, like a damn snipe hunt. Turns out that guy was fine but his friends were a bunch of assholes. So no, we ain't got time to hunt down every kid that goes missing when they got trouble at home."

"There wasn't any trouble at home." At the cop's lifted eyebrow and obvious assessment of her features, including her chest, Nell added, "Not with him. Not with us."

The cop made a face like, *If you say so.* "Well, I could see why he might be a little hesitant on coming home."

Nell could've spit right in his face.

"Most kids run away for a reason," he said. "They don't want to be found. But if we pick him up off the street, we'll be sure to let you know." That last part he added with a little singsong in his voice.

Nell headed toward the exit, head on fire from rage. They chuckled behind her. Nell hated them for that. She'd wanted to yell, *That's my boy.* But she hadn't. Because he wasn't. He was her nephew. And he only lived with her because she'd gotten his dad killed.

Nell wasn't sure who she hated more, the cops who had laughed, or herself, for not saying something.

"Fucking asshole," she muttered under her breath as she left the station.

Though it took all her willpower, Nell didn't run to grab her wrench from the truck, go back in the station, and beat the man to death.

Balled-up napkins from drive-throughs, dirt from her boots, tools, a quarter-full bottle of Coke, and an empty cigarette pack rumbled on the floorboard when she slammed the door to the truck. Though she knew the cigarette pack was empty, she reached for it anyway, hoping to find some full-freight, nonvape relief from the prickles of anxiety that had burrowed beneath her skin ever since her conversation with Ada at the picnic table. After looking inside the pack and finding nothing, she threw it back onto the floor.

As she drove by the front doors, she grabbed the Coke bottle, rolled down her window, and threw it toward the police station before darting off with squealing tires out of the parking lot and screaming, "Useless motherfuckers!"

After visiting the police station, she was unsure what to do. That was Nell's worst-case-scenario place to go. But there was one more place to check.

Nell parked in front of the redbrick Presley Savings and Loan building with the faded RC Cola slogan on the side, figuring it'd be best to park on the street rather than the side road. The front door had a message scribbled on the poster board in the window: **Thank you for almost fifty years of patronage, Woodrow & Sons**. She put a hand up against the glass pane and peered inside. What she saw reminded her of a field trip in elementary school to the Fort Smith Museum of History. If what she saw had been a photograph, the filter applied would've been called "dust and wood." All the scene lacked were mannequins dressed in thin cotton dresses and overalls. The contents at the back of the store were clumps of shadow from the lack of light. The counter where employees had bagged goods for folks held scraps of paper and a lone hammer, probably used to remove all the antique metal signs that used to hang on the walls. White shapes marked spots that sun and dust hadn't seen in years. Shelves that had dangerously combined household cleaners next to boxes of cereal now stood empty.

Nell turned away from the window and looked west toward Oklahoma. From where she stood, she could see all that was left of downtown. A line of brick and stone buildings stood on each side, many naked without their signs. Broken windows had been taped over. A few cars were parked in the spaces in front of one of the few restaurants and bars that had managed to stay in business. And a few boys on skateboards loitered in the small park dedicated to a wartime hero. She walked farther down the cracked sidewalk. The post office was still there, as was the fabric store, evidenced by the flyers in the window that announced the current yarn sale that ended on Easter. She turned away from the flyer and startled when the door to the bank opened and a handsome Black woman came out wearing a purple dress suit. Nell remembered her. The woman always had a giant laugh for the adults and a lollipop for the kids. The smile on the woman's face hung there a while as she tried to place Nell. When she was unable to, she waved and turned to lock the door. Nell said hello and checked her watch.

"Sorry, sugar. Didn't mean to scare you. I had to catch up on some things." She smiled. "Easier when everyone's gone."

"That's all right," Nell said and glanced back down the sidewalk at all the shops.

The woman got a sad look on her face. "Shame, isn't it?" She looked around at what was left. Then the woman smiled and pointed a finger at Nell. "You're Nora Holcomb's daughter."

"Yes, ma'am."

The woman smiled, pleased that her memory still served her. But then her lips turned down into a pitying smile. "You've got your mama's eyes." She stopped short of further comparison, given the latest news, Nell assumed. "You be sure to tell her I said hello." She didn't offer her name, and Nell didn't ask.

The woman fiddled through her set of keys and landed on a thick key to her car.

The sound of a bottle breaking drew their attention across the street. A couple of teenage boys slunk around a building, cigarette smoke trailing behind them. Pieces of broken glass glinted in the streetlights.

"Kids," Nell said, surprised at her ability to sound like a crotchety old woman.

The woman drew her suit jacket closer to herself. "I best be going. I suggest you do the same," she said and tipped her head. "Rough creatures hang out here at night."

The woman hurried off after their goodbye. Nell took one last look around her and started walking.

A bit farther down the sidewalk, she turned the corner where the boys had, carrying her keys between her fingers just in case. She probably should have grabbed her wrench from her truck, assuming someone hadn't stolen it back from her while she wasn't looking. The anger associated with that knowledge built up her confidence. If someone jumped out at Nell, she was prepared to hit them.

Around the back of downtown's main drag and Woodrow & Sons was a street that had no storefronts, just the back sides of the downtown buildings. Opposite those were sporadic buildings and bushes, chain-link fences around empty lots. She crossed that street and finally came to the one she'd not wanted to venture down: Sixth Street. When she was a kid, adults had warned all the children in Presley about the dangers of this place. Some used it as a bogeyman: *If you don't finish your homework, I'll drop you off on Sixth Street for the rats and junkies to eat you.* When she was little, it'd done the trick. But when she was a teenager, it'd been the place everyone was rumored to go for drugs and alcohol and sex. The city had shut it down many times, but it always popped back up eventually. Nell had even gone by there after she'd dropped out of high school and left home, but that had been one of those times it didn't exist. So she'd landed at the casino instead, which she preferred. She liked things like clean toilets and running water.

Nell took a deep breath and headed toward a lit barrel that a bunch of people stood around, probably ten in all. Along the way, she spotted a few people leaning against buildings. A car pulled up, idled while one of them leaned on the car, casting the others in its red taillight glow, and then they drove away. Nell's anxiety pulsed. She didn't want to think about how old they were, the danger they were putting themselves in, what might happen to them. Closer to the fire barrel, pup tents and sleeping bags dotted the ground, along with containers and other items that looked like trash at first but were clearly used for some function of street living. No one seemed all that surprised to see her. She must've looked like she fit in with her hands shoved in the pocket of her hoodie. Plus, she was taller than most of them. They were a mix of ages and ethnicities and body sizes and physical abilities. Without a word, they opened a space for her around the fire, communicating their welcomes with head nods. She stuck her hands out for warmth and declined when someone offered her a smoke. She wasn't sure how wise it would be to immediately start asking if they'd seen Elijah, but they seemed friendly enough, so she decided to take a chance.

After she'd asked about Elijah, they all looked at the photo she showed them and seemed thoughtful about trying to place him. A hell of a lot more thoughtful than anyone else had been. But the search was fruitless. No one had seen him.

"Sorry," a round-faced Latina girl with curly hair said. "Do you want to leave your number? In case he shows up?"

Nell hadn't expected any of them to have phones. They laughed at her surprise.

"Of course we have phones," the girl said. "You can't survive without a phone."

She gave her number to the girl and thanked her. She wished that she had brought along some snacks or something to give to them. Before she turned to leave, she asked the girl, "Do you worry about the Hunter?"

The girl kind of laughed and then went solemn, likely because Nell vibrated with anxiety. "Not really?" She looked around at the crowd of folks gathered around the fire. "We don't really fit the profile."

"What about Nikki?" There'd always been questions about whether she'd fit the profile or had been unfortunate enough to have an accident and get lumped in with everyone else, like Garrett.

The girl shrugged. "I don't know. We don't really talk about it. Or think about it. But we've gone on some hunts together, all of us." She pointed to the rest. "Kind of stupid not to, given it's free money. And we've got time." She laughed and then grew more serious again, perhaps remembering why Nell was standing in front of her. "We've been out here a while. None of us have seen him. If we had, somebody would've said something."

Nell considered and then shook her head, trying to calm down, choosing to believe the girl because it was easier to handle the idea of Elijah being out there somewhere without a serial killer on the loose.

"Do you need anything?" Nell asked before she turned to leave. The others had gone back to their quiet conversations. The girl had such a sweet face. Something in Nell broke a little at the thought of her being kicked out of her house, which she assumed had happened. Or she had run away. She couldn't have been more than fifteen or sixteen. "Do you have food? Do you need tampons? Water?" Nell's mind raced with things she could offer. She'd go down the street and buy it and bring it back. "Wipes? Anyone you need me to call? Could I take you somewhere?"

The girl smiled in a way that made her look more mature, yet tender. "I'm good. We take care of each other out here. But if you wanted to drop something off, I mean, we won't say no, especially tampons. They're so expensive. But I've been using the reusable panties anyway. They work pretty good." The girl laughed.

"How do you eat?" Nell asked, choking up as she said the words, thinking of Elijah out there all alone, who knew where.

"Some of us have jobs. Others ask for help from strangers or get SSI checks." The girl smiled again, this time in a knowing way. "We do okay." Tears crested and broke down Nell's cheeks. She couldn't control the low sobbing that made speech difficult. "Hey," the girl said. "It looks bad. But it's not so bad. We'll watch for your boy."

Nell could hardly handle the words coming from such a young girl. *Your boy.* That almost broke her in half. She thanked the girl, told her she'd come back soon, and rushed away, taking deep breaths to calm herself down now that the tears had come and seemed to have no desire to stop. She had to get back to her truck, away from what she didn't want to see, a place she didn't want to imagine Elijah living.

At the next street over, she waited for a car to pass before crossing the road. That's when she saw her, leaned against the wall with others. Laughing, smoking. She wore a pink, baby-doll-looking outfit. Cherubic except for that wicked grin on her face. There was no mistaking her.

The woman from the casino.

KAOK News Twitter Update

Elijah Holcomb, the son of the Hunter's alleged first victim, Garrett Holcomb, is rumored to be missing. This information has not been confirmed.

Twenty-Two

Nell

Friday, April 15
Early evening
Two days before Easter

Nell pulled the hood of her sweatshirt up, crossed the street, and walked toward the group. Unlike the group around the trash barrel, these people stopped talking and let their cigarettes burn to ash as they kept an eye on her the whole time. Nell knew she probably looked suspicious, but she didn't want them to see her face yet, so she tried to walk casually. But she didn't pause. She needed confirmation.

"Can we help you?" a white girl in a red bodysuit asked as Nell drew closer. They stuck their hands in their pockets, likely slipping their fingers around some pepper spray or maybe even a knife.

Nell held up her hands. "Sorry to bother y'all. I'm looking for someone."

"Well, I bet one of us can be that someone for the right price." The rest laughed with the woman.

Nell knew that voice. She knew that face. That body. She slipped the hood off her head.

“Oh shit,” the woman, Casino, said and took off running, but Nell was too quick for her.

Nell reached for Casino’s sequined jacket. She only wanted to talk to her. But the others grabbed Nell and tried to hold her back. A cacophony of voices yelled at Nell to step off or they’d ensure Nell never walked right again.

“I just want to talk,” Nell yelled and tried to shove them off her. One looked to be going for her hair, like they were in some barroom brawl.

“*Shit, shit, shit,*” Casino kept saying, looking left and right, as if seeking a way out, but they were backed up against a brick wall and a dumpster. It was her. No doubt about it.

One of the other women, a small Black woman wearing pigtails and a tight dress, held a hand up toward Nell, as if to prepare for an attack. Another friend, with red, red lips that framed a sweet smile, kept asking the woman from the casino if she needed to go, if Nell had hurt her.

“It’s the other way around,” Nell said and held up her hands. “I just want to talk.”

“They never just want to talk!” Bodysuit spat back at her. Then she literally spat at Nell’s feet.

Nell tried to shove around them to face Casino. “Please. We don’t have to leave. Keep your friends here. I don’t care. I need to know what you meant.”

“Oh shit,” Pigtails said. “Are you that woman from the news?”

“Yes,” Nell snapped at Pigtails. “Please.” She returned her attention to Casino. “I need to know what you meant.”

Casino still looked like she wanted to bolt. The others continued to ask Casino if she wanted them to call someone, not the police, other people, presumably tough, willing, and able to deal with Nell. Finally, Casino took a deep breath.

“I didn’t know who you were,” she said. The others waited with her, blocking Nell from getting too close. Nell took a step back in good faith. “If I had, I wouldn’t have done it.”

"She's right," Red Lips said. "Soon as we saw you on the news, she told us. She feels bad, but you can't blame her. She's just doing a job."

Casino looked a little exasperated at her friend talking for her and patted their arm as if to tell them to settle. Meanwhile, Nell tried to parse their meaning.

"What does that mean?" Nell asked. The others looked between Nell and Casino.

Casino looked almost ashamed to say more. To her friends, she said, "It's okay. I think it's safe."

"Is it?" Bodysuit asked without taking her eyes off Nell, the pitch of her voice drifting higher with doubt. "You don't have to play tough, baby."

"Yes, I'm fine," Casino said.

The others paused and then reluctantly left Nell and Casino to talk, but not without warning Nell.

"I've got my eye on you," Bodysuit said.

Nell's head spun with questions, but she didn't want to press too hard. She'd looked for this woman everywhere. She didn't want her to run away. Finally, after an awfully long stretch of awkward silence, Nell asked, "What did your friend mean, 'doing a job'?"

Casino blinked rapidly, scratched at her face, and looked to her friends off to the side. They were still close enough to grab Nell if necessary. "It was a job. That's all. I didn't mean nothing by it." She chewed on a nail. "This woman drove up one night. We don't get a lot of women out here." She looked like a preteen, in trouble for the first time and trying to negotiate the truth from lies. "She offered one of us money to help a friend. When we asked why, she said that her friend was going through a hard time and needed someone to help take her mind off it. She said that her friend was at the casino. She offered to drive one of us there, pay for our drinks and whatever, as long as we tried to show her friend a good time. Kind of like in the movies, you know?" Even though Casino's face was the same, she looked so different from the woman she'd met at the casino, less confident, more scared, younger. So young that Nell got a sinking feeling.

"How old are you?" Nell blurted.

The woman ripped the nail she'd been chewing and tried to subtly remove it from her mouth. "Twenty-one."

"Are you just saying that?" Nell asked.

The woman squirreled up her mouth, a tell. "No."

Nell's stomach dropped.

"I'm twenty-nine."

Nell felt like she was gonna pass out. She leaned over and put her hands on her knees. Finally, she got ahold of herself and faced the woman again. "You look so young," she said.

"I know," the woman said. "It helps."

She didn't need to say more.

"Who was this woman?" Nell asked.

Casino thought a minute and then shrugged. "I'm not sure. Just some woman. None of my friends wanted to go." She gestured behind her. "They didn't really believe it, and they told me not to. But there was something about the woman that made me trust her. And it was good money, so I said yes." She paused. "I fixed myself up different after I got to the casino. Put down my hair. Toned down my makeup and clothes with what I had in my bag." She laughed softly. "It felt kind of like a night on the town or on a blind date, you know? Not a job."

"How'd you know it was me?"

"The woman came in with me. We were kind of sneaking around. It was fun." She looked off in thought, as if remembering a day at the state fair as a kid or the first time she'd sneaked out of the house and gotten away with it. "And she pointed you out." Here, she got a look on her face that made Nell self-conscious. "You were kind of fucked up, and I didn't really want to go through with it."

"But?"

"But I needed the money," the woman said. "So much for the hooker with a heart of gold, huh?" She laughed self-consciously. "Sorry. But I've got bills to pay. A kid to raise on my own."

Nell hated knowing that she'd been a target for someone. But she hated—and was mortified—even more that she'd not been an object of desire but a joke, a fucked-up sad sack to make fun of.

"I wouldn't have gone through with it if you'd said no. I made sure you consented."

Nell shook her head. "Even though I was fucked up?"

The woman tilted her head. "I said kind of. You made the first move. You were the one who suggested we get a room. I was willing to go out back or to the restroom."

Nell could hardly believe the conversation. It felt like another out-of-body experience. "What would've happened if we hadn't had sex?"

The woman shrugged. "Nothing. She didn't ask me to have sex with you. That was all you. I did that because you were willing to get a room and drinks and food. Shit." She laughed. "You were cute. I liked you."

Nell shook her head, not understanding. "Why would she pay for you to hang out with me?"

The woman's demeanor changed, but she didn't say a word.

The thing that had gnawed at Nell for days bubbled to the surface, made it through the shock of finding the woman she'd been looking for and the confusion of learning that someone had paid her to seduce Nell.

"Before you left the hotel room, you said that it was a shame Garrett had to die." Nell waited for an explanation. "Why did you say that?" Tears welled, and her throat clogged with emotion. "Why would you say that?"

For the first time since they'd begun their conversation, the woman looked truly upset. She looked at anything but Nell. Her friends had gone back to their own conversations. A car pulled up and dimmed its lights, the hushed tones of negotiation the only sound, until the door creaked open and the car's engine faded.

"Please," Nell said, still crying, if softer now. She pulled out her wallet, held it out. "Take it. Do whatever you want." She swiped at her face. "Please tell me. Please."

The woman thought for a long time. She looked like she might even cry. Finally, she directed her attention back to Nell. "It's what she told me to say."

Text Messages between Matt Vercher and His Mom, Teresa Vercher

Mom: Did she say anything about the egg?

Matt: No. I told you. She was just fixing the shopping carts.

Mom: Why would she be fixing the shopping carts?! That doesn't make any sense?

Matt: I don't know. She said they needed to be fixed.

Mom: But why????

Matt: . . .

Mom: Maybe I missed something. Maybe that was a piece of the missing puzzle. Rod said something about "cages," and I was thinking he was talking about maybe the pet store over on Darby. But me and Sissy went over there and couldn't find a thing that was related to

Matt: MOM. STOP.

Twenty-Three

Nell

Friday, April 15
Night
Two days before Easter

Nell entered the casino convenience store and gift shop. A little bell announced her arrival. April, the cashier, looked up, elbows on the counter, scrolling through her phone.

"Hey, Streaker! I was wondering what happened to you." She leaned on one elbow and faced Nell. "You lose your job?"

"No," Nell said, but considering she hadn't been in to work in she didn't know how long, given she was out looking for Elijah, she couldn't be certain. "Not as far as I know."

April puzzled over what Nell said and then shrugged. "Let me know if you need a job. I'll give you a reference."

Nell laughed, which was about the first nonanxious or angry response she'd had in a long time. "Even after what you saw on the news?"

April shrugged again. "We're all a bunch of fuckups here. I think you'll fit in."

"I'll keep that in mind," Nell said and grabbed a pack of Combos from the shelf. She didn't want to seem like she only had one thing in mind, even though she did, especially after her chat with Casino on Sixth Street.

"Hey, you happen to know any of the security people over at the casino?"

"Why?" April curled her lip. "'Cause you think we all live on the rez or some shit? We're all related?"

Nell was taken aback by the reproach. She hadn't realized her question could be offensive. "I'm so sorry—"

"I'm just fucking with you." April laughed. "You looking for video of that night?"

"How'd you know?"

"First thing I would've done."

"Well, I've tried," Nell said.

April nodded. "So you've come to me."

Nell licked her lips and prepared for a speech.

"I gotchu," April said. "I'm bored anyway. Follow me." She proceeded to lock the register and then walk to the doors. After Nell exited, April turned the sign that said the shop was closed and then locked that door as well. They walked to the casino, sneakers hitting pavement the only sound. April seemed glad for the break. She lifted her head, closed her eyes, and took a deep breath. Once they arrived at the casino doors, April held the door open for Nell and bowed when she passed, reminding Nell of Ada.

"If you ever need a job, you should let me know," Nell said. "Assuming I haven't lost that job."

"And leave all this?" April said and flung her hands into the air.

They both laughed and walked side by side toward the penny slot machines. Before long, Homie appeared.

He shook his head at Nell, beefy arms across his chest. "I see you've recruited one of my sisters."

April snarled at him. "'Recruit,' my ass. I offered."

Now he shook his head at April and then nodded toward Nell. "She's bad news."

"She's all right," April said. "Just wants to relive the best night of her life here at the most luxurious casino in all of Oklahoma."

Nell wished the ground would open and swallow her as they laughed.

Finally, after their laughter paused, Nell said, "Please. I need to see the video."

April crossed her arms over her chest and nodded toward him. "Come on, Homie. Don't be a dick."

After a moment's more consideration, Homie motioned for them to follow him. They all walked between the slot machines and then around the high-roller tables until they reached a door with a sign that said **STAFF ONLY**. He waved a badge attached to a lanyard across a black box, and the door buzzed and clicked.

April tried to follow, but Homie stopped her.

"Come on, man."

"Go back to your store, little sis."

She grumbled.

"Thank you," Nell told her. "I really appreciate it."

April flapped a hand in the air in dismissal, but she had a smile on her face when she did it. Soon, the door shut and left the casino and all the noise behind them.

They walked in silence to the end of the fluorescent-lit hallway; not even their shoes squeaked across the linoleum, it was so quiet. But then a humming sound came to her ears and grew with each step. They stopped at the last door on the right, with the words **SERVER CLOSET** on it. He swiped his badge again, and they entered a dark room, which was the source of the humming. There were racks and racks of equipment with little LED lights and blue and white and yellow cables all tied up nicely, running from the front of the machines and up the wall until they disappeared into the ceiling.

He held the door open for her. "Where the magic happens."

She walked inside and waited while he talked to another Indigenous guy who sat at a small desk with several monitors and computers, a desk lamp, a coffee, and a breakfast sandwich. Nell's stomach rumbled at the smell of eggs and bacon.

"It'll be a minute," Homie said and pointed to a chair near one of the servers. "You can wait here."

She didn't complain or ask how long because he was doing her a huge favor. She hadn't expected it to take so long, though. At some point she fell asleep. The humming noise from the servers and the clicking of the guy's keyboard lulled her to sleep, but she kept waking when her head jerked to the side.

Finally, after four hours and no bathroom break because she didn't want to interrupt the guy, Homie returned.

He nodded his head at her when he entered the room and headed straight for the guy at the monitors. Nell waited impatiently while Homie examined something on a monitor she couldn't see from her chair.

"There," the guy said and pointed at the screen.

Homie leaned in close and then nodded. "Well, son of a gun."

Nell's heart raced as she waited.

Finally, he motioned her over.

The guy sitting at the computer didn't say a word. Sometime while she slept, either he'd gone out or someone had brought him a BLT and chips. It was all she could do not to reach over and take a huge bite.

Homie told the guy to rewind and play, which he did before he grabbed his half-eaten sandwich.

This time, Nell was the one who leaned in close to see the video. There in black and white was her truck. A timer ran down the seconds and the minutes of the night when Nell had entered the casino for the first time in years. Like Casino had said happened, someone, their back to the video camera, stalked the machines, slowly made their way toward where Nell sat pulling her lever over and over. Their face wasn't visible, only their back. When Casino returned from the restroom, the person pointed at where Nell sat on her stool. The person loitered around them, Nell oblivious the whole time, until Nell and Casino entered the elevator together. That's when the person left the casino, presumably to steal Nell's wrench from her truck for some reason Nell didn't know.

Finally the person patted their pockets and turned around to face the camera, seemingly having forgotten something. They wore a lightweight black cardigan and black pants, and their face was kind of fuzzy, but a server breezed by, lifting the cardigan to reveal a sparkly shirt.

"That bitch," Nell seethed.

KAOK News Report

With two days until Easter, the Hunt for the Golden Egg is in full swing and the fever is high for those seeking the grand prize of $50,000.

"We at KCLS could not be more happy with the Hunt this year," KCLS station owner, DJ, and Hunt creator Rod Halstrom told us at the Sherman's Grocery today, where the swag tent is set up and lucky winners can spin the wheel to win prizes, including a special clue. "Last year was so bad for so many of us. I'm thrilled that the Hunt is here to bring people together again. We all needed a reason to get out and get back together."

Others at Sherman's Grocery agree. "Even if our team doesn't find the egg," Belinda White, fifty-four, told us of her team, the White Winners, "we still had the chance to get out and get some sunshine—and show people that Presley is still here. And we're not gonna let anything stop us."

Alice Raleigh, however, was not pleased by the event. We caught up with her at Sherman's after she left the store with a cart full of groceries. "I'm just trying to buy food for the family I have left," she said. "But I walk outside, and I see these people laughing and cheering. And I drive down the road, and I see people looking at the ground. And I turn on the TV, and y'all are here with your microphones, shoving them in people's faces." She pushed her cart away from us before turning toward us again. "I'm disappointed in Sherman's for hosting Rod, and I'm disappointed in y'all for giving them so much airtime. Nobody seems to care about me, or Aaron, or our son. Or any of the other victims."

"Of course she's upset. It's an upsetting reminder," Rod said. "We at KCLS feel for the families. But there's been no evidence that any deaths are associated with our family-friendly event."

Others in the parking lot seemed to agree, as shouts went up around us and Eggheads stood in line to spin the wheel to win a chance at a last-minute clue. But as for the Hunter, Presley is holding its collective breath, hoping that this year the egg is found without incident.

Twenty-Four

Ada

Saturday, April 16
Early evening
One day before Easter

Ada whacked the brush that surrounded her with a long stick she'd found on the ground. She'd seen it and grabbed it, still mindful of that first time she'd gone hunting with Elijah and gotten lost in the woods looking for the egg because she'd been daydreaming about herself and Nell. Stupid. That day felt so long ago. Ada should've taken that as a sign to give up the Hunt. Or at least give up going with Elijah. She should've gone alone, but she'd let her fear get to her.

She turned at a sound behind her. It was probably a squirrel that had dropped onto the leaves to retrieve an acorn or something. She couldn't tell, given the darkness that had settled over the afternoon. It'd been bright all day. But of course it was cloudy now. When the sun did break from the clouds, it was mostly covered by the tree limbs above her.

She heard the noise again. *It's a squirrel,* she told herself once more. Or maybe someone else wandering around. Tricksters. She'd not fall for that again.

She shook the thought. *It's just a squirrel!*

She hadn't even had the opportunity to go out hunting with Anthony, like he'd said they would. Like they'd planned. He got called in to work because someone had tested positive for COVID. He told her he'd call them back, tell them he couldn't make it because of a family thing. But she told him not to worry about it. She'd once been a teenage retail employee. You never knew what messed-up middle manager you'd get who would make your life a living hell if you said or did something they didn't like. He'd felt bad. And that's not what she wanted. But she appreciated it all the same. She knew he would've come with her if he could have. That meant something.

Ada ignored the **No Trespassing** sign that'd been hammered to a tree, because it looked fake. Other Eggheads did that sometimes to try to keep other people out of the places they were actively looking. The nails were new, but the property wasn't. She and Anthony had been hunting this area for years. No one tended it. Usually, though, the tricksters liked to take down trespassing signs and make people think places were safe when they weren't. That's how the guy had died in 2017. Allegedly.

If there were accidents and fatalities, it was because of jokesters and people like that. Getting their kicks by creating victims, either by messing with people or their revisionist history of events. Ada and the older Eggheads knew that. New Eggheads didn't.

If there was one thing she couldn't do, it was accept that Elijah was gone. He had to be somewhere. Maybe on this property.

She hadn't intended to go much farther into the woods, but she had nowhere else to go and felt too low to go home to an empty house on a day off. She couldn't stop looking until she found Elijah. She couldn't live with herself if Elijah turned up dead.

She cut through the brush and kept her mind focused on her mission: find Elijah. It seemed like a foolhardy one. She wasn't sure what she thought she might find in the woods. The positive-thinking part of Ada's brain told her she might find Elijah curled up in Garrett's old sleeping bag on the ground somewhere in the woods, having run away out of embarrassment, that was all. Maybe he'd seen Nell on Sunday. Somehow. Somehow, he knew about the casino. Maybe he knew someone who worked there. Or maybe he had found Nell and her secret lover. Maybe they'd had a fight about her. Or maybe Elijah had suppressed his own feelings about the Hunt coming back and had finally broken down. Or something.

She racked her brain trying to figure out what could've happened. Why would he disappear on them, but then write those weird messages to both of them?

It was pointless. She'd never been good at predicting who the killer was in all those whodunits. It hurt her head.

At any rate, she told herself, there was nothing more to it than embarrassment or something else that had happened at home. Whatever had happened, Elijah had gone someplace where he thought maybe no one else would go. He was tricky like that. But the imaginative, darker side of her mind told her to be on the lookout for his clothing, or something worse. She shuddered at the thought and tried to get it out of her mind.

She used the stick to brush at trash on the ground, a habit from looking for the egg all those years, even though she was supposed to be looking for Elijah. There were soda cans and plastic bottles, discarded potato chip and bread bags, all manner of unidentifiable paper things. A few soiled clothing items here and there that filled her with dread when she came upon them. She poked at them with her long stick, exhaling deeply when she was presented with evidence that it didn't belong to Elijah. He'd never wear a Razorbacks T-shirt.

The sun crept lower in the sky, dropping the temperature all along its path. Night would come on fast, so she had to hurry. Before she'd locked the car, she'd hitched a hoodie around her waist and cinched it tight. She paused her search to pull it over her head but got stuck in the process. Then she heard a cracking noise again.

Fucking squirrel!

Her blood pressure and its corresponding beat under her skin intensified. She wrangled her head through the hole—one arm still stuck somehow, all bent and uncomfortable. Her breath came fast; her head felt on fire. She paused, searched the woods around her, and wondered how everything could look so much darker after only a ten-second struggle to wrestle her arm into a sleeve. Nothing moved. Nothing made a peep. Back when she'd bought the trailer, when Anthony was younger, she'd jumped at every little noise, terrified that someone was trying to break in and cause them harm. She'd had to draw the curtains tight and leave the lights and TV on in the living room while she slept, as if that might convince someone that she was at home with a lot of people. Not alone with a baby.

Vulnerable.

She wasn't that anymore. She kept going.

Daylight was faint. She turned the flashlight from her phone on to see better, to feel more secure about where she was walking.

For another thirty minutes or so, she was scouring the area when there, on the ground, next to a pile of dirt and rocks, nothing much to mark it, she saw a glimmer.

Gold.

She nearly gasped on her own intake of breath.

She eased closer to it. Closer.

It couldn't be, she told herself. It's not. It's a candy wrapper or wrapping paper. A child's toy, lost on the ground, picked up by a flood from Lee Creek and carried here, to its current resting place.

It couldn't be the egg. Could it?

She walked toward it like it was a timid animal, ready to launch away at the slightest sound. Briefly, the logical part of her brain screamed Elijah's name, like a reminder. But just as quickly, the thrill-seeking part of her brain shoved logic aside and told her to run. *Run toward it. Now. Before it's lost to the darkness.*

She slipped on the soft green moss along the way and nearly skidded to the spot like a baseball player headed to home plate. She laughed at herself, maniacal. Full of want and giddiness and dread that it wasn't what she thought it was.

She paused, caught her breath. Then she slowly reached for it. Removed it from the ground as if it were a land mine. Trying not to shake with an overwhelming hope that she'd found the egg after all these years hunting.

Ada had always had a picture in her mind of what the egg would look like when she finally found it. She'd imagined the scenario so many times, in all sorts of weather, in all sorts of places around Presley. But she'd never guessed it would look like what she held in her hands: a Popsicle stick that had been stuck in the ground, its spray paint of gold barely visible. For a minute, she wasn't sure if it was real or just her desires after such a long hunt for the egg tricking her into believing she'd actually found it. She turned the Popsicle stick over. In Sharpie, Rod, she presumed, had written: *Congratulations you've found the golden "egg" call this special number for your prize.* Just like that. No punctuation other than the quotation marks. No fanfare. Just chicken scratch. No wonder it took forever for people to find. It was a Popsicle stick in a haystack. And the number was smudged and illegible at that.

She had expected something fancy, like a Russian Fabergé egg with jewels on it. The least Rod could've done was use a plastic golden egg from the dollar store, but she supposed he'd spent all his creativity on the clues and then placing the "egg" just so. But this was some redneck shit. A total letdown. But not for long.

The Hunt wasn't about an actual golden egg. It was about the money.

That little wooden stick represented $50,000 and all the things that money could buy. Anthony may not need money for college due to his scholarship, but she could buy him new clothing to start him off right. Books if he needed them, since the scholarship didn't pay for that. She remembered they'd been so expensive back when she'd started her freshman year and then had to return all the books for what amounted to pennies when she'd had to drop out her second semester. She could buy Anthony a new car. Get rid of the old one he drove, which certainly wasn't a beater. But he deserved something new. He'd earned it. And maybe let him have a little spending money on the side so he wouldn't feel like he had to work and go to school to have nice things or go out to eat with his friends. And of course, Anthony would have a fit if she spent it all on him, so she'd leave a little for herself. She didn't need much, especially with Anthony off to college soon. Her grocery and electricity bills would be cut in half, at least. But she could treat herself. Get her nails and hair done. Maybe a massage, but only the kind where she didn't have to take off her clothes. Or maybe she could get one of those recliners that also had a massager built in, something like that.

She wiped the dirt from one end of the Popsicle stick and then cupped it in her hands like the precious object it was. She couldn't help but smile. But then she remembered someone else that she'd promised to split the money with.

Elijah.

She looked up to the sky and expelled a long breath. Someone would find him. Or he'd come home. And when that happened, she'd give him whatever she didn't give to Anthony. He deserved it. And she'd give Nell a new vape pen to make up for all the times she'd bummed off her. Buy her a proper dinner to apologize. She hoped it would make Nell smile, make her forget what Ada had done. The trouble she'd caused. She'd understand if it didn't, though. But it could. Right there in her hands was possibility. Hope. Good things.

A branch broke behind her. She turned, startled.

Shared Google Doc / The Hunt

VICTIMS #14 AND #15

On March 26, 2018, John Dalton, forty-five, Black, shot Alex Foster, twenty-three, Black, in the chest, having assumed Alex was an intruder on his property.

John, who worked at the paper plant, reported that he'd been having trouble with people trapping on his land without permission. One of his dogs had stepped on one and had to have its leg amputated. Neighbors confirmed that John's **No Trespassing** signs had been up for years and even pointed to the place on the tree where you could see where the sign had been. The three friends who accompanied Alex with Hunting that evening swore there were no signs and the cops confirmed it. John's wife, name withheld by request, also reported that John had been heartbroken about their dog's suffering and had vowed to find whoever did it and make them pay.

Unfortunately, John suffered a massive heart attack after the police left his home, presumably from the emotions of what had transpired that day, making 2018 the first and only double homicide attributed to the Hunter.

Twenty-Five

Ada

Saturday, April 16
Sunset
One day before Easter

Ada let out a giant breath and clutched her chest. "Jesus Christ. Are you stalking me?"

Somehow, even though the darkness had come on quickly earlier, now it seemed hung in suspension and lit Maggie's face as she walked closer to Ada. She wore a plain black shirt, pants, and shoes. No bedazzlement to be found.

"Why would I stalk you?" Maggie asked. "What are you doing out here?"

The last time they'd spoken was at the grocery store. Ever since, they'd passed each other in the hallway with stony stares forward, not gifting the other with attention.

"I'm looking for Elijah," Ada said. Maggie pursed her lips as if to contain a thought. "What are *you* doing out here?"

"I'm also looking for him," Maggie said and then seemed to swallow. Ada had seen Elijah and Maggie talking and laughing together at times, in the break room, when he stopped by to get something from Nell. Sometimes, Ada had gotten jealous, seeing them there. But that was ridiculous. "Did you see the posters I put up? Someone took them down. I replaced them this morning."

Ada had seen them here and there around town on electric and telephone poles. She had wondered who had put them up. Of course it'd been Maggie. She was the one who rallied around something, whether it was good or bad. She got people excited about things like holidays and other events around town. Wore goofy earrings, depending on the season. Kind of like the cheerleader for the factory. She organized fantasy football things and raffles. Made sure everyone knew that so-and-so's kid had a bunch of shit everyone needed to buy. She'd even done that for Anthony, back in grade school, for his band. Convinced everyone to buy expensive chocolate bars that tasted like a whole lot of nothing. But Maggie did it with a smile and without seeming to want anything in return. And now she'd done it for Elijah, something that Ada had suggested to Nell. But Nell had freaked out, so she hadn't forced it. Maggie didn't wait for permission. She did what she thought needed doing.

"I saw them," Ada said, trying to cover the fact that she had been looking intently at the ground a moment ago, not for Elijah but for the egg. "I thought maybe he'd be out here."

"Why do you think he'd be out here?" Maggie had a weird look on her face that made Ada uncomfortable.

Ada shrugged. "I don't know. I'm looking anywhere. Everywhere. Just in case." Something about being here with Maggie, outside the factory and not under normal circumstances, made Ada uneasy. The same way she'd felt when she'd run into her at the grocery store. "You must've thought it was a good idea. You're here too."

Maggie smiled and shrugged as if to say, *I suppose so.* Then her face resumed its normal nothingness. Her eyes glanced to the ground and then landed on Ada's hand. "What's that?"

Ada looked down. The Popsicle stick. She'd been so startled and then distracted by Maggie's appearance and questions that she'd forgotten she still held it in her hands.

"Oh," Ada said. "Nothing. Just some trash. Thought I'd pick it up while I'm out here."

Maggie gave her a quizzical little smile and tilted her head. She waved her hand at the ground, where so many other pieces of trash were lying around. "Might need a bag." She nodded toward Ada's hand, which had slipped the Popsicle stick into her pants pocket. "What's so special about that trash?" She smiled, wicked. Like she knew something Ada didn't. Or had figured out what Ada was hiding and was now playing with her. "Is that . . . ?" She let the question trail off, but that weird smile stayed plastered on her face.

Ada hated to lie. Not because she felt terribly bad or anything. She hated trying to keep facts straight. Lying was too much work. And what good did it do? Based on recent events, she could firmly say, no good at all.

"I found the egg," Ada said.

"Oh." Maggie's smile faded. "I thought you were looking for Elijah."

"I was," Ada said and then corrected herself. "I am. I just happened to come here."

"That's convenient," Maggie said. "Two birds, one stone. Well, one bird so far, I guess. Unless you've got Elijah hiding in your pocket too."

Ada didn't know how to read Maggie's response or what to do next. Something felt off about Maggie. Like she was undergoing some kind of Jekyll and Hyde transformation.

Maggie must've caught the look on her face. She paused a minute, and then she laughed. But it wasn't the one Ada was used to hearing at work.

That laugh. She knew that fucking laugh!

"Have you been following me?" Had she been the one in the woods that first time she'd gone hunting with Elijah? "You pop out of nowhere at the grocery store. And now here?"

"Can I see it?"

"What?" Ada asked, but then she realized what Maggie was talking about by the way she stared at her pocket like Gollum in *The Lord of the Rings*. Ada backed away from her slowly. "If you find it, you're not supposed to show anybody. Those are the rules."

Maggie offered a little laugh. "I don't think Rod's gonna mind. And you don't have to tell him, right? We're friends. You can trust me. I just want to see it. After all, I came this close."

"I thought you were looking for Elijah."

"I was," Maggie said. "I'm doing both. Like you."

"What about your crew? The others?"

Maggie shrugged. "Sometimes I go alone." She glanced at Ada's hand in her pocket. "It's just a little peek."

Ada considered that Maggie had followed her for days, weeks, maybe even years. "I know, but I don't want to take any chances. I can't afford to blow it. I've got Anthony to think about."

Maggie pursed her lips again and nodded, eyes to the treetops. The darkening had come on so quickly, but now they seemed suspended in time and space and dim light. Ada didn't like it one bit.

"I should go," Ada said and stepped around Maggie.

"I was so close," Maggie said.

Ada huffed air out her nose in acknowledgment. She was half-scared and half-annoyed, not sure which half to lean into. "I've been so close too. Ever since the first Hunt."

"I was right behind you. Maybe a minute or so."

"Because you were following me?"

Maggie gave her that weird smile again but didn't say anything.

Ada rushed off toward her car.

Ada got the feeling Maggie was still right behind her, even though she'd picked up her pace. There was definitely something off about Maggie, and Ada didn't want to stick around to figure out what it was.

Ada kept her hands shoved in her pocket, but she felt Maggie's cold fingers reach in and scrounge for the stick.

"Who do you think you are, sticking your hands in my pocket?" Ada lunged away from her and then turned, breath jagged from adrenaline and fear. But there was nothing to fear. It was Maggie. Former friend. Gossip. Factory office manager. "That's the kind of thing that'll get you put in the hospital if you don't watch it."

Maggie huffed now and gave a little smile, her chin tilted up in the air so that her eyes were tilted down, looking at Ada from on high. "I wanna see it."

Ada was confused, scared. But there was also anger underneath all that. "I told you no."

"Why do you have to be that way?" Maggie crossed her arms and pouted. "Give it to me," Maggie said and lunged at Ada, that weird smile still on her face.

"What the fuck?" Ada yelled and shoved Maggie back, but it didn't dissuade her. If anything, it emboldened her. Maggie came at her again, her hands like pincers, snapping at Ada.

"I said stop!" Ada shoved Maggie again, and she fell onto the ground. But she didn't cry. She started laughing.

"What the fuck is wrong with you?" Ada screamed at her.

Before Ada knew what was happening, Maggie had grabbed Ada's ankle and yanked it so hard Ada fell to the ground. Then Maggie was on top of her; they were scrambling in the dirt, in the darkness that had decided to finally wash over them. Ada punched and scratched and screamed. She grabbed Maggie by the hair, pulled some of it right out from the roots, her anger in that moment so intense she worried she might've taken Maggie's scalp along with it. But no matter how much Ada fought back, Maggie fought back more. She was strong, which terrified Ada because she couldn't believe it. How could this little nothing of a white woman get the best of Ada? A high school athlete? A tough girl? The one you don't mess with? But there she was, this animal on top of Ada suddenly, a gleam in her eyes, knees on Ada's shoulders.

The Popsicle, that "golden egg" between Maggie's teeth, little bits of spittle gathering at the corners of her mouth. How had she gotten it away from Ada?

Fuck this little former friend. This little nothing of a woman. Ada hadn't come all this way, hunted all this time, for Maggie to steal it from her.

Ada gathered her strength and launched her head toward Maggie's forehead.

Shared Google Doc / The Hunt

VICTIM #12

On March 25, 2016, the Bartels, white, arrived at Furniture World after a visit with their in-laws. The family indicated they stopped at the store as usual because the children were typically cranky after such visits and the store's free popcorn and massage chairs tended to settle them down. While the children played with the various settings on the massage chairs, their parents sat across from them on a sleeper sofa. The Bartels noticed an odd smell coming from the couch. Being "curious folk" by nature, the Bartels investigated the smell. Upon lifting the sleeper sofa, they discovered the decomposing body of a teenage boy.

The boy, Chad Jones, white, thirteen, had gone missing a few days prior. His mother and stepfather had taken Chad and his four brothers to the store to "get out of the house," similar to the Bartels and other Presley parents. At some point, Chad and his brothers were playing hide-and-seek, at which point Chad went missing, not to be found until the Bartels sat on the sleeper sofa that he'd become stuck in and reportedly suffocated. Asked why they did not report Chad as missing earlier to the authorities, the Joneses expressed that they did not want to "get the police involved in their business." Upon further investigation, authorities discovered a homemade counterfeit money operation in the home. The parents were taken into custody and the boys turned over to Child Protective Services.

We were unable to contact the family for further information. Several neighborhood friends indicated that Chad and his four brothers hunted for the golden egg every day after school, as did many of the children in their apartment complex. After Chad went missing, his brothers were told to "keep quiet" by their parents. But the brothers told their friends and looked for Chad after school instead of the egg.

All the children we spoke with said the brothers told them they'd seen Chad speaking to an unfamiliar person at the furniture store. The brothers believed that Chad had been lured into the mattress and suffocated by that person, the Hunter—a claim they could not prove but nevertheless believed and spread as fact to all their friends.

Twenty-Six

Nell

Saturday, April 16
Evening
One day before Easter

After seeing the video at the casino on Friday night, Nell had headed straight for work. She raced up the front steps and tore through the hallway to Lloyd and Maggie's empty office before entering the plant floor. Gunner looked up from where he was perched on a stepladder, monitoring all the women on Nell's shift.

"Oh, so you—"

"Shut the fuck up, Gunner," she yelled. "Where's Maggie?"

He held a middle finger to his ear and pretended that he couldn't hear her, mouthing, "What?"

She covered the floor, looking for Maggie. No one knew where she was, but they'd seen her earlier.

Fucking Maggie. Nell guessed she was messing with her. But why? Why would she pay someone to say those awful things about Garrett? To Nell? That's what she couldn't get her head around. She didn't figure Maggie to be the evil type, but what did she know about anything anymore? It was too much. Elijah, Casino, Maggie.

After waiting in the parking lot at work for Maggie, Nell finally gave up. She first saw the posters at the gas station while filling up the truck. They were everywhere. On telephone poles, at the gas stations that she'd gone to the previous day.

She texted Ada: WHAT THE FUCK? POSTERS?!

Ada didn't know what she was talking about, so Nell took a photo and sent it to her. **MISSING.** All caps. Right there at the top. And a photo of Elijah that Nell couldn't even remember taking or seeing smack dab in the middle. His name, his birth date, a note that he'd last been seen hunting with a friend at Chaffin Park.

She ripped down every single one she could find. Rushed around stores, just to be sure there weren't any hidden somewhere. She even went down the hallway to the Walmart employee break room and found a corkboard and scanned it before someone caught her and started asking a bunch of questions about her start date and her missing badge.

Why are you so mad??? Ada texted back. This is good!

Where is Elijah? The text came from Tessa. He's missing?! What is going on?!

Posters are good, Nell, Ada wrote.

They weren't good. They meant what was happening was real. It meant that Nell had to relive it again. That terrifying moment when she'd realized that something was wrong. Posters with Garrett's face had been plastered everywhere once too. Now that face was Elijah's.

Nell had searched all over for Elijah on Friday night through early Saturday morning—while swinging by work more than once and keeping an eye out for Maggie's car on the road. After a fruitless search, Nell had bought herself the largest volume of cheap vodka she could find and drunk it straight from the bottle because the last time she had wanted to do that when someone went missing she hadn't, and then Garrett had shown up dead anyway. So maybe, she'd reckoned, if she got wasted, she would wake up and realize it had all been a dream, or at least she could see if the outcome was different this time.

But on Saturday afternoon, she'd finally woken up from her drunken stupor in the casino parking lot and everything was the same as it had been the day before. She wandered to the casino gift shop for coffee. April gave it to her for free. Said Nell looked like she needed someone to be nice to her. Good kid. Way nicer to Nell than she figured she deserved. Nell had left her a twenty in the tip jar.

Finally, after sunset, the coffee and time did their magic until she thought she was mostly sober. But she drove slowly, with her hazards on, just in case.

After a while, she pulled up into her old driveway. The living room lights were on and cast a warm glow onto the grass. Their little house was surrounded by lots of other little houses that looked like theirs. Her dad had been so proud to buy it. She remembered him telling her and Garrett many times. Her mom's and dad's happiness and love had filled the rooms. Everything in their lives had been easy. They were normal, and nothing ever went askew. And then everything changed, and it was like a vine had come up from the ground and covered the house—everything within darkened. The only sign of life that little lamp at the living room window. One day, Nell thought, that's gonna go out too.

"Nell," her mom said and checked her watch. "What are you doing here so late?"

It was sometime after 10:00 p.m.

"I just wanted to see you," Nell said, trying to trap her tears.

Nell must've smelled like vodka because her mom held a hand to her nose. She tried to be subtle about it, but even her subtlety was obvious. "You drove here like that?"

"I stopped. Drinking. And then driving." Nell wanted to mention that the fumes probably hung on her, but she didn't think that'd go over well and she knew she had no excuse. "I mean, not entirely. Just tonight. I stopped the car to sober up. That's what I meant."

Disappointment clouded her mom's face.

"Who is it?" her dad asked from inside.

"Don't tell him," Nell said.

Her mom pursed her lips, assessed Nell, and then called over her shoulder. "Just Nell."

Nell grumbled. Her mom was never good at little white lies.

"Everything okay?" He paused, probably checking the time. "Do you need me?"

"Everything's fine." Her mom held a finger up to Nell and reached for something out of sight. An Arkansas Razorbacks blanket. "We're gonna sit outside a minute and catch up."

She motioned for Nell to follow her after she shut the door.

Her mom draped the blanket over their legs after they sat on the porch swing. Her mom's toes dipped to the floorboards and pushed off without thought. The action made Nell a bit woozy, so she used her toes to stop the swing. Her mom left and returned from a quick trip inside the house—no doubt with a stop at her dad's recliner for a quick debrief—and returned with a ginger ale. Nell downed the whole thing. On family vacations, she and Garrett both got car sick. Every time, their mom would hand them whatever carbonated beverage she had on hand and tell them to drink it all and try to burp.

Nell did and felt a bit better.

Her mom absentmindedly started rocking them again. The chain squeaked out into the night.

Nell pulled the edges of the red blanket up around her waist and tucked it beneath her thighs. She hadn't had anything to eat and was probably dehydrated, making her feel cold on top of queasy.

"You gonna tell me what's going on?" her mom asked. They didn't look at one another. They both stared across the street to the Avashias' house. It looked like theirs, down to the porch swing.

Nell burped again. She didn't know what to say. She never did anymore. They used to come out here and talk for hours, like a typical mom and daughter, even though Nell was anything but typical. But her parents had never made her feel anything but loved.

"How's Elijah?" her mom asked.

Nell wanted to tell her mom that he was missing, that she didn't know where he was, and it was probably Nell's fault, but she didn't want her to worry until she knew there was something to worry about.

"He's good, I think," Nell lied. But maybe it wasn't a lie. Maybe he was good and actually did have poor service or something. Or he really was mad at her. That was fine. That was understandable. He needed time.

"He at home?"

"A friend's house." That's what he'd told her. That's what she chose to believe.

Her mom nodded, the logistics sorted. "We saw the news."

Nell offered an awkward laugh because that was the only thing she could think to do. "Not my best moment."

"I'm guessing that's why you're here."

Nell slipped off her tennis shoes and tucked her legs underneath herself and the blanket. "I guess."

"I thought you'd put this self-destructive behavior behind you."

"I have. I'm just having a—"

Her mom sighed. "Every time I think you're good, you show up drunk."

"I'm not always wasted." Nell laughed and wiped her face. "Just, you know, once a year."

Her mom didn't laugh. "Getting wasted is not going to bring Garrett back."

The words stabbed. "I'm sorry. I shouldn't have come."

"That's not what I mean, and you know it." Her mom sighed deeply. "It's almost like you feel responsible for what happened."

Nell slipped her feet back into her shoes. She'd wanted to tell her mom so badly over the years. Wanted to come clean but she didn't know how.

"No one's responsible but the person who did it."

Nell tossed the blanket aside and stood.

"You come home smelling like a brewery, you don't really say anything, and then you leave. I barely hear from you. And I don't see you again until the next year. Same time. Every year. Like clockwork. The only way I know anything about how you're doing is from Elijah."

Nell paused. "You talk to him?"

"Of course we talk to him," her mom said in that exasperated way of hers that indicated she wasn't sure why she had to clarify what she'd said in plain English. "He's our only grandchild."

Wasn't her mom the one who had turned Nell away? Hadn't she turned away from Elijah, saying it was too hard to be around him? Had Nell made that all up? Had she been the one who held both of them back from her parents, not the other way around? Nell's nose leaked, matching the tears coming from her eyes.

"What's going on, Nell?"

She didn't know. Her thoughts felt amorphous and hard to capture on her tongue. "It's hard."

"I know it's hard. It's hard on all of us. But you make it harder," her mom said. "Don't you see that?"

Every part of Nell's head ached, and her lips trembled from trying to hold in the emotion.

"I don't know how to help you, Nell." Her mom shook her head. "I tried when you were younger. And when Elijah came into our lives, but you wanted to do it alone. But you're an adult now. And Elijah's about to graduate. Maybe it's time for you to leave this town. Start over somewhere else. Let go of this strangling grief you can't seem to shake."

Nell gasped, and all that emotion spilled out. "Aren't you sad? All the time?"

Her mom sighed. "Of course I'm sad. But I can't let it drown me. I'd never be able to go on."

Maybe that was the difference. Maybe Nell didn't know how to go on. Or want to.

Her mom looked at Nell for a long time. "I love you. We both do. But this place has nothing but hurt for you."

"Okay," Nell said and walked down the porch steps. There was nothing else to say. These same words had been exchanged between them so many times. Her mom was right: every time the outcome was the same. Every year Nell showed up, right on time. But this time, it was the worst it'd been. This time, Nell hadn't just fucked up—she'd lost focus on anything but herself. She'd not even noticed the calls from the school. Hadn't questioned where Elijah was or if he was okay or when he was coming home.

The farther she drove from her parents' house, the more her chest tightened. She clenched her fists against the pain, coughed to try to get it to stop—as if that could make it stop. As if anything could make this pain stop, this pain that felt honest to God like her heart had been scooped out with a spoon and her skin threaded back together over the hole with a staple gun. She glanced up and through the windshield, her eyes to the sky, seeking the comfort her mother found there in God and Jesus and the Holy Spirit.

There was nothing there but sky.

Group Text from Todd Browne to Curtis Matthews and Mark Phillips

Saturday, April 16

Who the fuck is Elijah Holcomb, and why am I seeing posters of him all over town?

Twenty-Seven

Ada

Sunday, April 17
Easter morning

"What happened to your face?" Anthony asked, all nonchalant, like maybe the giant bruise on Ada's forehead that morning was the result of a work injury. As if she'd come home like that even once before.

She walked to the fridge and grabbed a protein shake to go along with her banana. "I found the egg, and Maggie tried to steal it from me." She set the protein shake on the counter and then peeled the banana. "She attacked me, so I headbutted her and took off."

"Are you serious?" His mouth hung open. A video game character hung suspended on the TV behind him on pause, one thick arm in the air, the other holding a machine gun or some other weapon.

Anthony stood from the couch. Tossed the game controller aside. He looked shocked. Like, really shocked. For the first time ever. As if he was finally seeing his mom for more than the person who fed and loved and sheltered him. She couldn't blame him for that. But in that moment, she realized that she was finally ready, too, like Anthony. She had a whole life ahead of her still. Their love was still there. It wasn't going anywhere. He might not be her best friend anymore, the person he had spent all his time with at one point. But her boy would come back. He always did.

She laughed and walked to the door, banana and protein shake in hand. The first glimpse of sun shined through the little front window, warmed her skin. "Baby, I told you it was my year."

She had come home late the previous night. She had felt pretty bad about leaving Maggie there alone in the woods unconscious, even though she'd deserved it. Ada had considered it, but then turned her car around, fearful that maybe she'd accidentally killed her with a head-butt. She'd waited as Maggie finally came to and managed to get to her own car. Ada had even followed her to ensure she'd made it home all right. Would Maggie have done the same for her? Absolutely not. But if Maggie went to the cops with some cockamamie story, Ada wanted to be prepared. She sure as hell wasn't gonna go to the police. She knew better than that. Back at the house, she'd grabbed an ice pack for her head and taken photos of her injuries on her phone just in case, though.

And now she was ready to get her prize.

"I'll be back in a bit," she said on her way out. "Love you!"

Ada drove to the station with the radio turned up so loud it rang in her ears. She sang along. Felt like a Disney princess with cartoon animals singing along with her in the car.

She'd done it. She'd really done it. She'd found the golden egg.

The number on the Popsicle stick was too smudged to even try to guess at the numbers. She'd googled and then called the radio station several times on her way home the previous night from her fight with Maggie, but no one had answered.

In the radio station parking lot, she shut the car door and locked it with the key fob. Not many people were out at this hour on this side of town. She saw a few buildings with dark windows. An old strip mall that used to host name-brand stores but now featured arts and crafts booths and local tailors selling their designer knockoffs for half the price. Hardly any other cars in sight. The one stoplight down the road was red and then yellow and then green and then red again.

But she knew there would be an early-morning DJ. So even if Rod wasn't at the station, she'd be able to tell them to tell Rod that she had found the golden egg.

She'd found the egg. She alone. No one else had followed the clues or searched like she had, and for years! Everyone had laughed and talked about how she was obsessed. But she'd played the game, and she'd won. Their nastiness couldn't cut through that.

The station door was unlocked, so Ada walked in. The place smelled of fresh-brewed coffee and the mild scent of cigarettes that had probably clung to the carpeted walls since the '70s. She'd come here once in high school, on one of those career-day-type events. She'd been mesmerized by the room, the idea of bringing music into people's homes, talking about music all day. All alone. To yourself and yet to everyone. She'd listened to Friday-night dedications every week, hoping that someone would dedicate one to her. She and her friends had gone to all the events and tried to win free tickets to local concerts at the fairgrounds. The station had been so much a part of her life, not just for the Hunt.

And here she was again. She was so excited that she barely felt the headache from the headbutt. Anthony had texted several follow-up questions after she'd left the house, including how she'd learned how to headbutt someone like in the movies and if she could teach him. The only one she responded to was the request that she go to the hospital to ensure she didn't have a concussion. She agreed. She didn't want him to worry. She'd promised to go, but not before she'd claimed her prize.

"Hello," she called out, and soon enough a tall, lanky man she recognized from KCLS's Facebook posts popped out of a hallway.

He held up a hand and smiled. "Hello. What can I help you with?" She'd heard that voice so many times. Conrad Cooley! He was tall, dark skinned, and handsome, which she hadn't imagined! He sounded like a white dude on the radio.

She showed him the Popsicle stick, and he was about as excited as her. She was too excited, she realized. She should've kept the Popsicle stick hidden. Those were the rules. She'd said so to Maggie. But the number was rubbed off. What was she supposed to do? And he worked for the station, so she figured she could trust him.

"It looks like a piece of trash," Conrad said and laughed.

"I know! You've never even seen it?"

"No. But I'm not surprised. Rod is kind of cheap." He raised an eyebrow and smiled. "Ask me how I know."

"Well," she said. "I shouldn't have shown you what it looks like. Technically, that's against the rules."

"Your secret's safe with me." He mimicked zipping his lips and then crossed his heart. "I think I heard Rod back in his room if you want to go knock."

"His room?"

"Yeah. He basically lives here." Conrad pointed down the hallway. "He converted an old storage room into an apartment. Said it was cheaper than buying a house or renting."

"Oh," she said, not thrilled about the idea of going into Rod's personal space alone, but she didn't want to bug the guy or appear afraid. He probably had to get back to his job.

He turned away from her to head back to the studio, but he paused and faced her again. "Congratulations," he said, and it sounded like he meant it. "That's really cool you found the egg. And for the biggest prize yet! Seriously, that's awesome." He had a nice smile. And a great voice. She felt a flutter like she got sometimes sitting out with Nell on the bench. She didn't mind that feeling. And she didn't mind who it came from at this point. She didn't mind it at all. She'd have a free schedule soon. Maybe she'd fill it.

Despite her hesitation about being in Rod's personal space, she moved in the direction that Conrad had pointed and knocked on a door that had one of those battery-operated doorbells stuck to the wall with tape. She rang the bell. There was no answer, so she knocked. She knocked again and finally put her ear to the door after checking that Conrad wasn't watching, because that felt weird.

She heard little noises. A little like breathing, a little like gasping. She worried that maybe he had a woman with him and she was interrupting. But who had a bedroom at work? That was also weird.

"Hello?" she called out and knocked again. "Rod?"

Conrad came around the corner. "Everything all right?"

She jumped back from the door and tried to keep her heart from beating out of her chest. "I don't know," she said. She felt embarrassed suddenly. Like a damsel in distress. "Yes. Everything's fine. I think he might still be sleeping. I'll wait in the car a bit."

He smiled again, and she thanked him again. God, she felt like such a schoolgirl.

Outside, she waited in her car. She texted Anthony to let him know she was fine and that she had not gone to the hospital yet, but she planned to after she'd spoken to Rod. She wanted Anthony to know exactly where she was. Everything with Elijah had spooked her. Still, Anthony wasn't easily persuaded and kept harassing her about going to the hospital first. She decided to ignore the other texts he sent about it. She didn't need him dampening her spirits. What if someone else decided to show up and claim they had won the prize? And she wanted to get to Rod before Maggie had a chance to ruin anything.

While she waited, she also texted Elijah again. Nothing. And Nell. Also nothing.

She scrolled through Facebook to pass the time and navigated to Maggie's profile. She'd unfriended her a long time ago, but Maggie didn't lock down her info. Her posts were public and accessible to everyone. Nothing about the night before. The last post was a photo she'd taken of the missing poster of Elijah she'd designed, printed, and hung on a pole, asking everyone to be on the lookout. Comment after comment expressed thoughts and prayers that Elijah be found. And of course, everyone praised Maggie for putting up the posters. She had to get the attention. The post had gained traction, and somewhere down the lengthy scroll, someone whose name she didn't recognize asked, *Hey, isn't that the same last name as the first victim of the Hunter?*

Ada clicked off her phone. She didn't want to read any more of it right now.

There was nothing to do but wait.

TikTok Transcription from Christa Chung

DUUUUUUUUUDE. This one Black chick LITerally came into the store the other day looking for this kid, asking if I'd seen him. That was, like, Sunday? A week ago? And now he's fucking missing? Like, at the time, I was like, yes I saw him no he did not talk to me and I did not talk to him because I don't talk to every rando who comes into the store go away I'm trying to not actually do any work thank you please. But then I was thinking about it after I saw his poster, and then I was like, OMG WHAT IF I'M THE LAST PERSON WHO SAW HIM ALIVE?!? FUUUUUUUUUUUCK!

Twenty-Eight

Nell

Sunday, April 17
Easter morning

The stench hit Nell first.

She almost puked again. She lifted her head, and it felt like something was stuck to her face. She wiped along her skin and was left with wet chunks of paper in her palm. The **Missing** posters she'd collected were in the passenger seat, covered in vomit. After she'd left her parents' house, she'd stopped at a liquor store and had loaded up once more.

She eased off the hump of the console that she'd collapsed onto and settled into the driver's seat. She opened the car door, grabbed the posters, and tossed them onto the ground. She barely remembered how she'd ended up wherever she was. Back in the woods somewhere. Everything got hazy after she'd stopped at her parents' house.

She'd lost track of how long she'd sat in her truck. The sun had come up, and it had gone down. But she didn't recall how many times. Or if it was the vestige of a dream. But sunrise was imminent. She eased her legs out of the car and put a foot on the damp ground. Under her shoe, Elijah looked up at her from one of the posters. Goddamn, he looked just like Garrett.

Her head ached, her mouth tasted like garbage, and her stomach growled. Nausea came in waves, but she had stopped puking. She never was much of a puker, except in April, despite all the drinking she'd done when Garrett had given her her first fake ID and then after, when he'd turned up dead. Several years after his death, her cousin Cindy had told her they thought Nell would turn up dead, too, given how Nell had disappeared for a while after the funeral. Nell left home that night in her black pants and black shirt and never went back. She couch surfed for most of what would have been her senior year. Spent some nights in her car. By the time she finally showed up a month or so later, she'd gotten rid of the car and had taken the Chevy pickup Garrett had inherited from their grandpa. She'd spent the past couple of days in that pickup, hunting for Elijah.

She finally got out of the truck. Her bladder was full. She was grateful that she hadn't pissed herself in her drunken stupor this time. She squatted near the wheel well because all around her were trees. And she didn't really care if anyone saw anyway. Everyone in town had already seen her either near naked or naked, if they'd seen the original video that someone had posted on Facebook.

She wandered to the front of the truck and stood there a while, getting her bearings. In her stupor, she'd managed not to kill herself or someone else driving drunk like a fucking asshole. Trees surrounded her on all sides. The woods thickened and sloped to the bank of Lee Creek. It took her a minute before she realized she had navigated to the spot on that little two-lane highway where a deer hunter had found Garrett's body snagged up in the underside of a dead tree trunk, miles away from where Nell and Tessa had last seen him.

After Garrett's body was found, they'd come out here as a family with the cops after it was no longer taped off as an active scene. The day Nell and her parents walked the woods with the cops, the water had run strong. But now it was near a trickle, even with spring showers. Erosion had taken much of the bank too. But those changes in scenery didn't dim her memory. The cops hadn't been able to tell them how Garrett had ended up in the creek, only that he had. Even with drowning listed as his official cause of death, there had been noticeable injuries. But no one had any insight into how he'd gotten them. The river and creeks had flooded that year. Any number of things could've shattered his bones.

Nell was stone-cold sober. Maybe for the first time in a long time, if she was being honest. If it wasn't beer or wine or some other libation, then Nell drowned her pain with hard drugs then and weed now to keep her mind from going to the dark places where it liked to dwell. But out here in the wide, wooded open, without any of that, all her faults and fears and failings raced into her head and ricocheted off one another to create a jumble that ended with Nell sobbing on her knees in the mud. She was so thirsty. And empty. Her head pounded. Stars spotted the sky. She dry heaved onto the ground, the bitter stomach acid coating her mouth and making her gag until her whole body shook. She lay on her back and stared at the sky, everything in her depleted.

Her mind spiraled with what-ifs about the past and the present. Everything pointed back to despair that she was too late. For Garrett, for Elijah. Especially Elijah. Especially now. She'd lost him. The one person she'd promised she wouldn't lose. She'd gone to Garrett's grave site so many times after Tessa had asked her to take care of Elijah. She'd sworn to him: *I won't fuck him up, Garrett. I won't kick him out.* Elijah had gone with her to the cemetery. He'd heard her speak those words. After his initial kid-like confusion, he'd made fun of her in his teenage way. He knew that he always had a home. He knew how she felt.

She'd fucked up so bad. She'd fucked up so many times.

"Fuck you," she whispered to herself. Then she banged her fists on the ground. "Fuck you, you stupid, stupid asshole."

She sobbed, the tears spilling down her cheeks and onto the ground.

Elijah would never run away. That left only one other explanation for why he hadn't come home or answered the texts. Why she'd heard someone in the trailer and in the woods at night while at work. It had to be either Maggie fucking with her or it was the Hunter.

But Elijah would have had to be a participant with Maggie. He'd never go along with something so cruel, not even when he got mad at her. That only left one option.

Would the killer take the first victim's son? Was this the ending he wanted for them? Why was it Elijah the killer had wanted to torture? She was the one who had kicked Garrett out of the car. She was the one who had pushed her anxieties about what Elijah might say about her fucking his mother to the back of her mind, along with all the other people who would be disappointed in her. Then the only thing she'd been focused on was finding that woman. She hadn't even noticed that he'd gone missing. Ada had had to tell her.

A fire ignited within her, a desperation born out of her busted state of mind. The killer had Elijah. He had to have him. There was no other reason for Elijah to leave. It hadn't been his fault.

He hadn't left.

He'd been taken.

He'd been taken from her, like Garrett had. But she wouldn't let him. She wouldn't let him take Elijah in the same way.

She scrambled to her feet. Mud caked her jeans and shoes and hands. She twirled around the woods, Lee Creek babbling behind her. She gathered as much air into her lungs as she could. "If you want to hurt someone, take me!" she screamed. A few birds scattered from the treetops, but otherwise, there was only the trickle of the water, the sun casting a light glow to dispel the morning fog. "Come on, you son of a bitch!" She threw her arms into the air. "I'm the one who fucked up! Let Elijah go! I'm the one you should kill!"

Kill me, she thought as tears streamed down her face. *Kill me.*

"Kill me!" She barely recognized her own voice as it barreled out of her and into the air. "Kill me!"

She repeated the words until her voice was hoarse and she was on the ground again, but this time she curled her body tight. Her mouth still making the words but jumbled with the dirt and pebbles that her lips dragged into it with each utterance of the phrase: *Kill me! Kill me!*

She felt a jab at her shoulder and twisted in shock. She screamed and kicked at the sight of a man with a shaved head standing above her, wielding a knife.

"Nell?" the voice asked.

Her screams morphed to stuttering and tears as his vision came into view. Not a knife. A machete. And camo. And then the sun dropped just right and haloed around his head, lighting his face.

Garrett.

"Is that you?" she asked.

KAOK News Clip

In shocking news this morning, Elijah Holcomb, the son of Garrett Holcomb, the alleged first victim of the Hunter, is confirmed missing according to sources. Yesterday, several people reported seeing posters indicating that Elijah had gone missing, last seen hunting alone in Chaffin Park on Sunday morning, April 10.

In an even more bizarre twist, several witnesses reported seeing a woman going around town ripping down the posters. That woman is rumored to be Elijah's aunt—and Garrett Holcomb's sister—Nell, who was recently seen on video running naked through a casino.

"It's real strange," Stephanie Ross, a three-time Egghead told us this morning. "Makes you wonder if the Holcombs have something to do with what's going on every year. I mean, Garrett went missing and turned up dead, and now we get all this weird stuff happening every year since. Maybe he's alive. Maybe he's the Hunter."

Asked for a response, Nancy Barker said, "I'm absolutely horrified by this news. Elijah is a close family friend. He's been to my home, my church. Lloyd gave Nell a job and helped her get back on her feet after a long bout of self-destructive behavior after Garrett's tragic death. We consider them a part of our family. I hate to say it," Nancy said, "but I told you so. I told everyone. I'm absolutely shaking thinking about what Garrett and

Nell's mother must be going through. And Elijah's mother. This is a family in crisis." Nancy dabbed at her eyes with a tissue before continuing. "It's only a matter of time before the Hunt touches all of us, such is the reach of this tragic event. History told us that someone would get hurt during the Hunt this year. All that Rod and the city and local business owners had to do was listen. But like other lessons from history, nobody does. I'm not shocked."

The Holcombs were unavailable for comment this morning.

Twenty-Nine

Nell

Sunday, April 17
Easter morning

"It's you." Nell scrambled to her knees and hugged Garrett around his. "You're here."

He said something, but she couldn't understand. Her ears buzzed.

"I'm sorry. I'm so sorry." She wet the knees of the camo pants Garrett used to wear hunting with their dad. She'd recognize them anywhere. They had belonged to Grandpa Holcomb. The patches and tears were from the war. She hugged him tighter to herself. "I never should have gotten so mad. I shouldn't have stopped the car. I didn't know. I'm so sorry." She repeated everything in case he didn't hear. In case he didn't believe. But he was here, wasn't he? And he was crouched down with her now. He had her face in his hands. "I'm so sorry. I'm sorry I left you there. It's all my fault."

"It's not your fault." His voice. It was so young. Like it'd been when he went away to college, when he came back to town on the weekends. Like when he died. But he wasn't dead. She'd gotten older, but he'd stayed the same. He was here!

"It's all my fault," she said. "If I hadn't—"

"Nell. What are you doing here?"

"We went back to find you, but you were gone. I didn't know. Forgive me. Please forgive me." She collapsed onto the tops of her knees, kissed his muddy boots as he crouched before her. "Garrett. Oh God. Garrett. I can't believe you're real. I can't believe I found you."

"Nell. It's me." A hand at her back, patting her, like a child. "It's Elijah."

"Garrett." When she spoke, her lips brushed against his boots. "Garrett."

"Elijah," he said. "It's Elijah."

Elijah? Her brain wouldn't work, wouldn't make the connection, because when she lifted her head too fast, the spinning stars surrounded the head of her brother, of Garrett. Not Elijah.

She flung her hands to his bald scalp and felt around. "What did he do to you? Did he hurt you?"

Garrett pulled her hands away gently. "It's Elijah, Nell. Garrett's gone. It's me. It's Elijah."

No, it couldn't be. Garrett was here. He was real.

"Oh Jesus. Shit." She heard his intake of breath. "You're having a breakdown."

She held him away from her, still gripping his face in her hands, and looked at him until her eyes finally stopped feeling like they were jumping in their sockets. And finally, a visual came to her. Elijah's face. Just like Garrett's. Only his long black hair with blue tips was gone.

"Elijah?"

He held her hands with his. "Hey," he said tentatively. "It's okay. It's me."

"Where's your hair?" And then, she sobbed. "Where have you been?" She felt as small as a child. Scared of the dark, of being alone for too long while her parents were out at a restaurant for date night and Garrett was out with his friends before he let her come along. Her heart wrung out its anguish and shot it through her mouth and eyes. "I looked for you everywhere."

"I'm sorry," he said and then held her. His arms fit all the way around her. He had arms like Garrett's. Long, sturdy.

"Where have you been?" she asked again through galloping hiccups, not able to get enough air, having extinguished her capacity with her crying. "I was so scared."

"Oh God." He rocked her. "I'm so sorry. I didn't have service." He stroked her head, and she collapsed into him like a child would a parent. "I should have left to double-check my phone, but I didn't want to miss him. I thought you had gotten my texts. Fuck. I'm so sorry."

She squirmed out of his embrace and wiped at her eyes. "Where have you been?"

He looked about as sorrowful as she felt. "In the woods."

"Why?" she cried again, even though she didn't know how there was any moisture left in her body from all the drinking and crying and puking.

"I was looking for him."

"Who? Garrett?"

"No," Elijah said. "Garrett's dead, Nell. You know that, right?" He patted his chest. "You know I'm Elijah, right?"

She swiped at her eyes. "Then who are you looking for?"

"The Hunter," he said.

Shared Google Doc / The Hunt

VICTIM #4

On March 19, 2008, on a Friday night after one last hurrah hunt with her coworkers and then going for all-you-can-drink margaritas at the Chi-Chi's in Presley, Sarah Donaldson, twenty-eight, Latina, drove out of the parking lot toward the apartment where she lived alone. Sarah had recently moved to Presley from Hot Springs and was well liked among her marketing colleagues.

Sarah's coworkers did not hear from her over the weekend and assumed that she had called in to work on Monday. When they again did not hear from her on Tuesday, they reported their concerns to HR, who tried to reach Sarah at home. The HR associate continued to reply to Sarah's coworkers' concerns by letting them know that Sarah had been contacted. In the meantime, by Thursday, no one had heard from Sarah, so the coworkers went to the police station and asked them if a missing persons case had been filed.

On March 21, a hiker found Sarah's car parked in the woods, with no signs of an accident. When the police arrived, they found Sarah in the back seat.

When asked why Sarah might have pulled off to the side of the road, the police speculated that Sarah may have pulled over to sober up after the alcohol she'd consumed, and passed out, only to succumb to exposure, as listed in the death certificate.

However, Sarah's coworkers insisted that she had only consumed one beverage at the beginning of the evening and had promptly switched to water and then coffee for their shared dessert.

The coworkers also noted the HR person is no longer employed with their company after their complaints that the associate had not taken their concerns about their coworker seriously and had joked in a company email that Sarah had probably "gotten knocked up and left town."

Thirty

Ada

Sunday, April 17
Easter morning

Ada had been waiting on men a lot lately. She'd waited all these years to find the egg, and now she wanted her prize. She thought about wandering back into the station, but that felt weird. Through the windshield, she spotted a door. There was a mailbox there too. She went to look. A handwritten note taped above it read that only mail for Rod should be delivered there. Everything else was to be delivered to the station mailbox at the front door. Rather than going back inside and risking an awkward encounter with Conrad, she knocked on the door. Again, nothing. But this time it was hard to hear what might be going on inside because Easter-morning traffic had started up and cars were going by.

"Rod?" She knocked and checked the door handle. To her surprise, it turned. "Rod?" she called out again and eased the door open. Her pulse quickened. "Conrad said you might be in here?"

She peeked around the corner and drew in a sharp breath.

Rod was naked in the middle of the floor, covered in gold.

"Oh my God. Oh my God." She ran to him. "Rod?"

She felt for his pulse, even though she wasn't sure she'd know if she felt it or not. It's the thing to do, at least on TV. But what if that was all wrong like lots of things on TV and a normal person like her couldn't ever find the pulse without training? Yet she felt something pulsing under his skin, and she blew out a long stream of fear. Motion from the corner of the room startled her, and she collapsed backward onto her butt.

A tall man stood in a small hallway. His head was covered in a ski mask. His hands were covered in gold.

The Hunter.

KAOK News Twitter Update

All of us here at KAOK wish you a HAPPY EASTER! Happy hunting today, whether it's for your traditional egg hunt in the yard or the golden one hidden somewhere around Presley. Stay safe—and have fun!

Thirty-One

Nell

Sunday, April 17
Easter morning

"The Hunter?" Nell asked, clutching Elijah by the arms. "I thought you were dead."

"Why are you out here?" he asked. They were still kneeling on the ground, facing each other. "I didn't mean to scare you. There's nothing to be scared about."

"Why did you leave?"

"I left you a note," he said. Then he added, "And I texted, but I guess you didn't get those. So that's why you're here."

Elijah grabbed a log from the woods. He patted that, an invitation for her to sit. Then he gathered some stones to put in a circle and then wrapped a familiar blanket around her. Garrett's. The one he'd liked to take camping because it was army green and wool. She hugged it to herself. She hadn't seen it in forever, not since their last camping trip on Petit Jean Mountain.

"Where'd you find this?"

He carried some sticks in his arms and placed them on the ground. His army-green shirt had belonged to Garrett as well. It fit perfectly around his lean frame. "Grandma and Grandpa's house."

She breathed it in. "When?"

"A while ago," he said. He looked so different without hair.

"What happened to your hair?" she asked and sniffled.

"Everyone in Presley knows who I am. I didn't want them to recognize me." He stacked the wood into the shape of a pyramid inside the circle of stones and lit it like a pro, like he went out camping every weekend instead of sitting next to Anthony playing video games all day.

"Why?"

"You should eat first." He glanced up at her from where he crouched by his backpack. "Looks like you've had a rough night."

After a while, he handed her a hot dog. One of her favorite smells when they went out camping. Possibly one of the best reasons to go camping. She smelled it, suspicious. "I thought you were vegan."

"I am," he said. "It's a not dog."

She devoured it and didn't have anything bad to say about it either. He handed her a water bottle. She downed that in one go.

"What day is it?" she asked when the world finally stopped spinning. She had been out there a while. She'd probably lost her job. Her mom was right. She had to get out of that town. It was gonna kill her one day.

"Sunday. Easter." Elijah held out a dried-puke-covered poster on a stick. "You made posters?"

She shook her head. "I don't know who made them."

He looked confused. "Then why do you have so many?"

Nell didn't want to admit that she had taken them down. "I saw some and grabbed them for myself," she said, which was technically true.

"Sorry. I left you a note. I texted all of you."

"One text to Ada on Sunday. A note to me on Sunday, one text on Monday. Nothing to Anthony, and then you disappeared and didn't respond for a week. What were we supposed to think? You could've been hurt, and no one knew where you were." She sat a while thinking of other ways she could admonish him, but she was ravenous and woozy. "You got anything else to eat?"

"But I didn't get hurt." He rummaged through Garrett's old backpack. She'd had no idea he had all this stuff.

She tried to keep her tone even and quell the urge to knock the shit out of him for being such a little dumbass. "So, all this freaking out over nothing, huh?" she asked. "You just decided to pretend to be me and ditch school and go camping?"

He handed her a granola bar. "Not exactly."

She ripped the wrapping and finished the granola bar in two bites.

He poked at the fire and added another log. A rush of heat filled their space. "Like I said, I was looking for the Hunter."

She'd been too scattered to understand what he'd meant when he'd told her earlier. She finished the granola bar and threw the wrapping into the fire. "Why on earth would you do that?"

He leaned toward the fire from where he sat on a log he'd dragged over, elbows on knees. "I wanted to know if he was real." He tossed more wood on the fire. "I've been hiding out in the woods. Watching people. Waiting to see if I saw anything. If I saw him." He poked the fire again. "I'm sorry. I didn't mean to worry you. I just wanted to know if he was real. I wanted to know who killed my dad."

She coughed and chugged some more water he'd given her. For so many years, she'd fought the idea, believing like others that it was a myth. But she'd finally broken down and believed it. "And then what? What would you do if you found out?"

"I don't know," he said, staring right at her. "The not knowing? That's what sucks."

The not knowing felt like it had been killing her, slowly over time. She'd been too upset to do anything but fall apart after the cops couldn't definitively tell them how Garrett had died. But Elijah had gone out and done something.

"I've been looking for a while," he said. "Me and Anthony."

"Why didn't he say something, then? Ada and I were worried sick."

He held up a hand. "He didn't know I planned to come out here. That wasn't part of his plan."

"What was his plan, then?"

"Before the pandemic? Same as mine: figure out if the Hunter is real or a myth." He clocked the confusion on her face and continued. "We mapped all the victims by location and year. We dug into autopsy reports to see if they really died the way that people said. And we looked at all the death records for Presley and surrounding areas for the same year."

She'd watched enough documentaries and TV shows not to be surprised but impressed at their level of detail. "How'd you get all this information?"

He looked at her then, seemed surprised and not altogether unhappy that she was interested and wasn't furious with him. Or traumatized. "It's kind of been crowdsourced over time. When Dad was killed, it was 2005. A lot of people weren't even on social media then. But some were. Facebook was mostly for younger people. But a lot of the older folks didn't even get on that until about 2008 or so. So, for a long time, it was nothing but crickets, as you probably know." He waited for questions. She had none. "But then, in year nine, the Raleighs decided to make a stink about what happened to Annalee."

She grimaced.

"They have a right to question what happened," he said. "I don't know if you know, but they're pretty big time in Presley. Like developers or something. But they belong to the country club, so." She did not know. "When Annalee died that March, everyone had these messages on her Facebook page and Tumblr saying how sad and tragic it was and tagging it with things like #MentalHealth and #SuicidePrevention, which would absolutely not be cool with the Raleighs because they're pretty evangelical as well as being snobs."

"So?"

"So we figured they didn't want anyone knowing the truth because that would mean that Annalee's soul was basically done, zilch. Like, dancing with the devil forever. So, they jumped on the bandwagon and basically were like, 'Poor Annalee, the latest victim of the Hunter.' And then from there, as you know, we got to where we are now."

"But that's purely speculation," she said.

"Oh absolutely. We're not detectives or whatever. We were just having fun. We weren't able to get her autopsy results. And you can't exactly go around accusing people of covering up their daughter's death." He sighed. "Unfortunately."

She was amused and a little shocked at his dismissal of such a heavy subject. "How long have y'all been doing this?"

"Since eighth grade."

"Eighth grade!" She shook her head and sighed. "So? What's the verdict? Is he real?"

He stabbed at the ground with a stick, looking like an odd mix of a boy and a man. "I don't know."

He reminded her of a time when he'd studied so hard for an algebra test—she knew because she'd tried to help him—and he couldn't get it. Nothing would click. He came home and slammed his bedroom door. After she let him calm down a bit, she went inside and he showed her the D he'd gotten on the test. Sometimes, she'd told him, no matter how hard you try, things don't work out in your favor.

"I guess it was a waste of time," he finally said. "I just wanted to know if it was true. Like, maybe if I figured out the others and a pattern, I could maybe figure out what happened to Dad."

Nell's stomach plunged. She couldn't look at him. She'd just found him. They'd had this moment together. The first good one in a long time. She wondered how much more her heart could take. Her nerves were near shot. Surely her blood pressure in the past week alone had taken at least a year off her life.

Tears broke down her cheeks. "I'm sorry, Elijah." He looked on in confusion. "I'm the reason he's dead. I kicked him out of the car that night. I was mad. I got so mad at him. I wanted him to know that he had hurt me. I wanted to hurt him." She held a hand over her mouth, afraid to say more, but the words slipped through her fingers, so quiet, but so loud. "I loved your mom. But she didn't love me. I was so jealous of Garrett. And so hurt." Nell choked out the last words and sobbed again. "And so, so stupid."

Soon, Elijah's arms were wrapped around her, and Nell sat there, stunned and sobbing. She felt an overwhelming something she couldn't even put her finger on. Maybe because she hadn't ever felt it before. She didn't know what to call it, this rush in her body, like a blockage had been cleared and her blood and hormones and everything else could flow and work normally again.

"I didn't know he'd die. I would never have . . . ," she said between gasps. "We went right back. But he was gone."

Elijah grasped her shoulder, squeezed, and then walked away from her and the fire. Nell didn't know what to do, so she waited. After a while, he returned and sat across from her. His eyes were red, his face puffy. His head tilted toward the ground. But he let his eyes drift to Nell's. There was pain there. Sadness, still. But Nell knew somehow that it was temporary. That this pain between them would pass. And they could be something different to each other now, something easier and softer.

"We should probably go somewhere where there's some service and let people know you're not dead," Nell said, tentatively, thinking of Ada but mostly Tessa, who must've been out of her mind with worry.

Elijah nodded, and they had one of those brief but extended moments of looking at each other. And she knew that they would be all right.

Facebook Post: Marcy Todd

Sunday, April 17
Easter morning

It's Easter, y'all. Today's the day. Has anyone found the egg yet? We been looking all over. Except Maggie. She totally bailed on us. I haven't heard anything from her. But that's not unusual. Have y'all heard if the egg has been found? If it's not found today, does that mean the money goes to the next year's pot like in 2021? Or does it go to charity? HELP! I'm new to the Hunt this year, and I'm so confused! What happens now?!?!

Thirty-Two

Ada

Sunday, April 17
Easter morning

"No!" The Hunter held his hands out in supplication, but it didn't stop Ada's screaming. "No! Wait!"

She scrambled back toward the door, but the Hunter caught her legs. She kicked and kicked until she finally got him right in the face. He grabbed at it and held his eye.

A flash of sneakers passed her vision, and she heard a familiar voice yelling for the man to stop. Conrad. She rushed to her feet and joined him.

Conrad stood with a mic stand held high, shaking, his eyes full of terror. Ada grabbed a large green glass ashtray from a table and held it up. They faced the Hunter. He was still splayed on the floor, clutching his face.

The Hunter kept yelling, "Stop. I can explain!"

"Oh my God. Oh my God." Conrad had finally seen Rod on the floor, not moving. The mic stand dropped from his hands. "Oh fuck. Rod? Rod?"

"What are you doing?" Ada yelled. "Call 911!"

"Rod?" Conrad's hands shook. He looked from Rod to the Hunter and back again.

"Conrad!" Ada got his attention. "Call 911!"

Conrad nearly tripped out of the room, dazed.

"You son of a bitch!" she yelled at the Hunter. "Where's Elijah?"

The Hunter eased against the couch, trying to catch his breath. He clutched his chest.

"Don't you have a heart attack on me! Not before you tell me where Elijah is!"

The guy's breath came in spurts. He wrestled with the mask and yanked it up over his mouth and eyes . . .

"Lloyd?" The Hunter? The glass ashtray slipped from Ada's hand.

Lloyd leaned against the couch, mouth open and gasping. His bloodshot eyes glanced up at her. He whispered something, but she couldn't hear what.

"What the fuck?"

He whispered and shook his head. She couldn't help herself. She raced over to him and kneeled. She put a hand on his shoulder and rubbed it. What in the hell was going on?

"Is it your heart?" She spoke softly to him and tried to get him to talk, but he was in a near trance. But there was something about him that still seemed "in there." Like he knew exactly where he was and what was happening. But he was . . . ashamed?

"Conrad!" she yelled across the room.

He didn't respond.

She had dropped her phone when Lloyd startled her, so she reached for it and called 911 herself. She tried to explain the situation to them, but they had about as hard a time understanding her as she did understanding the information she was trying to relay to them.

"A man?" the woman asked. "Covered in gold?"

"Yes. Rod Halstrom. From KCLS."

"Is there blood?" the woman asked.

"No, gold." It didn't make sense. But Ada didn't know what else to tell them. "There's bruising. And a heart attack."

"I'm sorry. What?"

"Could you send someone over here?" she asked, agitated. "Now? Hurry!"

While she waited, she rubbed Lloyd's arm and told him to hold on. Just hold on, which felt out of sorts, given that from everything she had witnessed, he was the Hunter.

"Why?" she asked.

He couldn't speak and clutched his chest, breathing rapidly, his terrified eyes freaking out.

Out of the corner of her eye, she saw Rod's hand twitch.

"Oh my God. You're alive." She moved to where Rod lay in the fetal position. "Rod? Are you okay?"

She wanted to cover him in a blanket or something because seeing him there like that on the floor made her uncomfortable on his behalf, but she didn't know if she should. She'd already trampled all over what was possibly a crime scene. She didn't want to ruin it further.

A thought intruded: *I hope this doesn't ruin my prize.*

She felt terrible about that. Truly awful. One man, a victim, was in and out of consciousness and decorated like a golden Easter egg, and the other, a killer, was clutching a golden hand to his chest, struggling for air. She hoped the ambulance or cops would get there soon. The longer she waited and realized what she was sitting in, the more anxious she became, like she was supposed to somehow fix the shit show she'd walked in on, and someone might die if she didn't figure it out, fast.

She focused on Rod. He didn't move again, but he was still there. She rubbed his head and whispered things about help being on the way, even though she wasn't sure they were, and *You're gonna be okay*, which she also wasn't sure about. While she waited and rubbed Rod's head, she was able to fully survey the room.

It'd been torn up as if Rod and Lloyd had struggled. There were empty gold spray paint cans all over. A black plastic garbage bag, the kind contractors used.

The kind they used at the factory.

"Ada," Lloyd said behind her. She was shocked to hear him speak. His voice was so quiet. He was still struggling.

"Why did you do this?" she asked.

He whispered something that sounded like, "Is he okay?" That scared her because Lloyd was not the type of man who would or should be here, looking like a shell of himself. He was kind, he never yelled—except the previous Thursday—he went to church and had a family whose photos littered his walls.

"He's gonna be all right," she said through her tears, choking up. "You're gonna be all right too."

Lloyd looked irritated and stared at Rod. "Not him." The words were strained. His face got red; sweat poured from his brow. "Not him!"

"What?"

"Not him!" he yelled, and then it looked like he'd been hit by lightning or something because he jerked a bit and then kind of slumped. His eyes were still open.

Suddenly, there were people all around them. There were shouts and questions and exclamations like she'd exclaimed when she'd first come into the room. There were clicks from cell phones, and someone tugged at her arm, asking her what had happened. A team of medics surrounded Lloyd, and then a team of medics and cops surrounded Rod, who was still unconscious. But Ada wouldn't budge. She wasn't moving. Not yet.

Outside, she could hear Anthony shouting her name. He should be home! Safe!

"Ma'am," someone said.

Anthony shouted her name again. She followed his voice and saw him there in the parking lot through the bodies that rushed in and out of the room. Anthony trying to get through. And Elijah next to him.

Elijah! He'd been found! And Nell, her arms wrapped around him, looking frightened. Other people moved across Ada's line of vision.

"Ma'am. You need to leave. Now."

Ada pushed the person's hand off her arm and turned to face Lloyd.

"Lloyd, who? Who are you asking about?" She screamed it at him as someone tried to yank her away and out of the room. "Is who okay?"

Lloyd looked up at her, his eyes shiny and drooped, his shirt soaked. No words came from his mouth, but she could see what he said before the medic put an oxygen mask over his nose and mouth: *Elijah.*

Shared Google Doc / The Hunt

VICTIM #1: UPDATE

On April 18, 2022, Garrett Holcomb was removed from the list of the Hunter victims after Lloyd Barker admitted that he had been involved in the hit-and-run accident from which Garrett died in 2005.

According to the taped confession that led to his arraignment and subsequent guilty plea to involuntary manslaughter and improper disposal of a body, Lloyd had been a "desperate man" on the night he had run down Garrett. He and Nancy had gotten into a fight over Nancy's "unnatural and close friendship" with her manager at the HVAC company where she worked as an accountant—an accusation that Nancy has vigorously denied. Lloyd had been a man on the verge of a marital and spiritual breakdown, he said. In such a "broken state of mind" that night, he'd gone to the casino and proceeded to "drink and smoke and gamble away our savings."

On the way home, drunk and falling asleep at the wheel, he veered off the road and hit what he thought had been a deer. Lloyd had been distraught to instead find a human being. In shock and worried about what might happen next, Lloyd had carried Garrett down to Lee Creek and placed him in the water, "like Moses, and returned him to his maker." Lloyd then drove toward home. Once near his house, he ran the car into a tree and walked home to Nancy, where he told her about the drinking and gambling and the car—but not how he'd hit and killed Garrett with his car, both Lloyd and Nancy insist.

No investigation of the car accident was conducted, as Lloyd did not report it.

After Garrett's death, Lloyd turned his life around. He and Nancy made the decision to get saved and rebaptized. They traveled to Hot Springs and were remarried in a quiet ceremony. He'd wanted to come clean about what he had done many times, but he didn't know how. Lloyd said he took an interest in Nell after meeting her in the Cherokee Casino restaurant. He had seen her on the news and knew that she was Garrett's sister. As part of his "transformation," he offered Nell a job at Mayflower Plastics, where he was plant manager. When Elijah was eventually taken in by Nell, Lloyd believed that "the Lord had given me a way to make amends for my crime." In the ensuing years, Lloyd showed Nell and Elijah "kindnesses" through gifts and allowing Nell several concessions at work when she "fell on hard times."

Despite all that, Lloyd admitted that he'd been perpetually scared of getting caught and his anger grew toward Rod Halstrom every year the Hunt continued. Lloyd had done his best to shut down the Hunt, ensuring no other "innocent pedestrians" like Garrett were harmed. Like Nell and Elijah and all the Holcombs, Lloyd had lived under the weight of Garrett's death and the town's subsequent classification of Garrett as the Hunter's first victim. The only relief, he said, was in 2021, when the Hunt was canceled. But with the ongoing pandemic, the pressure of work with supply chain issues, the return of the Hunt in 2022, and upon hearing that Elijah, Garrett Holcomb's son, had gone missing, Lloyd confessed that he had "snapped."

On Easter Sunday, April 17, Lloyd arrived at KCLS wearing a black ski mask and clothing to hide his identity. He "tried to reason with Rod" about shutting down the Hunt and it not being too late to "get right with God." Rod allegedly laughed in Lloyd's face, at which point Lloyd began his assault on Rod. Despite being "in shock" at his own behavior, Lloyd decided to "take advantage of a bad situation." He found gold spray paint in Rod's closet and proceeded to strip Rod of clothing and paint him gold, in the hopes that when found, people would think Rod had been attacked by the Hunter, thereby ending the Hunt for good. He insisted that he only meant to scare Rod, not physically harm him in any way.

Asked their thoughts on the situation, the Raleighs said that the incident between Lloyd and Rod was the latest in a long line of tragic incidents associated with the Hunt, none of which they wanted to be a part of. They had allegedly split from the church in 2014 after "Nancy had co-opted our grief over Annalee and turned it into a sideshow." Asked their feelings on everything that transpired with Lloyd, they told us, "We have nothing to say about those people. We are still grief-stricken over Annalee's death. All this attention has done nothing to bring her justice."

Nancy asked people to try to understand and to forgive Lloyd.

Lloyd currently resides with Wally McAuley and others at the Tucker Unit, managed by the Arkansas Department of Corrections.

Epilogue

Nell

Tuesday, May 17
Midnight
One month after Easter

Maggie hadn't shown her face at work, not after Juanita—who never wanted to get involved in their work squabbles—told Maggie that she might want to leave town when Nell came in to work looking for her. Where Maggie was now, no one knew. If they did, they weren't saying. But Nell doubted anyone cared. Janie, Phonesavanh, and Viv were pissed off that Maggie had gone hunting without them on the night she'd attacked Ada, so they wanted nothing to do with her.

Nell never did get to confirm why Maggie had pulled that stunt with Casino or if she was the one behind that business with the wrench. She hadn't mentioned any of that to Ada. Or to anyone. She figured she ought to count her blessings, given Elijah hadn't turned her away after learning that she'd kicked his dad out of the car the night he died. This younger generation seemed to know how to weather storms better than she had at their age. She decided to try to take a lesson from him on this one. Ada, however, was not in a forgiving mood.

"We all know she stalked me. But that woman also tried to kill me!" Maggie hadn't actually tried to kill Ada. But who knew, maybe Maggie would've killed Ada over the egg if Ada hadn't headbutted Maggie into temporary oblivion, for which Nell was impressed. Ada mentioned that Maggie had had it out for her, showing up at the grocery store and laughing all weird in the woods. Ada swore it was Maggie out there. Nothing could convince her otherwise.

"Good thing she left town," Ada continued. "If I ever see her walking these streets, I'm gonna beat her ass into next week."

"Not if I get to her first."

"I hear that." Ada sucked in a long draw of Nell's vape pen. All that prize money from the Hunt, and she still wouldn't buy her own. "And where does she get off, making those posters of Elijah without your permission?" She looked off to the side a minute before going on. "She probably helped the Hunter." Ada smacked Nell on the arm. "Hell, what if she is the Hunter?" She looked to the lot full of their coworkers' cars and shook her head. "I was probably next in line."

Nell laughed. She knew Ada loved the attention.

Ada had gotten all gussied up for the interviews. She'd done well too. Looked good and mostly behaved herself. Everybody at work had cheered and clapped and paid her more attention than she'd probably ever had in her life. They'd all wanted to know what had happened, precisely, to the minute. She'd been the one who had walked in on the person everyone had believed was the Hunter, in the middle of killing his latest—and greatest—prey.

Before they could wisecrack some more about Maggie and which poor person she was probably stalking now—a new favorite topic of theirs—the door to the plant opened. Chris, the new plant manager, a white guy in his late twenties, took the steps two at a time. He'd come from Illinois. A promotion. One of those ambitious types who worked till midnight, hoping that someone in management might notice what was going on in Presley, Arkansas.

"Evening, ladies!" he said and waved.

"Evening," they said brightly and waved in unison like a couple of Stepford Wives. He didn't pay them any mind. Just dashed off out of the parking lot as soon as he could.

"I don't like the looks of him," Ada said. "Who wears a polo shirt to a factory?"

"He's all right," Nell replied.

"If you say so."

Nell kind of missed Lloyd, if she was being honest. She didn't approve of what he'd done, obviously. But she could understand how guilt could weigh so heavily on someone's mind that they kind of went mad. In a way, they were both responsible for what had happened to Garrett. At the sentencing, Lloyd had told Nell that was not the case. He was the sole person responsible. But before they took him away in handcuffs to the back for further processing, he'd said she should consider heading to church with Nancy sometime, think about forgiveness. For herself. This from a man headed for prison. She guessed she'd heard worse advice. She'd probably go. She figured Nancy needed the company now that Lloyd was gone, and the Hunt too. Not to mention the Raleighs publicly turning on her. No doubt Nancy would find another cause. She had the spirit for those.

No one could've guessed that the man who'd given Nell a chance with a new job, who had treated Elijah like his own family—buying him presents and teaching him and talking to him about guy stuff—had been the one who'd killed Elijah's father.

Outside the courtroom, Nancy swore up and down that she'd had no idea what Lloyd had done and that her verbal and social media attacks on Rod and the city were born out of a passion for people and safety. Of course she stood by her man.

Ada thought that was a load of crap and said so.

Lloyd and Nancy were forever tied to the last Hunt for the Golden Egg put on by KCLS in Presley, Arkansas. The brainchild of Rod Halstrom.

Last anyone heard, Rod was in the process of selling the station to a Christian-music conglomerate. He'd moved out of town and was working as a small-town DJ, somewhere a little like Presley, Nell suspected, with the woods and ever-present precipitation this time of year.

Was Lloyd the Hunter?

Lloyd swore up and down that he had only killed Garrett, and by accident. But a lot of people didn't believe him. No matter what he or Nancy said.

So was the Hunter even real?

No one knew. The cops investigated—allegedly, like everything else in Presley—but had turned up nothing but new rumors. People in Presley loved their villain and weren't ready to say goodbye, at least not until the next Easter rolled around. When Nell had asked Elijah more about what he'd seen out on his "camping trip," he'd said, *A bunch of drunk assholes.* Nell figured she'd have to wait and see with the rest of them. At least this time, she could be on the outside instead of the inside of a rumor.

While they sat at their little bench outside the factory, Ada moved on from Maggie and proceeded to recount the latest gossip from her manicurist. Apparently, she had a special one now and even knew her name. Ada's nails did look good, though. Bright, bright pink. A color Nell never would've guessed Ada would pick out from a wall of options.

Ada admired their gloss in the factory's outdoor floodlights and told Nell about how Conrad, the guy from the radio station, had called her up to ask if she wanted to go out and get to know him, considering their "shared trauma."

"As if I have trauma? Shit, I'm a hero. He damn near ran out of the room. I had to call 911 myself. Useless. He had one job! Couldn't even do that." Ada laughed and shook her head and went back to admiring her nails. "I can see why you don't fool with men." She waited for Nell to say something. When she didn't, Ada punched her in the arm.

Nell winced and then guessed at what Ada would say. "Because men are fools?"

"Amen," Ada said and laughed. "Lord help me, I hope I didn't raise one too." She shook her head again. "This last year with Anthony has made me wonder."

Nell doubted that very much. Soon, Anthony would spend his days on a campus in Texas, training to be the next engineer or computer wiz. Or what have you. He would make a name for himself outside the town whose story had gone viral across the state. A fool? Hell no. Not Anthony. Elijah, though? Well, Nell couldn't really cast stones. But when he'd finally heard about what had happened at the casino, he'd laughed and laughed. Little shit.

No matter how many times Elijah told her he'd been careful, and he never meant to hurt her or scare her, he did. If he'd known Nell would "freak out," he never would have gone out. That's what he'd said. Nell wasn't sure she believed him. She'd seen enough of how people could twist a few random facts to create a fully believed truth. She guessed she could give him that. And she gave him her forgiveness, even though what he'd done was a real shithead move. They'd not put any details in the papers or on the news about Elijah spending the night out in the woods stalking the Hunter. His being a minor. And a missing gay kid who got eclipsed by the capture of a presumed serial killer. She figured that was too much for everyone to digest all at once. Everything but Lloyd had fallen to the cutting-room floor.

Knowing Elijah, he'd be in New York City soon, telling all the boys at the bar about his weird-ass relatives and life in Presley, Arkansas. He wouldn't be wrong.

"Speaking of fools," Ada said, "you got any more mystery women hiding out in the woods?"

Nell laughed but eyed her. "Why would I hide them in the woods?"

Ada cleared her throat and pretended that her phone was buzzing. "I should get this."

"Mm-hmm." Nell had wondered more than once if Ada had ever seen her sneaking out into the woods to see Tessa. Now she knew.

Nell and Tessa had kept their promise not to tell Elijah or Ada or anyone else about those brief, heady months they'd spent together while Tessa built up the courage to reconnect with Elijah.

Nell missed Tessa. Of course she missed her. She'd always miss her. But Nell had gotten those months. And Tessa had gotten the thing she'd wanted most in the world: she and Elijah were talking. Elijah's missing person status had spooked Tessa into action. It had been rocky at first, and there were still a lot of hard feelings. But it was a step. A first of many, Nell knew.

Ada stretched her arms into the air and popped all her joints before she placed her arms back on the table. "So, I guess we're both back on the market, then."

"Back?" Nell teased. "I didn't know you'd ever gone off it."

Though it was dark, Nell caught the blush on Ada's face.

"I'm just saying, you never mentioned anything to me. Don't get weird," Nell said and poked Ada's leg. "I didn't know you'd been dating anyone."

"Well, I don't know if I'd call it dating." Ada held up a finger. "Get your head out of the gutter. That's not what I meant either." She laughed. "I'm on the apps. I talk to people."

"The apps, huh?" Nell bit down on her bottom lip, trying to keep the smile off her face. "Okay."

"Okay?" Ada frowned.

"Okay," Nell repeated, but she couldn't hold in her smile.

Ada fussed with the plastic wrapping on her Coke bottle, tearing it off and then slowly unwinding it. Her blush was full blown now. "I mean, I haven't been on a date in a while. A proper date," she added.

"Like letters and sodas?" Nell asked as the lyrics to her favorite Liz Phair song popped into her head.

"Letters and sodas?" Ada looked thoughtful for a while, and then her eyes drifted to Nell's lips and back. "Yeah. Something like that."

Nell was glad that the Hunt hadn't offered enough prize money for Ada to retire and that Nell hadn't given her enough of a reason to stop talking to her. Nell would've missed the punches on the arm, the will-they-or-won't-they gossip, and the way that Ada's warm thigh felt against hers that night on the bench. A familiar tingle worked its way up from Nell's toes.

If life hadn't happened the way it had, for both of them, Ada wouldn't be sitting there next to Nell. She wouldn't be looking at Nell in a way she hadn't looked at her before, without turning away. Without a punch or a punch line.

"I'll take you on a proper date," Nell said at last, daring Ada to look away.

Ada held Nell's gaze briefly before she got shy and then tried to compose herself. She stood and began her saunter back into the plant, leaving Nell out there on the bench to watch her walk away. Ada spun to face Nell and offered a cheeky grin. "All right. Let's go on a date."

"All right," Nell said, smiling. "I'm gonna make you pay on our second date, though. Considering all that loot you got burning a hole in your pocket."

Ada laughed in a way that Nell hadn't ever heard her laugh before. Like she imagined she'd probably laughed before she'd come on at Mayflower Plastics. Before she'd gotten married so young. Had Anthony. When she'd been soft, by Ada's own account. Semisweet, Nell had countered, never fully. Shy, but only for a moment, before that boldness of hers kicked in.

Nell almost asked her to stay out there with her a little while longer, but she let Ada walk away without tugging at her attention like a preteen in love. Something told Nell that there would be plenty of time for all that. And there was something about sitting out there alone. Nights like that, she felt like she could feel Garrett there. Though it made no sense. He'd never been to Mayflower Plastics. But she guessed that wherever she went, he might go too.

She missed him. She'd always miss him. But now she thought maybe she could learn how to look forward to new things too.

Shared Google Doc / The Hunt

Modified August 17, 2022

This is the last entry I'll make because you're off soon. I know you have more important things to do than research Presley's alleged serial killer. Listen, you're not the only one with a life! 🙂

One thing I wanted to share before I go, though: this summer, I got bored. I know, you're shocked. Maybe even more shocking is that I didn't text you. But I knew you were busy. (As always, but I've learned to Let Go and Let God, as they say in AA.) This started as my project, anyway, so I guess it's fitting that I call the time of death.

ANYHOO, before I do . . . I was bored, so I decided to read through all the entries we made up until 2021 (the pandemic really put a damper on our productivity). It was fun to see how far we'd come. How much we'd learned. And how professional we sounded! Thank you for indulging my initial idea to turn this into a documentary. I still think it would make a fucking-awesome HBO limited series. Maybe I'll keep working on it offline when I have time in my BUSY schedule. Don't worry. I'll give you *some* credit. 🙂

So yeah, signing off from this particular document forever, so fuck the professionalism. But before I do, there was one thing that stuck out to me . . .

So 2013 was the year that everyone started freaking out about the Hunt. Yes, I know, the Raleighs refused to believe their darling Annalee would choose a world without them (I've met them, btw, so you can probably guess what I think about that). But you know what else happened that year? The pipeline burst. I know, I know. You're thinking: *Thank God I stopped working on this with you before you became a conspiracy theorist like the rest of the world!*

All I'm saying is . . . maybe that has something to do with people thinking that bad shit happened, not realizing that there could be something else going on? The pipeline ran into town and pooled in the streets and yards. That shit is toxic, obviously. They evacuated something like twenty residences, but there are a lot more people than that in Presley who inhaled the fumes and probably drank that shit in their water. (Maybe into Lee Creek, which feeds Presley's municipal water system? Yes, I looked it up. Who knows? Probably! But I'd get sued if I said so publicly. Not that they'd listen to me. But think about it.)

One other thing I noted in some of the research I did (you know how I love my research!) is that they don't even know what the long-term health effects on humans are from pipeline spills, only short-term, like respiration issues and headaches. And remember how everyone talked about how all they wanted to do was nap? What if one of the effects was psychological as well? What if the spill also created a great mass delusion of what would be relatively normal events? Could that explain why some people believed in the Hunter and others didn't? Or was it another case of people being easily manipulated into believing something totally absurd?

Just thinking out loud.

SIGH. Kind of a bummer that we STILL don't definitively know who the Hunter is, or if they even exist, after all this work. That was the goal after all. But alas, life is not a binge-worthy HBO limited series with DEVASTATINGLY handsome Hollywood actors playing working-class heroes like us and an ending wrapped up all snug as a bug in a rug. (I just puked all over my brand-new Savage X Fenty mesh tank, so you know). But nobody knows who Jack the Ripper is, and look at all the attention that bitch STILL gets. #Werk. Jk, he sucks, OBviously. Or she? They? We'll never know. Of that I'm certain.

I went to see Lloyd, btw. I was curious about prison life. He looks good, considering. He says hello. He cries every time he sees me, though. Total drag. I'm like, *dude, I forgive you. Let it go.* Oh, Wally McAuley also says hi. He was a little bummed we couldn't get him out of jail. Shrugs. We did our best. BUT I GUESS OUR BEST WASN'T GOOD ENOUGH. Lol. Not sure you'll get the reference. BUT YOUR MOM WILL. Make sure you tell her . . . and I didn't say it to Wally's face, OF COURSE! But I was straight up thinking: *Maybe your drugs did interact in a bad way? I mean, you hated Big Phil! Your neighbors CONFIRMED that shit.*

Ugh. Adults, amirite?

Speaking of, your mom and Nell are now delivering care packages to the teenagers down on Sixth Street. Apparently, Nell made friends with them when she thought I was dead or missing or whatever. HOW CUTE ARE THEY? I COULD PUKE. By the way, still not over how you did not cover for me on that one. Like, duh. Of course I was gonna camp out! It's like you don't even know me at all. But then again, I guess you didn't last year. Lol. Jk. I'm only still a little tender about it. But they're, like, buying all these tampons and giving them combs and T-shirts and shit. And I'm like, um, just give them some fucking money, hoesssss. Anyway . . . they're having the time of their lives and not missing us at all. HOW VERY DARE THEY? Pretty sure they're about to become "roommates" now that we're gone. About time. Jesus, so puritanical. *But you didn't hear it from me!!!!*

ANYway. I guess that's it for now. At least until someone else mysteriously shows up dead in Presley in April 2023. But with no deaths in the year of our Lord 2022, I think we have our answer.

Until then, signing off. For real this time. Have fun in Texas. If you become a famous engineer or founder of some multimillion-dollar corporation, please don't forget to thank me or I'll legit kill you and ensure no one knows what happened. I'm, like, an expert now. I'm serious! Lol. I'll miss you. If you ever find yourself in Eureka Springs, hit me up. (I know. I know. It's NOT New York, but it's the gayest place I can find for now that doesn't require me to sell my organs to survive.)

When you come visit, we'll find another serial killer to track. Or maybe we'll just pick up where we left off with the Hunter. Like old times.

Xoxo, bitch. ☺

Friday, April 7, 2023
Two days before Easter

Maggie leaned against the car window, letting the cold slip from the glass and onto her head.

She'd had a lot to drink.

After she'd left work around 8:00 p.m., she'd headed to a bar in Hot Springs, where Mayflower had transferred her after all that nonsense with the Hunt. Lloyd had finally gotten what he wanted. And Nancy. Though not how they'd planned. Ada and Nell had gotten a restraining order against her for attacking Ada. And for that casino business, which was only a joke! No one knew how to take a joke anymore.

"No one knows how to take a joke anymore," she said out loud, the words more slurred than she thought they ought to have sounded. She'd only had three margaritas. She wasn't a lightweight.

Aaron laughed, which was nice, to be honest. Aaron Raleigh, in Hot Springs. What were the odds?

Earlier that night, he had cried, too, when she'd broken down in the bar after she'd recognized him, leaning her head on his shoulder. She thought maybe he was stalking her, wanting revenge or something for her part in promoting the Hunt. I mean, she couldn't blame him. His daughter had died. So she cut Aaron off before he could harass her and make a scene. God, she hated a scene. Unless she was a spectator, of course! Before he could say anything, she'd asked for forgiveness and told him that she didn't mean anything that had happened.

"Did you kill my little girl? My Annalee?" Aaron asked.

Maggie's lips were a little numb, that first sign of a good buzz coming on. But a tremor of fear also went through her, the way he said it. So accusatory. "No!"

"Then there's nothing to be sorry for," Aaron said, which honestly was a shock. She wished that Ada had reacted the same way, but Ada held on to a grudge like no one Maggie had ever seen. Oh well. Her loss!

And now Maggie was in Hot Springs, and she had been forgiven by Aaron Raleigh. Her side of the street, as Ada liked to say, was clean! And so she and Aaron were having a right good time, talking shit about all those people in Presley. He didn't even believe in the Hunter! Nancy was the one who'd started all the hullabaloo and dragged his wife, Alice, into it too.

He and Alice sound like they're on the fritz, FYI. She giggled to herself.

"Why Hot Springs?" he asked her as he popped a piece of spearmint gum in his mouth. That made her worry briefly that he might try to kiss her, or something more. They'd left the bar, and he'd stopped his Tesla on some bluff that had probably once been considered lovers' lane by boomers. Aaron was a good-looking man, to be sure. He had that hot salt-and-pepper George Clooney thing going on. He got manicures. He was a pillar of the community. A man who went to church. But then, he was in the country club. He was a developer of subdivisions and all sorts of gaudy houses for rich people with no taste.

Sure, she'd fuck him. Right after she'd sobered up. She didn't want to forget a thing. Maybe she'd even get a photo of him on her phone. She'd never done that. Maybe now she would. Everyone in Presley thought she was so lame. That she had no life. They had no idea.

"Hot Springs," she said and shrugged against the car window, barely able to open her eyes or keep track of when they'd left the bar and ended up here. "It's where they'd take me. Work."

At the bar, he'd been so easy to talk to. She admitted that she'd only paid someone to follow Nell, to say those things to her, because she was jealous of Ada and Nell's friendship. She hadn't expected Nell and the woman to have sex and Nell to have a naked breakdown! She roared and then laughed, the frozen-margarita glass she held empty save for melted ice, and in grave danger of crashing to the floor.

"They act so holier than thou. Better than me. I didn't plan it out or anything. It was purely spur of the moment. I saw Nell at the casino, after she'd called in sick to work." The words were a boast. Then she got a little sad. "We were friends once, you know? Me and Ada. Close friends. The best."

Aaron patted her arm. "Friendships are hard."

Some friendships weren't meant to last. At least that's what he'd told her. It made Maggie feel better about the inexplicable anger that crackled within her. She wouldn't explode, no, not like that. Not like the stereotypical Other Woman in the movies, the Glenn Close character in the stained tee, clicking lights on and off.

She noticed him sniffling next to her in the driver's seat. She had thought she'd heard him whispering, *Annalee. Annalee.* Which was a little unsettling.

"Are you okay?" Maggie asked, her words slurred and slippery.

He swiped at his face and smiled at her. "We should get fucked up tonight."

To be honest, she already felt a little fucked up. She wasn't sure why. She'd had those margaritas, but this felt different. Weirder than what she was used to, and she'd had a lot of experience in college getting fucked up. Getting into bar fights with her sorority sisters and then lying about it the next day to their house mother.

Maggie blinked slowly and nodded once before she smiled. "Mr. Raleigh, why on earth would you want to get fucked up with me?"

"Why do humans do anything we do? We're human? We aren't logical. We do things because they feel good." He laughed and pulled out something shiny from his pocket. Maggie stared at it, tilted her head, felt like she was in a fun house at the fair, wondering at the shiny object in the distance, drawing closer, wanting to know, wanting a piece of it. He stared at it for a long time. Maggie couldn't tell if it was a knife or a pen or something else. But she wasn't scared. Somehow, she wasn't that.

"I want to feel good. Just once," Aaron said, the pain in his voice haunting and low. "Don't you?"

It was so weird, she thought. Almost like he was asking her consent. Which shouldn't be weird. Consent should be great. It should be fun.

The Consent Killer.

The words popped into her head for some reason. Maybe that's who the Hunter really was. Someone that everyone loved. Because he asked. He asked so nicely. And she couldn't help but laugh, thinking of Aaron Raleigh, victim's father. Hero of tiny white dogs. Serial killer.

Sure, Maggie. Whatever. Besides, she was in Hot Springs now. This wasn't Presley. The Hunter only hunted in Presley.

And then she looked at him looking at that shiny whatever in his hand, the edges around everything blurred. And God, she really hadn't felt this good in so long.

"I do, Aaron. I do want to get fucked up with you."

It felt good. Good, good. Sitting there with him, knowing that the crackle of anger she'd carried with her for so long would be gone for a while. And if she was lucky? Maybe forever.

Because that's the kind of night it was, sitting there with Aaron Raleigh. The kind of night that sparkled. The kind that eclipsed all other nights.